GW00676349

Please return/renew this item by the last date shown on this label, or on your self-service receipt.

To renew this item, visit **www.librarieswest.org.uk** or contact your library

Your borrower number and PIN are required.

4 6 0329316 1

THE LANDSCAPE OF MURDER

THE LANDSCAPE OF MURDER

Michael Jecks

SEVERN
HOUSE

First world edition published in Great Britain and the USA in 2024
by Severn House, an imprint of Canongate Books Ltd,
14 High Street, Edinburgh EH1 1TE.

severnhouse.com

British Library Cataloguing-in-Publication Data
A CIP catalogue record for this title is available from the British Library.

ISBN-13: 978-1-4483-1093-7 (cased)
ISBN-13: 978-1-4483-1094-4 (e-book)

All Severn House titles are printed on acid-free paper.

MIX
Paper from
responsible sources
FSC® C013056

Typeset by Palimpsest Book Production Ltd.,
Falkirk, Stirlingshire, Scotland.
Printed and bound in Great Britain by TJ Books,
Padstow, Cornwall.

Praise for Michael Jecks

"The light tone is perfectly matched to the gripping plot"
Publishers Weekly on *Portrait of a Murder*

"Plenty of action and all-too-plausible suspects hidden in a
thicket of duplicity" *Kirkus Reviews* on *Portrait of a Murder*

"Superb . . . a fast-moving and gripping plot"
Publishers Weekly Starred Review of *The Merchant Murderers*

"The comical hero provides an amusing instrument for
exploring the mores and history of the period"
Publishers Weekly on *The Merchant Murderers*

"Plenty of historical detail, loads of twists and turns, and a
hilarious tale of criminal ineptitude"
Kirkus Reviews on *Death Comes Hot*

"The novel's energetic pace never flags"
Publishers Weekly on *The Dead Don't Wait*

"Steeped in the rich, bawdy background of 16th-century
London . . . Enough suspects and red herrings to keep mystery
fans intrigued"
Booklist on *The Dead Don't Wait*

"Entertaining . . . Jecks brings the seamy side of Tudor
London to life through rich, atmospheric descriptions of its
taverns, brothels and streets"
Publishers Weekly on *A Missed Murder*

"Diverting . . . The main draw is high-spirited Jack, with his
Bertie Woosterish commentary. Fans of offbeat Tudor
mysteries will clamor for more"
Publishers Weekly on *Death Comes Hot*

About the author

Michael Jecks is the author of forty-nine novels, including the acclaimed *Last Templar* medieval mystery series, modern spy thriller *Act of Vengeance,* and eight *Bloody Mary* mysteries. A former Chairman of the Crime Writers' Association, and founder of Medieval Murderers, he lives in northern Dartmoor.

www.michaeljecks.co.uk

This book is in fond memory of
Donald Richard Gadd – 'Don'

A lovely guy – and wherever he is now,
the engines will all be working perfectly.

and

For Sheila and Lois

Prologue

I t was my companion who actually discovered the body: 'What's that?' she said.

It looked like a clump of dirty washing in the dark under the trees. Just a loose jumble of rubbish, as though someone passing had emptied a bin-bag of old clothes into the thick undergrowth well beneath the trees. Weeds and nettles had been flattened under the weight of cotton and fleeces, some shreds of material caught by the brambles.

But there was something different about this pile of clothes, and as we drew nearer, my companion gave a little gasp. Or maybe it was me.

The clothes may well have been discarded, but so was Rick. Because he still inhabited them.

That was why Megan gave her shocked, 'Oh, my *God!*' and that was what I would tell the police later. *She* found him, not me.

There is, I believe, a more or less unwritten rule that someone who discovers a dead body once is fine, but someone who makes a habit of finding them is likely to attract a considerable amount of attention from the local constabulary. I had discovered a dead body the previous year, and I really didn't want to gain a reputation as always being in the vicinity when an unpleasant death occurred, or to have the police wasting time investigating my life and interests. I have enough on my plate just trying to afford the electric bill.

However, this discovery had a similar impact on me.

It was she who first saw him, but it was shocking to me because I had spoken to him only a couple of days before, and he had mentioned suicide. That, I think, meant it hit me much harder than it did her. Not that she wasn't knocked back by it, you understand. It's just that I felt guilty; my first thought was, I should have realized he was serious.

Yes, I really felt bad about his death, the poor lad.

Maybe it was just that: guilt; then again, perhaps it was because he was so young. A lad of seventeen or eighteen has all his life ahead of him. It should be carefully guarded and hoarded, not thrown away like, in this case, a pile of old clothing. Rick Parrow was – to all intents and purposes – still a boy. He was spotty, lanky, like a teenager still shooting upwards, good looking in a sort of pasty, skinny, over-tall sort of way.

And now he was dead.

I suppose *What's that?* is the sort of comment you hear every day but, even so, this was one of those occasions when it sounded wrong. Her voice had a slight tremble to it. It was not the words that mattered so much as the tone she used, as though she had already had a premonition.

As, I suppose, I did too.

ONE

T he last months had been hard. After the excitement of the previous year, life had returned to some kind of normal. I had tried to put behind me the sheer terror of my brief sojourn in Devon. I wanted to forget the county, the dead body, and all the unsavoury characters I'd met, and tried to return to paying the bills by the careful application of paint to canvas. Yes, I was gaining a reputation as a portrait painter – that's good, right? Nick Morris, world famous artist.

Wrong. I was merely a noted painter of cats.

I have nothing against cats per se. In my time I have owned a couple, and both were friendly, amiable fellows who would happily spring on to my keyboard when I was typing, or walk idly over a wet palette and leave colourful paw prints all over the carpet (thank you, Sophie). But there is something about other cats that leaves me battered and scratched. My latest scar that day was a long, itchy and ragged line almost from wrist to elbow, thanks to a feline felon called Suki. That really was far too gentle a name for the vicious brute. Every time I saw her, she launched herself at me – and not with friendly affection in her green eyes; only resentment, hatred, and the sort of concentration I daresay she would show when stalking an errant fledgling freshly fallen from the nest.

Suki was the sort of cat who would roll over in a display of friendliness to permit her stomach to be rubbed, only to suddenly launch four paws'-worth of claws like so many sackloads of flick-knives, and try to eviscerate the poor sap who had trusted her. Yes, that was how my arm, and shirt, had become ripped.

I did not like Suki.

When I took up my paintbrushes in earnest, I had not thought I would become an instant millionaire, but I had hoped to achieve some sort of financial stability. I was no Hockney or Warhol, but there were plenty of artists making a reasonable living, and with my business acumen and experience I saw no reason why I should not emulate them.

Sadly, to date my attempts to achieve financial security had failed, and it should be stated that it was not for want of new orders.

Apparently the cat lovers of south London were enthusiastic about having their moggies rendered in oils. They could keep the leering brutes fixed on their walls for all time, to remind themselves of the multiple victims slaughtered by their moggy mass-murderers – and the poor berks like me who had been taken in and scarred by their apparently welcoming slashers.

That is why, when I had a call from my friend Geoff Hatch inviting me to lunch, I was glad to accept.

Geoff had enjoyed a long and successful career in the City. He could afford lunch for me – which was more than I could manage just then.

Geoff had taken me to various decent restaurants over the years, but that day he took me to a French bistro off New Oxford Street. It was small and authentic, in a truly Parisian manner, by which I mean it was decorated with as much disregard for its clientele and fashion as any in Paris. Grubby lampshades kept the illumination to a minimum; the expense of washing tablecloths was reduced by virtue of plastic coverings printed with a sort of 1970s red check pattern, while the cutlery would have been sneered at by any lorry driver in a greasy spoon – an expression that was perfectly matched by that of the waiter when he caught sight of me.

Once, several years ago, when I had travelled to New York on business, Geoff had recommended a specific . . . I won't call it a café, since that would insult the average Burger King, but it was a place where reasonable salt beef sandwiches could be obtained. However, as I should have anticipated, Geoff's main reason for sending me there was the quality of the staff, rather than the menu. Yes, the sandwiches were tasty, but it was the rudeness and arrogance of the serving staff that was memorable. They threw plates down before their customers as if disgusted by their choice. It was apparent that, if they had the inclination, they could all have been working in a prestigious restaurant, and it was the good fortune of the clients that they deigned to bring them anything. They demonstrated the purest form of contempt for those sitting and waiting patiently, scowling and growling when asked how long they'd have to wait – and they say in America the customer's always right. Anyone believing that should try going there and complaining.

Here in the French restaurant I suspected a similar atmosphere and stiffened my sinews. If this fellow was going to treat me to Gallic insults, Geoff had chosen the restaurant, and he was also going to have to spend prodigiously for the pleasure of seeing me insulted.

He caught my not-terribly-subtle glance about me. 'Don't panic, Nick. The food is better than the decor,' he grinned.

I did not find him reassuring, but when the waiter returned with a bottle of more than acceptable wine, and then presented with a flourish a basket of the most perfect small sourdough rolls, I began to unbend a little. The arrival of olives, rock salt and olive oil, together with a little plate of French sausage cut into irregular chunks was enough to persuade me to reserve judgement.

The wine was really very good. I sipped appreciatively, eyeing Geoff over the glass's rim. 'You look like shit.'

'Don't sugarcoat it or pull your punches, Nick.'

'But you do. You have pouches under your eyes and you've lost your Trumpian orange tint.'

He treated me to a fixed glare. 'I think you mean the healthy tan from my visit to the West Indies.'

'Didn't look like it.'

'Just because you rely on the Costa del Sunray Lamp, don't assume everyone else is the same,' he said, with a certain snappishness.

I lifted my glass in salute. After all, he was paying. 'Come on, then: give. What's this all about?'

He toyed with his glass, selected an olive, fiddled with his napkin, gazed out through the window, and generally succeeded in giving the impression of a man reluctant to come to a painful decision.

I wasn't persuaded. Geoff was a banker, a man used to dealing with all kinds of unsavoury characters in his daily struggle to survive on a half-million-pound salary, with multiples of that in bonuses. I knew him. He was not easy to embarrass.

'Well? If you don't want to tell me, that's fine, but let's order before the chef's visa runs out.'

He gave me a sour look. 'Unfeeling bastard.'

'That's not true. My belly is feeling distinctly empty.'

'I have a client—'

'Bully for you. That's good. You *can* afford lunch.'

'And he is in a spot of trouble.'

'Hold on! The last time we had a conversation like this, it ended up with me nearly getting murdered by the Russian mafia! If you want me to—'

'No, no. It's nothing like that,' Geoff said, waving his hand in an unconvincing attempt at placating me. 'Look, let me tell you about Derek Swann.'

I'll give you the gist of his story rather than relating the whole thing verbatim. For one thing, he was curiously hesitant in his manner, which was unlike him. His explanation was full of 'ums' and 'ers' which made his tale more than a little tedious, and he grew quite repetitive as he spoke. You don't need to hear that kind of nonsense. So, instead, here are the edited highlights.

Derek Swann was one of those Thatcherite businessmen who achieved great things in the late 80s. He took advantage of new laws making life troublesome for unions, benefited from government privatizations, invested wisely, took positions on the boards of several companies, and basically made himself a shedload of money, much of which was apparently legitimate – at least, it was according to his banker.

Swann had set up Derek Swann Electronic Export and Trading, or DeSEET UK, which soon morphed into a software programming company specializing in government contracts. Never particularly cutting edge, the business expanded nicely until the crash in 2008, when his investments suddenly disappeared, along with so many others' during the banking crash.

Undeterred, Swann wound up two of his companies, and from the ashes created a new business, focusing on artificial intelligence, cleverly named DAIS UK.

It seems that this new venture was even more successful than his others. He had taken it to the City, received a fortune from excited investors, and soon rebuilt his fortune.

'So what's the problem? Don't tell me you think he's ripping off the Mafia, or getting involved in drugs like—'

'Nothing like that, no. The thing is, well, I've got to know him as a friend over the years, and he has started selling up. It's not like him. I suppose I'm worried about him.'

By this stage we had finished our meal, and I sat back with that comfortable satisfaction of having done myself well on the vittles, asking the waiter for a large brandy. Well, you have to take advantage when a friend is in dire need of assistance and buying you lunch. 'You're trying to tell me that you have some fellow-feeling for another human?' I said, and I may have sounded a little cynical.

'You know me well enough to know I'm not like that.'

He was right there. I'd met a few of his colleagues over the years, and I'd have to have been desperate indeed to want to join them for a meal. Geoff was less greedy, less political, less obnoxious than many of his peers in banking. Still, I didn't think he'd lose sleep over a client behaving erratically or even foolishly. So long as his bank made money and he made his annual bonuses, he would be content.

I think he must have seen my expression.

'Yes, I'm a bit worried about him. Is that so unnatural?'

'Geoff, you're a banker.'

'A banker with a heart, old son,' he said, hurt.

'A banker,' I repeated. 'No need to qualify the comment. So what has this to do with me? You must need something, since you're picking up the tab.' Not that it was a patch on the sort of lunch he would enjoy with friends in the City, I could have added, but I didn't because I'm not unkind. And he hadn't paid yet. There was always the risk that he might withhold his wallet when it came to paying my share. I sipped my brandy. It was lovely.

Geoff sighed. 'He's selling his home. His wife has left him, taking a fair chunk of his money, and he's decided to chuck it all in. He has a marvellous place up in the Peak district, a Georgian house on the outskirts of Ashbourne, and he's decided he wants a painting of the property to remind him of it when it's gone.'

'Is he broke?' I asked suspiciously. I had been stung before by enthusiastic businessmen who wanted their glorious piles to be painted, only to discover too late that they had lost everything, the house was being repossessed, and they could not buy me a beer, let alone pay my – very reasonable – fee. The last time it happened, I had managed to contact the new owner of the property and sell it to him, although at a knock-down price. As he said, I was hardly going to find another buyer who wanted a painting of someone else's house. That one still rankled.

'Broke? God, no! Why'd you think that? He's selling his business in artificial intelligence, he's already sold off his software firm providing accounting software to small businesses, just after it was approved by the Treasury, and made a mint on that deal too. That one paid off his wife. The AI firm will make a shedload of cash. One thing you don't have to worry about is getting paid.'

Which, I admit, was a relief. My bank balance could do with a little expansion. Suki was not going to reward me to the same sort of extent as a millionaire having his ancient pile depicted for posterity.

'Oh, all right. I'll do it.'

Thus it was that, a few weeks later, in mid-May, I found myself nursing the old Morgan up to the Peak district. Within a few hours, I was rumbling up the driveway of a small park which held a number of little holiday chalets.

The drive had been tedious. For ease, I had taken mostly the motorways, and the old moggie was not at her best on such roads. It's a bit loud, which is tiring, and then there's buffeting too, when the wind attacks from the side. I'm far happier on decent old roads with plenty of bends. The migmog enjoyed taking corners at a canter, and I never lost the thrill of pointing the long bonnet at an approaching turn and feeling the rear axle bounding under my seat with the enthusiasm of a skittish pony.

Lush green rolling hills, the occasional glorious crag poking up through thick foliage, drystone walls or hedges criss-crossing the hills, new leaves the colour of fresh lemon yellow mixed with a little French ultramarine, all just crying out for a paintbox and brushes. The temptation to stop – make a couple of quick sketches and perhaps throw a little pigment on them – was almost overwhelming, but I had seen that the weather forecast was good for the whole week, predicting sunshine every day. And after the drive up, I really did feel the need for a hot bath or shower. You know how a car's windscreen will get smothered in insect corpses? A Morgan driver's hair is also a fly magnet. A shower was necessary just to try to scrape all the dead flies and other bugs out of my hair.

I had rather hoped that Swann, being a wealthy businessman, would have offered a spare room in which an impecunious artist could install himself; but no, there was no such offer made, and I was left to make my own arrangements. At least I had the internet's recommendations. A certain web browser suggested local bed and breakfasts, but I chose instead a chalet in a holiday park. It struck me that was considerably more cost-effective than staying at a B&B. That would involve buying a meal every lunchtime and evening. Better – cheaper – to get in groceries and make my own packed lunches and dinners. There was also the possibility of a painting attracting a paying audience who wanted a memento of their holiday here. I can dream.

I registered with a delightful receptionist, who boosted my ego with her expressed fascination about having an artist at the park, parked the migmog, and began to fetch my bags.

The chalet was fine – small, compact, well-appointed and comfortable. The walls were all unpainted pine, reminding me of an Austrian holiday from years ago, with a small hallway, and to the left a fair-sized sitting room with two sofas, and kitchen. On the right were two bedrooms – I picked the one with the double bed – and opposite the door was a bathroom.

It took little time to arrange my belongings, pour a celebratory whisky, and take my seat on the deck before lolling in a hot bath, and I was just finishing my whisky when a cheerful voice called out, '*Hallo!*'

The caller was a robust-looking woman of about sixty-five or so, with a pleasantly round, pale face, and surprisingly dark hair that looked rather over-optimistic compared to her wrinkles. No, I don't judge, but I am an artist. One thing I have always been able to do is assess people, and this was definitely a woman with character imprinted on her features. She rattled as she moved. At least, she didn't herself, but the seven or eight bangles on her wrist did, as did the large necklace of brightly coloured irregular shapes too. This, I thought, was a flamboyant woman. She must be an actress.

Naturally I assumed, mistakenly, that she was speaking to me. She wasn't.

There are some people who can seem quite fey. They will anthropomorphize dogs, cats or inanimate objects. She was one such. Her greeting was not for me, but for the migmog, and as

I watched, she walked over to her and ran her fingers lightly over the headlamp housing, down to the wheel arch and along it in a gentle caress. And her face . . .

I don't quite know how to put this, other than in its simplest terms. When I take my Morgan to a garage, I can tell which mechanics are interested in her. They will walk over, wiping hands on grimy cloths before carefully sliding free the bonnet catches and lifting the side panels to gaze with awe at the engine sitting inside. They are the sort of engineers I want to look after her. They are fascinated by her, they want to get to know her, all her foibles and imperfections. They are epicures of the motoring world and my moggie was for them a six-course Michelin meal.

I understand such people. For me it is the same with a decent landscape or face. Many faces do nothing for me. I see nothing of fascination. Just as a car mechanic can see a modern Ford and barely give it a moment's notice, but brighten at the sight of a series of tappets to be adjusted, so I can pass by most people without interest, but occasionally will see one with features that stand out and startle me. This was one of those women.

Seeing me, she walked to the deck's rail and gave my migmog an approving nod. 'It's good to see a real car,' she said. She was carrying a towel, and from the look of her damp hair, had just been for a swim in the pool behind reception.

'Thank you,' I said.

'So rare to see a real car nowadays. I used to have one, back in my misspent youth, a lovely bright green four-seater. I miss that.'

'You sold it?'

'Yes. Had to when my husband Ron fell off his perch. Damn fool left me with nothing, and I had to get money to keep the house. The only thing I could sell was the car. Have you had her for long?'

'Several years.'

And that was how I met Megan Lamplighter. We bonded over Morgan ownership.

After a brief conversation, and a long, covetous stare at my migmog, she left, just as a small group of motorbikers appeared.

There were three of them, one on an obscenely loud, low-riding machine with handlebars that pointed to the sky, and which looked to my jaundiced eye almost impossible to steer. I was unsurprised to see the Harley-Davidson logo on the tank.

The rider himself was clearly a wannabe cowboy or sheriff. From what I could see of him beneath his olive green crash helmet, he ran to a long moustache which fed back into his sideburns like a 1970s Elliott Gould. However his physique was more like Spiderman's. His biceps were so slim, it was a miracle he could drive that machine at all. I just hoped he wouldn't drop the bike. If he did, he'd have heart failure to try to lift it again.

The thought brought to mind a day, God knows how long ago now, when I was a teenager, and standing waiting for the traffic lights to change. Waiting at the red was a very proud man sitting astride a huge monster, a Benelli Six. The six cylinders burbled on tickover, and I was utterly enthralled. For that moment, watching that king of the road, that master of all he surveyed, I was suddenly afflicted with a jealousy so intense, I knew life would hold no joy until I too owned a Benelli Six.

The proud owner clearly noticed his juvenile admirer, and as the lights changed, he pulled in the clutch, clicked down into first, and revved the engine. It roared, spluttered, and died, and I was treated to the sudden expression of horror and anguish on the biker's face as his pride and joy stalled and slowly toppled over, bearing him to the ground.

That, and watching him desperately try to pick it up again, persuaded me that motorcycles were really not for me.

As the Harley-Davidson and its T-shirted road warrior rode past, two other bikers followed in his wake. These were different, refined bikes. Both riders were clad in sensible leathers, both with lowered, darkened visors on full-face helmets, and both purred past almost silently compared with the Harley, although I saw that both heads swivelled to eye the Harley as they passed. Professional biker jealousy, I guessed. Or perhaps contempt.

Then, as they rode up the trail to their own rooms, the Harley rider reappeared, but not on his deck area or in the window. He was on the grass in front of the chalet and, as I watched, he stared after the other bikers.

I watched him with some bemusement. It takes all sorts to rent a holiday chalet, I reflected, as I went inside to run a bath and think about supper.

TWO

The next morning was a perfect May day. I fumbled about in the kitchen in my old dressing gown and prepared the essentials.

There are some things which someone working from home has to accept. One of these is that the daily commute alters, and does so in a not terribly subtle manner. For example, when I used to work in computing, I was always the first to drop into the coffee bar under the railway bridge opposite the Blind Beggar pub, where I'd collect the first shot of caffeine of the day, along with an egg and bacon sandwich, which I would eat with extreme care, leaning forward so the yolk wouldn't drip on my silk tie. Egg yolk doesn't add much to the decoration of a paisley pattern.

If your travel to work involves mostly clambering out of bed and walking along the hall to the studio, opportunities for a double espresso with warmed milk are rather reduced. It took me a little time to invest in a decent coffee pod machine, but it never seemed to make coffee hot enough for me, and before long I threw it out and bought an Aeropress. This, ever since, has become my travelling companion, as well as my go-to machine for coffee at home. Don't even think of mentioning instant coffee to me. There are few more repellent abominations.

The Aeropress is a simple design. A large cylinder with a close-fitting piston. You pull out the piston, shove in ground coffee, fill with boiling water and stir, then fit a cap with holes and a filter over the top. Upend it over your mug of choice, press hard on the plunger, and it dispenses perfect coffee. As a sideline, if you accidentally purchase a box of mangled tea leaves instead of bags, you can use the press as a tea brewer and strainer as well, I recently discovered when I bought a box of loose-leaf tea instead of tea bags, necessity being the father of invention, or whatever the saying is.

I made myself a coffee, then took it outside to the deck and sat facing the sun on one of the easy chairs.

The birds were almost deafening. I could feel the warm lick of the sun on my face, and the coffee was superb. Idly thinking about the work I would have to engage in, and my first meeting with Derek Swann which was due later that morning, I was unaware of anybody else in the park. It was as if I had the whole place to myself. Well, myself and the birds.

'Morning, there!'

I nearly spilled my coffee. In the adjacent chalet stood my friend of the evening before. Megan stood waving a *Hello* magazine to attract my attention. I have to admit, the last thing I wanted just then was a conversation. On occasion I can be friendly and sociable, but never before my first coffee, and rarely before I've managed to get outside of a couple of rashers of bacon, some eggs, and ideally a vat of mushrooms. However, it was impossible to be rude to someone as enthusiastic as my neighbour.

She was soon sitting on my deck, the magazine on my table. 'Ugh,' she said, looking at the cover photo. 'She really thinks people will believe she's a blonde? Look at her eyes, look at the colour of her eyebrows!' She hurled the magazine away as I passed her a coffee.

Megan must have been a beauty when young. Even now, she called out for a pencil and sketchbook. She was not model-perfect. She had none of the classical attributes, the high cheekbones, straight and narrow nose, large doe-shaped eyes, or anything of that sort. No, she was unremarkable from that perspective, but what she did have was *life*. It sparked from her. It fizzed in her blood, and made her every action and gesture enthralling and intriguing.

I learned that she was a writer, specializing in crime stories and romantic novels set during the American Civil War. She was here, apparently, in order to find some peace and quiet to write her latest tome. I tried to indicate that I also had work to do. My comments fell on deaf ears.

'Nothing irritated me so much as lazy grammar,' she said, launching into a clearly favourite topic. '*I was sat,* instead of *I was sitting.* Do no teachers teach English any more? One is an action, *I sat,* while the other describes a status in the past, for God's sake.'

'Yes,' I said.

She gave me a brief glance. 'Sorry, it gets my goat. All right, I'll relax. I do love it here. I come every year at the same time,' she said. 'There's nowhere better for me to be able to concentrate. I go walking, swimming and type away for hours. I can relax and exercise while still getting the work done.'

'You aren't married?'

'Why, fancy your chances, darling?' she said with a roar of laughter. 'I have been, yes, but not now.'

I gave her a questioning look.

'Not divorced, no. First was Ron, bless him. He was a lovely man. Died when he was thirty-two. Bloody heart gave out. I was distraught. Then I married Peter, and had ten glorious years with him, before he went and died, too. Same thing: dicky heart. Both of them were heavy smokers. If I could, I would ban all smoking. I used to be a nurse before I gave it all up to write, but if I could have got the chief execs of all the tobacco companies, I'd have stuck them in a room and forced cigarette smoke in till they choked. Those bastards kill off bloody good men like Ron. I mean, if I could, I would stop writing and live on my pension, but the way things are, I can't. Neither of them left enough to support me, so I'm stuck having to keep on working. I'll still be working on the day I die, I expect.'

'The joys of self-employment,' I said.

'Yes. Bloody tax. It's all youngsters decide how much we can afford to pay, and they're all on thousands a year, guaranteed monthly, with a guaranteed pension too. They have no idea what it's like living without monthly money. I get paid twice a year, and *then* I have to pay back my advances before I earn a penny! God, I sometimes wonder why I'm a writer!'

'I thought . . .'

'Don't say it,' she groaned, putting a hand to her brow dramatically. 'Everyone thinks authors are rich. I blame Joanne Rowling or bloody Rankin. Most authors earn half the average wage – under fourteen thousand – and a large percentage get less than the minimum wage. If I wasn't so ancient, I'd look for a real job. Stacking supermarket shelves or something.'

'You aren't ancient! Didn't you want to marry again?'

She turned to me, and the humour had gone. 'When you've lost two lovers like that, you don't want to go through that sort of loss again in a hurry. I couldn't bear it. So, no, I won't marry again.'

A man rode past on a little Japanese lawnmower, engine chugging merrily. The birds were making a hell of a row in the trees overhead, and a rabbit appeared on the lawn near a play park at the bottom of our slope. We drank our coffees in silence for a while. Then, Megan suddenly frowned and peered. 'What's he doing?'

The 'he' was a slender youth who stood at the entrance to the chalet park, nervously peering about him.

My chalet was at the bottom of the park, angled at some forty degrees from the road that meandered up the hill. If I leaned back, I could gaze in the same direction as him, and when I did, I saw the chalet with the Harley-Davidson parked outside. The owner was leaning on the rail of the deck, staring down the roadway, I assume. It was hard to tell, since he wore mirrored aviator sunglasses. I had no doubt it was the Harley's rider, though. He was dressed in army fatigue-style circa 1955: khaki trousers and T-shirt, and boots that must have taken an age to lace, since the eyelets ran halfway up his shin.

As I watched, the biker stood upright, his hands on the rail, and then he gave a sort of hesitant wave, as though anxious not to be seen, but still wanting to attract the youngster's attention.

Megan hadn't seen him. Her gaze was fixed on the boy still. 'What is he doing here? I don't recognize him,' she said as the youngster set off up the hill past us with a sudden intensity.

'I don't know,' I said. From the map which I had been given on arrival, there were some seventy chalets in the estate, and I hadn't had the time or inclination to go peering at all the people renting them. Megan leaned over and gazed after the lad.

I have to admit, it did look odd. He was walking like a trainee actor told to walk 'normally' – by which I mean he looked entirely self-conscious and unnatural. His arms were thrust into his pockets, as if in imitation of confidence, but his gait was somewhere between a trot and an amble. It was as if he was desperate not to call attention to himself, which of course meant he attracted any wandering eye. 'He's just a teenager who's got into a row with his parents, I expect,' I said doubtfully.

'You think?' There was a sharpness to her voice. I guessed

that she has suspicions about the biker. Then she seemed to
remember I was there, and settled back in her seat, once more
the writer. 'I'd say he was a thief or local hooligan. Look at him!
Did you ever see a more guilty-looking fellow? He has it written
all over his face.'

'Do you often let your imagination run away with you?' I
protested. 'He's just a youngster. Lads his age always look guilty.
It's part of being a teenager.'

'You think so?' she said, but her gaze was fixed on his back
as he walked up the hill. 'And just look at that man! If he's not
a fence for stolen goods, I don't know what he is!'

While we watched, the boy stopped in front of the Harley
rider, and then walked round the side to the chalet's door. Soon
he was inside, and the biker remained standing at the rail. He
took one last, long look at the roadway, and then his attention
moved to me. It was deeply disconcerting. I felt that look like a
mallet to the skull. I ignored him and returned to face Megan.
When I glanced back again, he had gone.

Megan gave a sigh of satisfaction. 'I told you so. A thief and
his fence – or a dealer and his distributor?'

I had little time to worry about her imagined villains. Today I
was to meet Derek Swann. When I had dressed, I carefully stashed
paints, brushes and sketch books into a convenient messenger
bag, took up my old metal easel, threw the lot into the moggie's
footwell, and was soon on my way.

Derek Swann had suggested we meet at Tissington because it
was not far from his house, and I got the distinct impression that
this was more of a job interview than a casual chat about my
approach to painting. He wanted to see what I was like and, to
be honest, I rather liked that. If I were buying a puppy, I would
want to meet the parents of the pup as well as the breeder. This
man was buying a painting, and I suppose at the back – or even
at the front – of his mind was the question whether or not I was
some kind of Kandinsky who would turn his house into a cube
of concrete with occasional splashes of colour, or whether I would
give it the respect he wanted, and give him a faithful representation. It struck me as perfectly sensible, although I would have
preferred to meet him in London if there was any risk that I

wasn't going to win the commission. It was a long journey to Tissington, after all.

The weather was perfect, so I drove with the roof off. When driving a moggie, it's always a good idea to keep the lid off. Not because the fresh air is delightful, but because clambering in and out through the tiny doorway when the roof is fixed is an exercise in advanced yoga.

At Tissington, the entrance was glorious: two tall gateposts led into a broad pasture with trees lining the road. The road took me down a slight hill to the village itself, and I had to stop to take it in. It was an archetypical English village.

Village pond? Yup. Ducks? of course. Stone walls? Naturally. Pleasant cottages with their own vegetable gardens? What do you think?

Perhaps I didn't make myself clear. This was the archetypical English village from a far-distant past. I expected smock-clad peasants to wander past. It was, in short, perfect, even down to the church, the vicarage and Jacobean manor house. I was just surprised that there was no actual castle in evidence. No doubt all these delightful houses were constructed from the demolished castle, if there had been one. Somehow I felt sure that there had been. It just seemed the sort of place that called out for a castle.

There was a left-hand turn towards the manor house, and a series of parking bays, with a café opposite. I reversed into a space and climbed out, mentally identifying the best buildings to be included in any paintings. I was pretty certain that some preliminary sketches while I was here would prove to be useful, and potentially worthwhile. I could paint, have prints made, perhaps some postcards of village scenes, and have the village shop sell them. If I kept 60 per cent, with 40 per cent going to the shop, I would be content.

An artist is, after all, a self-employed businessman. We need to keep an eye open for the next opportunity. Especially if it doesn't include feral felines.

Tissington, that morning, was a hive of activity.

There was, I was soon to discover, a 'well dressing' that week. Well dressing? You haven't heard of it? I cannot say that I am surprised. Neither had I before then.

It was, I was informed by the garrulous waitress behind the

bar of the small restaurant, an ancient ritual. Every year the villagers gathered to decorate the wells in the area in a form of pagan ritual to bless them and the springs feeding them. And in Derbyshire there are a lot of wells.

I have heard that it's because, during the Black Death, the area was miraculously unaffected while the people all around were ravaged with the disease. Tissington lost no one, and the prevailing view was that it was the special quality of the water from the springs and wells that protected the people living there. Naturally they wanted to bless the wells and thank them, so every year the priest holds a service on Ascension Day in the church, and then the congregation trails around all the wells and he blesses each one. Rather a nice way to thank them, I thought. The decorations stay up for some while, although I assume not for too long, because each decoration is made of flower petals and other natural colourings – no inks, paints or oily messes to upset the balance of the wells. But that, I guess, means they are short-lived.

It sounded a cheerful kind of bucolic celebration, rather like Morris dancing or dancing round the maypole, but involving less beer. Certainly the people in the village looked very happy with things. That is, all except one. To my surprise, I saw a boy sitting on a bench with the worries of the world on his shoulders. It was the same lad I had seen going to see the Harley Hell's Angel, or whatever Megan's supposed fence of stolen goods was.

It was hard not to notice him. He kept covering his face in his hands as if despairing, and after a while just sat with his head bent. I really felt my heart go out to him. I bought a coffee in the café, ordered a Derbyshire oatcake with ham and cheese (it sounded intriguing) and, as soon as I could, sat down, opened my sketchpad and started to draw. The first scene that caught my eye was the boy on the bench. He looked so miserable, so deep in morose thought, that I wondered whether he might make a suitable book cover or some other illustration. I was almost done when my oatcake arrived, and while I was thanking the waiter, the boy rose and walked off. I eyed him sourly. He would have made a good focus for me, had he remained just a little longer.

But there were other views to distract me. First the scene over the manor house itself, then that of the bulk of the church with its square tower, which took a lot of shading to make sense of the shadows from trees. Turning slightly, I could sketch the hill alongside the church, a pleasant pastureland with interesting lumps and undulations in the grass, which seemed to indicate an old building or ancient hill fort or something. It was missing something, so I gave it some context by adding a couple of figures at the bottom of the hill; then put in my Morgan, and a few of the other vehicles parked alongside. Irritatingly, a red Porsche appeared and parked next to the migmog, blocking the view somewhat. Still, it would do, I thought, and had just settled back to consume the oatcake and coffee, when a voice interrupted me.

'You must be Nick.'

I found myself confronted by a genial-looking man in his late sixties, from his appearance.

Derek Swann was an ageing hippy. He had a tousled mop of white hair over a face that was long rather than round. He didn't look like a man who would be a pirate at business. His stone-coloured walking trousers were faded; his shirt was one of those multicoloured Nepalese-style shirts with a 'grandad' collar and no cuffs. He wore Birkenstock sandals, but I was relieved to see no socks. I have seen too many hippies with that kind of affectation for comfort.

He had the sort of thin skin that made him look like a habitual smoker. I had known quite a few men like that from my sales days, but Swann didn't have the tell-tales common to heavy smokers. One guy I knew with similar grey colouring had been proud of smoking sixty cigarettes a day, and his right hand and wrist were stained a hideous nicotine yellow. Another man I knew, old enough to have pure white hair, had his hair stained yellow. Derek Swann had none of that. In fact, he looked quite healthy – for a smoker.

He grinned, showing a bright set of teeth that must have cost him a fortune, and held out his hand in a friendly manner. I have experienced many handshakes in my time, but this was one calculated to inspire trust. He didn't go for the emphatic forearm clutch with his left hand, but just stood shaking my hand for a short while, four distinct operations up and down, and then releasing me. He peered at me with blue eyes the colour of a summer's evening.

'I like to think I'm a good judge of character,' he said. 'You'll do!'

'Well, that has to be about the quickest interview I've had,' I said. I didn't add that I'd have preferred the interview before driving hundreds of miles.

'I've learned over the years that the important part of an interview is the first twenty seconds or so. The rest of the meeting tends to be me justifying my decision to myself, so now I save time and just go with my first gut feeling. I hired a new business partner last year when we met at Glastonbury – I go there every opportunity, the vibe is superb; I love the mix of different genres of music there – but I had to hire him after seeing him for only a couple of minutes.' He suddenly looked slightly anxious. 'I hope you don't mind?'

'If you commission me, I'm happy,' I said.

'Geoff said you had a Morgan. He seemed to think you were mad.'

'Yes, he does. His tastes run more to Porsches and Ferraris,' I said. 'But then, I think he's mad to be stuck in an office for silly hours every day. And the migmog has character, and that counts for a lot, I think.'

'So do I,' he said, and then it was straight to business. I refused his offer of a second coffee, so he ordered one for himself and joined me at my picnic table. A double espresso duly arrived for him, and he opened a little portfolio with a series of photos inside, turning it for me. 'I thought it might be useful for you to see what the place looks like. I've pictures from all angles, so you can get a feel for the house, but this is the angle I'd really like you to capture, if you think it would work for you too.'

'I'm surprised. Geoff said you were into computers and software.'

'I am – so I know how easily people can hack into them. For example, it was a policy of mine that no senior managers would have email. We all met up for coffee for general talks; when there was an issue, we would actually visit each other in our offices. Email generates emails, with everyone trying to include everyone else just to cover their arses. Most are irrelevant. If I need to speak to someone, I'll do just that – speak to them.'

I went through the photos. They showed a house with dark stone, set on three levels. If I had to guess, I would say that it was not an ancient pile. More likely this was early Victorian, with servants' quarters upstairs. There was a wide terrace area, a rose garden, and the house enclosed these like a protective horseshoe.

'Did you get a helicopter for these?' I asked about a couple of pictures which were obviously taken from the air.

'No,' he chuckled. 'I like playing around with drones. I have one which is superb, as you can see from the quality of that photo. I mostly use it on the coast, taking videos of the sea and sunsets. It's a brilliant tool. Some people play golf, some people relax by going fishing, but for me, you can't beat going somewhere wild with a drone and making videos. I love it.'

'One of those hobbies I haven't tried,' I said. 'The house looks stunning.'

'It was built a couple of hundred years ago,' he said. 'I just love the look of the place, and its history.'

'What sort of history?'

He held a hand out, taking in the church before us, the café, the manor house in one broad gesture. 'Look at all this! A lovely little village, unspoilt, calm. Yet it's not always been such a quiet backwater. The FitzHerberts own this entire village still, and they weren't always peaceful folk. There was a battle here in the Civil War, you know. Only a short time before Naseby and the destruction of King Charles's army. The Royalists were thrashed here too. You could say that this landscape has been washed with blood. My old house is not like that. It's a much more recent property, and it's never seen war and death. I rather like that.'

'I can imagine,' I said. I have never liked the idea of older houses with their own ghosts.

'Don't get me wrong,' he continued, 'I do love places like this. That manor, it's idyllic, isn't it? Big, bold, assertive . . . and strong, as if it's been here for all time, let alone four centuries or so.'

'Where will you go when you've sold up?'

'Geoff told you, eh? Oh, I have a place just down the road from Noël Coward's in the Indies. Lovely house, and the climate is warm all year round. It's something special to wake up and look across the bay, stare at the Blue Mountains in the distance, walk through the trees to the swimming pool or the sea, and pick ripe bananas or mangoes on the way. England is in my soul, but

I do get fed up with the rain here. I'll miss the place, of course. But nothing lasts for ever, does it?'

'I suppose not.'

'Have you been to Jamaica?'

I shook my head regretfully. 'One of any number of places I've always wanted to visit and never quite had the money,' I admitted.

'You should get the money,' he said seriously. 'You only live once. This isn't a rehearsal. If you *really* want to do something, you can do it. And better to do it while you're young enough to enjoy it still. Promise me you'll scrape the money together and get out there. Hey, when you do, you can stay for free with me on the estate. I can promise you a wonderful time there, and who knows? Maybe you'll paint your very best picture out there.'

There was a distant roar, and I knew it had to be the biker from the chalet up the road from me.

Sure enough, a few minutes later the Harley appeared at the bottom of the road where a triangle of grass marked the end of the road past the manor house. The Harley turned into the road and burbled its way up, past us sitting on our picnic bench, on up to the manor, and past it, the military helmet swivelling left and right as he went. He slowed at the benches, and I wondered whether he was looking for the boy again. At the top of the road, he reached a junction on the right, and took that, disappearing from view, his engine opening up a little as he climbed the rise to the top of the hill.

'You see that?' Swann said. He was pointing behind me towards the lumps in the ground I had been sketching in the pasture not far from the church.

'An old ditch?' I hazarded. I've seen plenty of earthworks in my time.

I was looking over towards the scene he indicated, and as he did, I saw the boy reappear up at the side of the church. He stood up near the tower, before slowly descending by the main footpath. Soon he was back on the bench where I had seen him before, once more resting with his head in his hands.

'No, not a ditch. There's a moat there, I think. It is where the original Norman castle stood. I believe it was a motte and bailey castle, which was gradually increased to become quite a large home. Back in the sixteen hundreds or so, the owner decided it was too cold and draughty, I expect, and built the new manor house. But the lines of the old walls are still there, if you know where to look.'

'It's a shame there's nothing to see,' I said, and I meant it. There's little sells quite so well to American tourists than elegantly collapsing ancient castles or manor houses. As I've said, an artist has to be looking out for any opportunity. Meanwhile my attention was more fixed on the seated boy than the field by the church, but I managed to draw my eyes away and concentrate on Swann.

He continued, 'Hardly surprising. I daresay, if you were interested, you could find all the original stones from the castle in the manor over there, or in the other houses all around here.'

We chatted about his house for a while, leafing through the photos he had brought, and as we did, I became aware of the sound of a motorbike again. As it grew, I looked back towards the triangle of grass, and sure enough soon I saw the Harley-Davidson again, slowly running down the road and turning back up it towards us. I shifted in my seat to watch as the bike made its way past the café and on to a section of hard-standing near the boy on the bench, where the rider stopped, his feet on the ground as he turned the ignition off. He put both hands to his helmet and removed it, settling it on the fuel tank before placing the bike on the kick-stand and dismounting, walking towards the boy. He stood over the lad, and I saw the boy lift his head from his hands. He expostulated, his arms gesturing wildly, first this way then that, and I could not help but wonder at the cause of his emotion.

Soon the discussion was over. The boy stood and gave a resentful and rejective push with both hands towards the biker before striding off up the hill towards the main road.

The Harley rider stood transfixed for a long moment, watching the boy go, and I was struck by how still he was, like a man who kept his own emotions under control. It reminded me of the story of a psychopath who had stood as his wife berated him, unaffected by her angry passion, until he suddenly punched her. It was enough to kill her, and when asked why, he simply said that she was starting to irritate him.

He turned, and I saw that he was wearing the mirrored shades again. He reminded me of a South Carolina cop from a movie, but scruffier. I felt his gaze wander over the road, down to us, up left to the church, and then back to us again.

'Shit!' Swann hissed.

Swann rose suddenly, and hurried away down the grass towards his Porsche, leaving me gaping. Without even glancing towards the biker, he sprang in, slammed the door, revved the engine and drew away in a swirl of dust. The engine sounded divine, I have to admit, although I would prefer the full-throated roar of a V8 in a Morgan. Not that I'd ever own one – not with my income. However, I wasn't thinking of Morgan Plus 8s or the current crop of Plus 6s. I was much more intrigued by the biker, and his impact on Derek Swann.

Talking of whom, he glanced at me curiously as he walked past to the café. I was still staring after the Porsche, now disappearing round the bend at the bottom of the road. Idly, I picked up a pencil and made some basic outlines on the page just to clear my mind. What on earth had made Swann behave like that, I wondered?

I started with a fresh study of the church, before turning my attention to the pasture. Soon I had an overview of the field, the well to the left, the lumps and bumps of ancient walls or something, and I was just shading it all in when I was interrupted.

'Excuse me, can I join you?'

It was the biker. He had two cups in his hand, and a cardboard box with something – a sandwich or salad, perhaps.

For all that Megan had been convinced he was a criminal of some sort, all I saw was a man obsessed with the Sixties and Seventies. He had all the dress sense of a Vietnam veteran, but with a leather waistcoat. He presented the sort of image that would usually make me move away along a bench. There was that aura of sweat and engine oil about him. I've always heard that Harley-Davidsons were terrible, leaking, old-fashioned bikes, more suitable as decorations than as a means of transport. This one, with the high 'Easy Rider' handlebars certainly looked uncomfortable. When the man made his way to my picnic table, I quickly decided to finish my coffee and leave.

His accent was pure Home Counties, not American, which somehow grated, given his dress sense and bike. I quickly said, 'Oh, of course. Yes, but I'll be going soon.'

'I saw you this morning,' he said. 'You have the Morgan? Lovely cars, those. Yours looks a sweet little thing. Here: have a coffee.'

A brief gust of wind brought with it no scent of oil or sweat, only a pleasant sandalwood aftershave. 'I really have to be going soon, I—'

'Come on! Here, take it!'

He was insistent, but not offensive. It was just that he was one of those men who automatically assumes that the world will fall into place around them in the manner which they expect. Not from arrogance, but more because, logically, the world should see that it was the natural order of things. He wanted me to stay here to chat with him, and clearly that was the right thing for me to do, in his world. That I might have urgent business did not occur to him. Not that I did, of course.

He set one before me, and dropped two sachets of sugar and a carton of cream beside it. 'Didn't know how you'd take it,' he said almost apologetically. He glanced at my bag of paints and sketchbook. 'You're a painter?'

'Yes, I dabble with paints.'

'I always admire guys who have that creative flair,' he said. 'So many people now use their brains and hands just to control the remote for the TV, or make some gormless comment on social media. To be truly creative, that is a gift.'

'Thanks.'

'What subjects do you usually paint?'

It was rather pleasant to be sitting in the sun chatting to a man who admired my chosen career. I have to admit, I warmed to him. 'I'm mostly a landscape artist, although I can turn my hand to portraits or anything else,' I said, adding, 'whatever takes my fancy – or whatever is likely to pay the best!'

He laughed at that. 'That's the way to work. Make sure that every day is fun, but most of all, that every day pays well enough to keep you in beer and potatoes!'

'What do you do?' I was careful not to mention drugs or youths who could distribute them around the community.

'Me? Oh, a bit of this and that. Mostly, I try to see the country. You know, most people get to see lots of Spain or France, but how many know that we have some of the best country in the world? Look around here, and going north to the Dales – it's

beautiful country, as good as anything you'll see in Tuscany or
Brittany. But no, everyone has to travel abroad, as if anywhere
else is going to be an improvement.'

'Well, if you go abroad, you're likely to have better weather,'
I pointed out.

'Yes, and win a malignant melanoma. I'm happier here. Besides,
when you're on a bike like mine, the thrill is in the road itself.
You must feel that. It's when you throw yourself into a corner and
accelerate out of it that you feel alive. Sitting on a French motorway
doesn't have the same sense of danger and excitement.'

'I suppose not.' I didn't feel qualified to comment on the sense
of danger I would have felt riding a motorbike in French traffic.
'I've never taken the migmog abroad. Perhaps one day. I'd like
to take her up to the Alps.'

'Yeah, I'd imagine that would be fun. I went up to the St
Bernard Pass on the Harley once. Made the engine sound all the
better for going through the tunnel there. Amazing sounds and
sights. I saw you were talking to Derek Swann when I arrived
just now, by the way. How's he doing?'

I was tempted to say that my client was none of his business,
but I was intrigued. 'You know him?'

'I'd hardly know his name else, would I?'

'He seemed anxious to leave when he saw you arrive.'

He grinned. It made me think of an alligator telling a joke.
There was amusement there, but also a threat. 'He would be. He
stole everything from me.'

My new companion's name was Jerry – Jez – Cooper, I learned.

'I had my own software house, and it was moderately
successful. Back then, in the early two thousands, there was a
lot of money to be made. I started out with the worries about
Y2K – you know, the year two thousand disaster. Everyone was
convinced that every major computer system would collapse
because of old software and systems, and businesses would fold
just because they had old machines and programs. Of course it
didn't happen, and although there were thousands of guys like
me sitting around and waiting for the end of the world, we'd
already reprogrammed all the kit we needed to, and there were
very few issues. But I made a lot of money, which was great, as

a twenty-something. It gave me a taste for systems and management, and I gradually moved into new developments.

'What really interested me was the way the internet was taking over, and how it affected companies. So I set up my own little business, tracking companies' social media and seeing how their posts affected their sales. They put out a couple of messages on Facebook, and I looked through the responses and gauged how people were reacting. As social media took off, I had to expand, and took on more and more staff, until by twenty fourteen, I had a team of thirty-two, and we were turning over about fifteen million a year. I was making good money.'

His smile remained in place, but now it was definitely more alligator than cuddly bear.

'And then I met Derek.'

He stirred coffee contemplatively for a little while. I watched him closely. He had a sort of closed-up look about him, like someone concentrating on an unpleasant task to come, but determined to go through with it.

'He persuaded me to join him in a couple of ventures. It looked like a sweet deal, and he got me to work with him, and then . . .' his eyes took on a colder, far-away look. 'Then he stiffed me. He brought in new members on the board who were all his cronies, not that I met them. They were all based in Jersey. Still, they voted me off. I had been managing director with thirty per cent of the merged business, but soon I had nothing. He'd even taken my client list. The firm moved to Jersey, and that was me done.'

I had heard of plenty of other, similar scam artists, but it seemed curious that Derek Swann would have behaved like that. The man seemed pretty straightforward to me. I didn't say that. There are times when it is fair and reasonable to express doubts in support of a friend, and then there are times when, by doing so, there is a distinct risk of getting your nose redistributed over your face; this was one of those times.

'What happened to you?'

'I had to learn to cope. For a while I went round to old clients and told them what had happened, and then I tried to put things together to start up again, but it wasn't too easy. He still owed me money from when we'd been collaborating, and that cost me the house. He left me with nothing. I had to sleep on friends' floors for weeks, but managed to get back into freelancing. I took the first decent contract I could, and worked in banking for a while, and then went round the world to get my head in gear. I spent a year bumming around on a beach in Thailand. It was great,' he said, his eyes gazing past me, through the church behind, and apparently picking up a beach café on his internal video. 'I rested, enjoyed the lifestyle, swam a lot, learned Muay Thai, and how to relax and meditate . . . yeah, it was good.'

I coughed to attract his attention again. 'So now you're gainfully employed, anyway. That bike must have set you back a fair bit.'

'The Harley? I love it. That was some money I made while out in Thailand. All very boring, but it helped me when I was really hard up, and it allowed me to fly home. As for *gainfully employed* – well, I have projects keeping me ticking over. The main thing for me is, getting things sorted. I have some debts to repay.'

I didn't question that. His eyes had gone sort of filmy, and he was staring over my right shoulder. There was no need for me to follow his gaze. From his expression I knew he was no longer dreamily viewing a Thai beach; no, now he was staring at a parking place which only a short while earlier had been taken up by a Porsche.

'Thought you'd like to know the sort of man you're dealing with,' he said. 'If he suggests an arrangement, just remember, anything he wants to put to you is fine, but it's cash up front with the bastard. He's one of those guys who has no scruples, no morals. No sympathy for other people and how his actions affect them.'

He left me soon afterwards, striding purposefully to his bike, looking neither left nor right, mounted the machine, set the helmet on his head, and was soon roaring away down the road to the triangular 'Give Way', and off, but as he went I couldn't help but notice that his head moved boustrophedon, as if looking for someone.

I sketched pensively, thinking about his words. However, his allegations were no reason to drop my commission with Swann. I put him from my mind.

'Wow, that's sick!'

I glanced round to discover I had an audience of three youngsters. When I say that, I mean young adults, not pre-teens. The boy who spoke was probably seventeen or so, and had just completed a growth spurt, from the look of him. He was taller and skinnier than he should be, with an expression of fascination as he peered over my shoulder. A girl with glorious, curling auburn hair stood at his side, one hand on his shoulder, while their companion was a dark-haired boy. These last two looked a little older, probably because their bodies had filled out a bit.

I rather hoped that 'sick' was in some way a positive comment.

'Thanks,' I said, trying not to sound too smug. After all, which creative doesn't like to be complimented?

'You like drawing?' the girl said in that tone that said she was being polite, but wouldn't it be better to find a shaded hedge to drink some cider? Not with me, of course, but one of her swains. I was far too ancient.

'I'd be a sad man if I didn't,' I said. 'It's how I earn my living.'

'Really? That's neat!' the first boy said.

'You drawing, like, the church?' the girl said. She was bored.

'I was thinking more of the field there. All those earthworks stand out well, don't they?'

'It's just grass,' she said, as if explaining to a moron. She took an e-cigarette from her pocket and inhaled, blowing out a stream of hideously sweet-smelling steam. It reminded me of bubble gum. I half expected the fumes to be pink.

'It was once a building or something,' I said.

'Yeah?'

The first boy nodded. 'They say there was a battle here. Long time ago.'

'What, like, *Lord of the Rings*, eh?' she giggled.

'Yeah,' the dark-haired boy said, giving her a stern look. He was clearly the local history nerd. 'It was a Civil War battle. The village had come out for the king and there were all these Royalists around here. But the Roundheads came and beat them so they all ran.'

'I see,' I said, beginning to add some details to my sketch.

'They say the Royalists left all their stuff here,' he continued. 'All their money and stuff.'

'Yeah? That's, like, great! Has anyone found it?' the girl said, suddenly genuinely interested. No doubt a treasure would allow her to buy more vapes.

'Nah, course not, Pen! Don't listen to Al. It's just a story, isn't it!' the first boy sneered, and shortly afterwards, he and the girl wandered off, no doubt to seek a sheltered nook where they could drink cider in comfort. Or lager, or some other form of adulterated alcohol. The dark-haired boy remained at my side for a few moments, looking from my picture to the earthworks. 'Stan and Penny don't like history. I do. It'd be good, if someone could find it, all that money,' he said ruminatively.

'I daresay plenty of people have tried to over the years,' I said dismissively. 'It's unlikely to be here still, sadly.'

'I suppose,' the boy said. He left me to join the other two once more.

After they'd gone, a man at the next table hailed me. 'Do you mind if I take a look?'

'No, feel free,' I said.

'I couldn't help but wonder what you were drawing,' he said, gazing at my efforts. 'You certainly have an eye for perspective. That's excellent. Interesting history, too.'

'The earthworks?'

'Yes. Those youngsters were quite right about the battle. The legend of money hidden there in a secret chamber has been circulating ever since.'

'What do they say?'

I glanced up the road, to where the trio were chatting to a familiar figure. It was the boy again. Since Harley Man had ridden off, he had returned. He looked sulky and resentful still. I felt rather sympathetic – when I was his age, I daresay I'd looked pretty much the same. Absent-mindedly I sketched the quartet in on my picture. They gave a sense of proportion to the scene.

My new friend continued, 'Oh, well the manor here was built in the sixteen hundreds, it's Jacobean. The old castle was on that hill opposite. You can see why: the well would have been near the castle; they would have built it on higher land, too, which that was. All in all, I'm sure the stories of a castle are right.'

'And the treasure?' I had to work fast. The girl was already turning and tugging her boyfriend's arm to draw him away. I quickly turned the page and made a larger sketch. A dark pickup truck behind them gave a pleasing contrast to the composition.

He chuckled. 'Hardly a great treasure, but the story goes that the king's men were carrying a large sum for paying troops and buying food, and were going to meet the rest of the army near Naseby. It's said that the old castle's cellars and some outbuildings were still apparent, and one of the Royalist officers had the clever idea of burying the money where the Parliamentary men couldn't find it. They found a cellar in the ruins, installed the money, covered it over with rocks and things, and then, during the battle, the officer in charge died, and the others were killed on their way to Naseby, or immediately after it. No one alive remembered where the money was buried.'

'And no one has found it since?' Too late. They were making their way up the hill now. I set the sketchbook aside reluctantly and concentrated on my companion.

'No. There are occasional hopeful types who have tried to dig for it, but they get short shrift when they do. No one likes strangers wandering about and prospecting on their fields. You can't blame them.'

'The prospectors or the locals?'

He chuckled again, but didn't comment.

By mid-afternoon I had completed three more sketches, one of the old site, one of the new Georgian mansion, which I hoped might interest the owner, and a third of the church, which it has to be said was hardly photogenic, but I reckoned I could tart it up a bit with a little careful use of highlighting. Perhaps the white outline of the top of the building, emphasized with the judicious use of gouache, to bring the building forward slightly . . . it would take some further analysing and thought. As a church, it was remarkably boring – more like a blockhouse than a religious sanctuary.

On a whim, I walked up the path to the church door. It was only a small building, compared with other churches I have known, and I sat at the bench outside the door and gazed about me for a little. It was a delightfully peaceful spot. A house opposite caught my attention – possibly the vicarage or rectory? – and I idly made a very quick sketch to see how it would best be represented on paper, and soon decided I would need to have some human figures to show its proportions a bit better.

Glancing up the road, the trio of teens were still talking with the lad from the park, and I made a very rough representation of them, the girl as a colourful, slim figure blowing out a streamer of smoke, her two friends standing near her, the resentful one looking down at the road, hands in his pockets, head slightly forward and almost submissive in appearance, like a puppy cowed by a small pack. It was such a striking pose in front of the other three that I edited my sketch and made it more detailed. The three left him soon after and walked up the road away from me, the dark-haired historian peering over his shoulder a few times as they went. Meanwhile the other fellow stalked over to a bench and sat down, his head in his hands once more. It was his favourite pose.

He was such a picture of abject misery that it was really quite touching. Watching him felt like voyeurism. I snapped the cover shut on my sketchbook and, rather than stay watching him, I went to the door and entered the grim-looking church.

It has to be said that I am not religious and do not know much about the interior of churches. This one looked quite old to me – but then even Victorian churches look pretty ancient. However, it was lovely. Stained-glass windows left the interior dark, but not dingy. The stonework was a lovely yellow ochre, where it had not been painted white. On the floor, on the walls, at either side of the altar were memorials to members of the FitzHerbert family. On the right were some glorious stained-glass windows, one with a picture of a rainbow over a watery scene with a beautifully depicted hill and trees, and an inscription reading, *I shall set my bow in the cloud, and it shall be for a token of a covenant between me and the earth*. Below it was another picture, this time of Noah's ark, with a mention of the dove coming back from her flight with an olive branch in her beak. It was a lovely setting, and although I'm not religious, I could appreciate the calm and peace in that room.

I left feeling refreshed. It was a happy artist who walked down from that hillock to the roadway.

How could I tell that it was the last time I would feel such ease while staying in the Peak District?

It was tempting to go and have another coffee, but I held that off as a treat for another day. Instead, I walked to the Morgan. On the way, I saw the boy again. He was still sitting on the bench, and if I had ever seen a fellow looking more harrowed, I couldn't remember it. He wasn't weeping, but it really did look as though tears were not far away.

What do you do in such situations? In the past I have seen people like that in cities, and my inclination is to want to go to them and offer a comforting word, or perhaps a manly hug – but of course I wouldn't dare in most situations. This boy had something really troubling him, but the easiest way to get insulted, or possibly accused of unwanted homosexual advances or some similar horror, is to go to a complete stranger and offer sympathy when it wasn't needed or wanted.

However, there was something about this lonely lad that seemed to beg for adult intervention. While I may not be the best adult in the room generally, I was the only one available just now.

I went to the car and stowed my painting gear before going to sit next to him.

His response was hardly welcoming. He glared at me sharply, then shifted a little up the bench, away from me.

I sniffed and carefully avoided his eye. Gazing before me at the old stable block (recently converted, I later discovered, into a wedding venue), I made an effort to ignore him. Instead I took out my sketchbook and started a pen-and-ink sketch of the building. You never knew, after all. Someone might want a postcard of the place where they were married.

He studiously paid me no heed, but averted his head, staring over towards the café again as though fascinated by the view. I sketched, occasionally taking a quick glimpse of his profile when I thought it safe. Then, naturally, our eyes met.

OK, it wasn't across a crowded room, but it did give me a chance to give him a smile. He didn't glower at me this time, but instead gave me a sort of grudging acknowledgement, as though we were in a lift. You know how it is, as the doors shut, those inside will stare fixedly at the point where the doors meet and not even remotely near to anyone else standing inside. Those at the back, whose view of the doors is obstructed by other people, will focus their attention on the shoes of all the others, or gaze at the ceiling tiles. What is it about modern life that makes everyone so nervous of meeting another's eyes?

Anyway, his sharp nod was enough for me. 'Lovely day,' I said.

He gave a grunt.

'I hope you don't mind,' I tried, 'but you look like you have something worrying you. Is there anything I can help with?'

He looked at me, then back towards the café, and a little cynical twist came to his mouth. 'Yeah. Do you know how to commit suicide?'

And with that, he stood and marched away, past the café, and on towards the pond.

As you can imagine, that was rather a conversation stopper, even if he hadn't left the bench. I think it's fair to say I gaped. Not quite like a salmon taking a fly, but my jaw had definitely dropped, and I was left looking more than a little gormless. I watched him walk away, little more than a boy in faded denims and a pale blue hoodie with a strange symbol like outstretched wings on the back. They were composed of horizontal bars in white, with a five-pointed star in the middle where they joined, a fairly modern kind of design, which I assumed was taken from a game or some brand he liked. But that soon flew from my mind as I absorbed his words.

That was not what I had expected to hear. A lad like him, young, with all his life ahead of him, should have been happy enough. He had access to beer, after all. And women. And he must have been on the cusp of his twenties, a period I still remember with some (occasionally embarrassed) pleasure. Yes, I had worked for some companies that really were worse than they might have been, but the fact was that I had enjoyed a lot of socializing with friends and family, and although I had periodic misadventures, such as companies folding and owing me a lot of money, for the most part I enjoyed my time. To see this fellow in such a miserable situation was curiously depressing.

I was quite abashed by the sight and by his words. Did I think he was serious? *No!* Who would expect someone to be planning deliberately to commit suicide when that young? Many, I know, but he didn't strike me as genuinely having a desire to end it all. Rather, he reminded me of friends I have known who have had some kind of misfortune, and who have reacted with extreme language as an aid to getting over it. It's like a safety valve on a steam train. Either swearing or extreme statements can help people absorb a grim situation, process it, and then get on with resolving or bypassing the issue, putting it behind them. It seemed to me that this lad was in that kind of position. He was in the middle of accepting whatever had suddenly landed in his path, and he was evaluating the problem before getting round it.

It's one of the hardest aspects of growing up, isn't it? Learning how to process and progress.

So I put it to the back of my mind and carried on working.

I was back at the chalet late in the afternoon, and was sitting down with a guide book of the area and a cup of tea when a cheerful voice called to me. It was Megan.

'Hallo, darling! Saw you there, and thought you looked like you needed a drink,' she said, brandishing a bottle of very acceptable red. I tend to go more for cost-effectiveness when I'm looking at labels, and this type would have been equivalent to three of my standard bottles.

'It's a bit early,' I protested, but I was already too late.

'Come on, get glasses,' she commanded, and soon she was with me on the terrace. I fetched two glasses, and while she poured, she peered round at Jez Cooper's chalet. 'Who's that?'

'Who's who?' I replied.

Glancing back at Jez's chalet, I saw an aubergine coloured pickup parked nearby. I returned to my seat. 'He is permitted to have friends, you know.'

She was not happy with that, but after a while of staring pensively at the truck, she returned her attention to me, but still brought the conversation back to Jez Cooper, or 'That Biker', as she called him. I had to admit I had met him, and relayed the conversation with him about Derek Swann.

'What will you do?' she asked.

'Eh?'

'Well, I mean – if this chap Swann is the sort of man who would stitch up a business partner like that, you don't want to work with him, do you?'

Inwardly, I sighed. This was the perennial difficulty. It's hard to explain to people that, when you are paying alimony, have an expensive flat to run, a Morgan which needs woodworm treatment, and an income which is largely based on paintings of cats, turning down money is not something that appeals.

I tried to explain.

'It's not as if I am certain Cooper is right. After all, many businesses fail. Sometimes because the directors fall out, or just basic incompetence on their part. With someone like Cooper, maybe it was his own fault that his business collapsed? I only have his word, after all. And Swann struck me as a decent sort. I can't afford to throw up a good commission just because of unsubstantiated allegations.'

'No, I can see that. I wouldn't give up a newspaper article for no reason if I thought I could get a hundred quid for it,' she said musingly. 'But you do have the other problem. That biker and the boy this morning. I don't know, but they certainly looked hugger-mugger, didn't they? Do you think we were right? Maybe our madcap biker is actually dealing in drugs and the boy is his runner?'

She sat back with a look of satisfaction on her face. 'You mark my words, that boy is already out at the school gates flogging pills or powders to the little brats of the town. I've heard about these situations, you know. A novelist has to do a lot of research, especially when writing about crime. You take that man on his bike. He can ride about the area with impunity, taking orders for his drugs, and then head off to London for a brief jaunt, and be back in a few hours to pass over the drugs and take the money. Simple scam, really,' she said, looking wistful.

'There is no evidence to suggest he's doing anything of the sort,' I said.

'Nonsense! Meeting that boy was suspicious in its own right, and then you only have to look at him.'

'Would you write a story based on him on flaky grounds like that? He could sue you,' I said. It was a relief for me as a painter that my work would rarely lead to problems. Some clients, admittedly, would complain and demand a refund if they weren't happy with my work, but at least there wasn't the risk of being sued for all my worldly possessions.

She screwed up her face quizzically. 'Well, I might take a little care before writing it up,' she admitted. 'I'd have to change the location, his name, what he looked like, and all that sort of thing before any editor would accept it. Of course, if he were dead, it would be fine. In America it's possible to be sued for defamation, under their rules, even when the person libelled is dead, so I understand. At least here in Blighty we only have to worry about the living demanding compensation.'

I was intrigued. 'So do you often use actual events in your stories?'

'Oh, yes. I mean,' she poured more wine into both our glasses, 'I don't go about looking for actual crimes and think, "Oh, golly, I have to use that." After all, there will always be other members of the family to think about, and they might get offended if I were writing about their son or daughter as victims in a novel. You know, putting my words into their mouths and so on. I wouldn't want to think of someone doing that to me, were I to have a child killed. However, I can't deny that sometimes there is a particularly gruesome murder, and a part of me will be crying out to use it. Because that is my job. I am here to look at death and make it understandable. And give people closure. Horrible word, I know, but one aspect of crime stories is that they impose logic and justice on an unjust world. I think we provide a useful service in that manner. What are you doing?'

I had picked up my pencil and a sketchpad.

'I was just thinking I could—'

'Well, you can stop thinking that right now,' she said sternly. 'I am here to enjoy a quiet snifter with you, not to become your latest artistic conquest!'

I set the pad aside and settled back in my chair. It was a shame, because she was eminently paintable. Her vivacity and enthusiasm shone through every pore, and I would have dearly loved to get her on paper. However, just now, I was into my third glass of wine, and the bottle was already sadly depleted. My sketching skills would be tested to their limits were I to try to paint her in this condition. Regretfully I decided I would have to wait for another opportunity to persuade her.

When she left, the pickup had gone. What of it? Jez had entertained a visitor – that was all.

THREE

There are mornings, and then again there are mornings. You know what I mean. Some days you wake up and the sun is shining. It's not even six o'clock, but you feel wide awake and keen to get on with things. The birds are singing, and all is right with the world. God is in his heaven and all that.

However, although that morning was bright and clear, and the birds were making a racket in the trees by the chalet, it was one of those other mornings.

It wasn't the wine. Megan had helped me finish a second bottle, but after that I had ruthlessly booted her out before making my way to a fish and chip van which had appeared down near the reception area. With a slab of rapidly congealing cod slathered in crisp batter, accompanied by a pile of chips that looked as though they could have been used to fill gaps in one of the local drystone walls, all reeking of the vinegar I had liberally splashed over them, I had returned to my chalet.

I guess it must have been about nine o'clock when I sat down to eat, and I was a pig. When I was young my parents taught me the essential life skills, and one of them was 'waste not, want not'. Sadly, in today's world, that is more an invitation to Type 2 diabetes than an injunction not to throw away food, but that evening I was firmly on the side of the old aphorism. I stuffed myself stupid, drank a strong coffee and went to bed.

Thus it was the next morning I felt heavy, lethargic, unrested, and more than usually thick-headed and woolly.

I drank two glasses of water, made a strong coffee in my Aeropress and carried it out to the deck, where I gazed about me with the bitter resentment of a man who needed at least two more hours of sleep.

Determined to make the best of things, I had brought Swann's photos with me, and spent some little while glancing through them. With the main view he had indicated, I began to make a few sketches. Only roughs, trying to get the perspectives right, making some calculations with a ruler and marking up on a sheet of A4 where the main shapes stood. I'd have to view the place at different times to see how the shadows moved, and when would be the best time to paint to bring out the lines and shades of the walls. The time of day when painting a picture can have a dramatic impact on the overall effect.

While sitting there, I happened to look up. A rabbit had bounded out of the treeline bordering the park. All around the park were tall sycamores, oaks and beeches, which protected the grounds from onlookers and the wind. Underneath, for a depth of twenty to fifty feet, was a tangle of thick undergrowth. One section, where the trees covered an area at least a hundred feet deep, there was a pathway cut in through the greenery where people could take their dogs and children in for adventure trails. I liked that path – the air in beneath the trees was thick with the scent of wild garlic.

In among this verdure there must have been a lot of rabbit warrens, from the amount of droppings I'd seen all around. At least it meant the grass was cropped reasonably well without the need for too many petrol mowers.

It wasn't the rabbit that caught my attention today, but the boy from yesterday. He was standing down at the exit from the park, staring up at the chalets with . . . what? Perhaps it was my imagination, based on my own feelings, but I reckoned he hadn't improved since the day before. He looked like a teenager who's just been told he can't go out to a party because he's still grounded after the last time. You know the sort of look: glowering at the injustice of it all, scowling at the world. I could almost hear him saying, 'It's so *unfair*!'

He stood there, glaring about him as though daring anyone to challenge him, but then he took a step forward, grimaced, took a step backwards, turned to face the exit as though about to flee, and then turned back again, indecision written all over his face.

No, this was no mask of bitterness: this was partly fear, partly embarrassment, perhaps, and reluctance.

My suspicions about Jez Cooper and his business grew. This lad looked full of self-loathing. Perhaps he had been blackmailed into working for Cooper? Although I had tried to defend Cooper while talking to Megan last night, there was no denying that there was something odd about him. For one thing, he looked like an extra from a particularly low-budget film, which wasn't necessarily a criminal offence, but did make him stand out. Why would a drug dealer want to be so obvious? They would try to conceal themselves in the masses, surely. Yet this man was making his presence as obvious as possible.

Of course, I had seen nothing about him to suggest that he might be dealing in drugs. There was only the fact that he had a youth turn up at his chalet early in the morning – and his admission that he had spent a fair amount of time in Thailand, which was itself indicative. I've known various people who went there, and it wasn't generally for the water sports – unless they were looking for some more exotic sexual adventures. From my admittedly not extensive research, by which I mean an occasional flick through *The Guardian*'s pages, Thailand was noted for drugs and tourists seeking alternative realities in the sun with cheap beer.

The boy came to a decision. He launched himself up the hill with the determination of a last soldier in a platoon running at the enemy. Except he wasn't running, but striding. I watched him approach, and smiled a 'Good morning' to him.

If I had hoped to engage him in conversation, I was to be disappointed. He threw me a grim nod, but said nothing and continued up the hill. When I leaned back to get a glimpse of his destination, I saw that Jez was standing at the rail of his own deck, just like yesterday. As I watched, the youth stopped near the chalet and the two stared at each other without speaking. Then Jez nodded, turned around and walked in through his French window. The boy stood a moment longer, and then made his way to the chalet's door. He disappeared inside, and I relaxed in my seat.

There was something going on between those two, and I was sure it was something underhand.

That impression was not helped by the sudden shouting in the chalet, and the appearance of the boy in the doorway. He leaped down the stairs, turned and shouted, 'Just leave us all alone!' before stalking away down the road.

And Jez Cooper stood once more at the rail of his deck with his reflective sunglasses glinting in the sun.

* * *

I was about to pack up and leave the chalet to meet Derek Swann at his house, when there was a brisk knock at my door.

'Oh, hi,' I said.

Jez Cooper pushed the door wide and stood in the little corridor. 'You seem very interested in me and my business.'

'Eh?' This was a different Jez. He seemed keen to pick a fight.

'Yesterday and today you have been keeping your eyes on me and my visitor. Why would that be, I wonder? Maybe you've been paid to watch me? Has Derek said something? Or do you just happen to be a busybody who is interested in other people's business?'

'Who would pay me to—'

'Why are you watching me?'

'I'm not – at least, not on purpose. I'm just interested in people. It goes with being an artist.'

'Well, in future, keep your eyes on your paintings and not on me,' he growled.

It was only then, I swear, that I noticed the size of his hands. He may have been dressed to look like a low-rent Rambo, with the muscles of a Pekinese, but it occurred to me, looking at him, that he was wiry. I may have underestimated him. His muscles may not have been as pumped as Sly Stallone's, but now I looked at him, I realized his hands were oversized. I have to confess that being a significantly lighter person, the way that his hands kept clenching was oddly hypnotic. I could almost feel his fist crashing into my head. He had mentioned the day before that he had learned Muay Thai. I vaguely recalled hearing that discussed as some form of martial art and, looking at his wiry frame, I suddenly felt quite sure that tangling with him would be painful.

That, apparently, was that. He nodded at me in a sort of significant manner, turned and walked out, leaving me with my sense of resentment at the world in general redoubled.

'What the sodding hell was that all about?' I asked the world. The world didn't reply.

The house was even better in the flesh.

I gazed up at it from the migmog after drawing to a halt. It was not one of those enormous manors that loom over the land-scape like medieval castles, all grey stone and threatening little windows as though they're scowling. This was built as a family home, with pleasant, warm stone that almost glowed. The windows were obviously designed to let in a lot of light, and the whole frontage gave the impression of smiling down at me welcomingly. By the time I had extricated myself from the Morgan, Derek Swann was at the top of the short flight of steps leading up to his front door.

'Nick, good to see you again. Come on in, come in!' he said.

I left my artists' materials behind and followed him. The entrance had double doors. 'Handy for the removals firm,' I said.

'Eh? Oh! Yes, it'll make it easier to get everything out,' he said. We were standing in a large oblong reception hall. In front of us, a broad staircase led upstairs to a halfway landing, where they bifurcated, one branch heading left and the other . . . you guessed it. The stairs were carpeted in red, while the hall's floor was a glorious oak parquet set in a herringbone pattern with a gorgeous reddish patterned rug at the bottom of the first step.

He saw my gaze and grinned. 'Don't step on that with dirty shoes,' he said. 'It's genuine Isfahan silk.'

He led me past doors to left and right, took me out behind the staircase to a short passage, and from there into a bright room which had no end wall, but instead gave out to a conservatory with views over the garden. Rattan furniture stood scattered about, the seats strewn with thick, comfortable-looking silk cushions. Derek Swann settled into one. A series of prints that looked Arabic were hanging on the walls, along with framed documents that had elegant, flowing writing from right to left. 'You've spent a lot of time in the Middle East?'

'A fair bit. They have as much need of decent software as any Western country. I'll tell you what, let's have some coffee first,' he said, and pressed a button on a little box standing on a small glass-covered rattan table. A few moments later a young woman appeared, and my respect for Derek Swann increased accordingly.

She was a slim brunette, with large, luminous eyes of a pale blue-grey I could have got lost in. When she smiled, she lit up the whole garden. Her hair was neatly plaited in two, and hung down either side of her face, framing the high cheekbones of a Greek goddess, and while her mouth was a little on the thin-lipped side, when she smiled it sent a bolt of electricity right to the places other smiles could never reach.

'This is Adela Grzenda,' he said. 'She is the housekeeper. If you need anything while you're working here, she'll get it for you. How do you take your coffee?'

It took a few moments for me to re-hinge my jaw, which had almost fallen to the floor, and to mutter something about a filter coffee with milk. With another laser-smile, she disappeared.

'She's been here with me for a couple of years now,' Derek said. 'A wonderful woman. Bright and keen, and very efficient. She not only looks after the house, she can take dictation and has a really good business sense.'

'Does she stay behind when the house gets sold?'

'That sounds extraordinarily sexist,' he said.

'Oh, I didn't mean . . . it's just the next owner, finding a housekeeper, someone reliable, I mean, um.'

'Still, I don't know what she'll do,' he admitted without enthusiasm. 'I have to say, I'd like to look after her, but it depends on who buys the place, doesn't it?'

All I could think at that moment was, if he had a brain in his head – or elsewhere in his anatomy – he would find a way to ensure that she remained with him when he travelled to his sun-drenched seaside home.

He waved at a thick seat and I sat. 'Have you had an opportunity to look through the photos?'

'I had a good look last night and this morning,' I said. A devil made me add, 'Until I received a threat from a man who seems to know you.'

'Really? Who would that be?' he said, and there was a pleasant, enquiring expression on his face, but it didn't touch his eyes. They were suddenly cool and measuring.

'A guy called Jerry Cooper.'

'Jerry? I don't . . . Oh, you mean Jez! Ah, yes, he was a sad case. He had a thriving little business, which was doing really well until 2014. I bought him out, and we had to let him go. Poor Jezza never got over it, I'm afraid.' His face took on an introspective look as he stared out over his pristine flat lawns, to the rosebeds beyond. 'He was quite broken by it all. Jez was one of those guys who could not accept that fate is like that.

Sometimes, in business, you have to accept that you've basically failed. Your idea wasn't compelling enough for the market, your sales approach was not successful, or maybe your ability to control finances was flawed. These things happen. But the main thing is, to pick yourself up again, and try a different idea. Too many folks out there think that when they fail it's all someone else's fault, that they've been taken for a fool, or they've been betrayed. I'm afraid Jezza falls into that category. He just couldn't accept that his idea was overdue and the competition had beaten him to it. Then, when I was in discussions with him, it was clear that he was not going to break out of his old business practices.'

'What were they?'

As I asked, Adela reappeared. She moved with the lissom grace of a ballet dancer, and we were both silent as she approached, set down a tray on a low table, and poured two cups of coffee from a silver pot. Then, to my immense regret, she smiled, backed away two paces, turned and left us to it.

'His business practices? Oh, mostly they involved working flat out every morning, and then taking the afternoons off. He and his team would go to a local pub at lunchtime, and stay there all afternoon. To his credit he always picked up the tab, but that was no help when two of his lads got into a crash. One of them was killed on the spot, but the other was badly injured. You know how they define these things now? They call them "Life-changing injuries". What a bloody foul description. The boy was only twenty-four, and now he's in a wheelchair with a broken back. He'll never recover, and nor will his wife. They were both pissed after playing silly games in the pub with Jez, and I hold him responsible for their injuries. But to him, it was all the fault of other people.'

'I got the impression he blames you for a lot of his bad luck.'

'Yes, well, as I said, he's one of those guys who cannot accept his own responsibilities. He alone was the architect of his firm's failure, and his marriage.'

'He's married?'

'He *was*, yes. I think the drinking got to her. Especially after the crash. She felt terrible about that. After all, a small company is like a family. You soon find that you are fully engaged with the employees, just as if they were your own children. He lost the company, and then his wife as well. They were estranged, and then she got the big C. Cancer. It was a terrible disaster for him. But that doesn't mean he has the right to start blaming other people. It was all his own making.'

'It was you he blamed, then?'

'He took a pretty extreme attitude towards me, yes. I didn't want a loud confrontation yesterday, which is why I left when he turned up on that bloody bike of his. Now, enough of him. Let's talk about the best angle to paint the house.'

The rest of the day was spent happily ambling around the grounds before deciding that my first impression was perfectly right, and then setting up my easel and paintbox with the best view of the place.

I have a small, lightweight chair which I carry with me when I'm painting, and I set this up and sat back, staring at the view.

There are several things to take into account. I've already mentioned the sun, but there are other aspects, such as, how large should the house be? Did I want the building to dominate the entire canvas, or should it take up, say, the bottom left section, maybe a sixth to a quarter of the available space? That way, it gives an impression of how the building sits in the landscape, gives a feel for the relationship between the house and its gardens. Then again, how much of the sky should be visible? Should I sketch in the trees and line of the lawns, the flower beds, rockery and pergolas to bring the viewer's attention back to the building itself, or even reinvent the grounds to make them more artistically attractive?

In the end, I decided to delay actually putting brush to paper, and instead took up my softest pencil, a 6B, and sketched out some alternatives, testing how to position the house, how to fill in the background and gardens, and then using the lead to create contrast and give the picture more balance in terms of tone.

'How are you doing?'

I tried to spring to my feet, but it's hard to spring from a camping chair – that could break the frame – so instead I carefully rolled myself upright and gave Adela a smile. The one she gave in return was dazzling.

'I – um – well, you can see what I've been doing,' I said, holding out my sketchbook.

She took it and studied the four outlines, flicking through some of the other pictures.

'Which do you like best?' I asked.

'They are all very good. You have a good eye for the view,' she said critically, holding the pictures at arm's length and peering at the house. Like that, I really wished I had another sketchbook so I could draw her. With her arms held out, her shoulders were arched backwards, and there was a beautiful curve that ran down to her buttocks. She was all smooth, gentle arcs and bows.

Don't judge me. I'm a ruddy artist. It goes with my job. And if you were there, you'd have been entranced too.

'Thank you,' I managed. My voice was not quite a squeak.

She passed the book back. 'How long will it take to paint?'

'Oh, only a day or two. But I hope to stay and complete some more paintings while I can. It'll make it easier to justify the cost of the journey,' I wittered. Yes, I was babbling, but really, it was hard not to.

She smiled. 'I hope you enjoy your time here. There is much beautiful countryside.'

'You aren't English, are you?'

'No, I am Polish, but I have lived here years. I was at university.'

'Where was that?'

'Oxford,' she said. 'It is a lovely city. I enjoyed my time there.'

'Yes. Dreaming spires and all that.'

She looked slightly confused, but smiled anyway, bless her. 'Yes, well, it was less spires and more field and laboratory work for me. I studied archaeology, in particular bone fragments.'

'And now you're a housekeeper?'

'Derek is very generous. He allows me much time off. I enjoy festivals, and he lets me go whenever I want. Glastonbury, Boardmasters, Chippenham – I try to visit as many as I can.'

'You're keen on music, then.'

'Of course. I love all music. And I adore the countryside, too. I often walk about here with a metal detector and see what I can find. There is much to discover. This landscape is ancient, and there are fascinating finds all over. Look at the view here,' she said, waving a hand vaguely over the land before us. 'Is this not better than a laboratory?'

'I don't know. I haven't been in a lab since school,' I said truthfully. 'What will you do when Derek moves to Jamaica?'

'He has told you he is to sell this house and go? Well, when he does, I will stay here. I will hope to get a job with the new owner, perhaps. If not, well, I will find another job, I expect.'

'You have worked for him for long?'

'No, only a year. Thirteen months. He has been a kind man to work for, a man I can trust.'

She smiled, and again the countryside was flooded with sunlight. Or that's how it seemed to me. Soon she was gone, leaving only a faint odour of summer flowers on the air.

'Morris, get a grip,' I muttered to myself. 'She's half your age.'

Which was true, but that didn't stop me thinking about her for the rest of the day.

I was back at the chalet at four in the afternoon, pretty contented with my efforts. The sketches had been approved by Derek, and I had his agreement to the one I really preferred, which showed the house three-quarters on, with the building at the left third of the page, the front of the building facing to the right of the picture, and with a good broad sky. I had inserted a few darker trees behind the house to bring out the colours and tones of the stonework, but apart from that it was faithful to the actual location. Yes, I was happy.

'Hard at it?' Megan called. She was walking past with a towel over one arm, her hair still damp from a swim.

'Yes, it's been a successful day. The main themes are sorted, and I've got the preliminaries in outline.'

'That's good to hear.'

As she spoke there was a roaring in the main road passing the park, and I heard two engines, both decelerating through the gears. Then the bikes turned into the driveway and came past us. It was the same two bikes I'd seen on the day Jez Cooper turned up. These were much more appealing than Jez's easy rider: one was a BMW, from the little roundel on the tank, while the other was a Yamaha, I think from the badge. It looked weird, the fuel tank a great lump, rather like the lines of a hump-backed whale, curving down to the saddle and up again at the back. Panniers on both made them look clumsy and ungainly, but I've never been fond of motorbikes. I like the feeling of having metal all around me. I'm old-fashioned enough to rather dislike the thought of pain being inflicted on me.

The two bikes gently purred up the road past us, the BMW's rider turning to look at us as he passed by, not that we could see anything. His helmet was black, and the visor tinted to conceal his face. The man behind him had his helmet's visor up, and he grinned at us, and then they were gone.

'You'd never get me on one of those things,' Megan said. 'I was on one once, a long time ago, and my man of the time was driving. So as we pulled away from friends, I turned to wave goodbye just as he turned the throttle. With only one hand to hold on, I almost fell off the back of the thing. Terrified me! Just as his driving did, I suppose,' she added reflectively.

'You don't go for the feeling of danger you get on a bike, then?'

'If I want danger, I'll write something sarcastic about Brexit or Just Stop Oil. That always wins enough rude responses to more than justify my jaundiced view of the British and increase my sense of danger.'

I laughed. 'Fancy a cup of tea?'

'I'd prefer a glass of something warming.'

'Wine or whisky?'

'That would make a good start,' she said affably.'

'I saw you had a visitor this morning,' she said a little later.

She had been to her own chalet to deposit her wet swimsuit and towel, and now she was sitting on my deck with a large glass of red wine and a slice of red Shropshire cheese.

'Yes, he dropped in just as I was going to go out,' I said.

'Just a social call, I suppose,' she said. There was a twinkle in her eye.

'Almost,' I said. 'I suppose I could tell you that he was keen to tell me all about the well dressing, or a little about the history of the area?'

'You could, darling, and I'd call you a foul excrescence and hopeless liar.'

I chuckled. 'All right, then! He came to warn me about watching him. He seemed to believe I was keeping a close eye on him.'

'And on the boy, I suppose?'

'Oh, I suppose so.'

'Did you hear them shouting at each other?'

'Yes, and I saw the lad run from the chalet, too.'

'It means I was right,' she said eagerly. 'He is involved in something illegal.'

'Oh, there's nothing to say that . . .'

'Why else would he come and threaten you like that? No, it's obvious that he's a bad 'un. Well, the thing now is—'

'No, not me.'

'You mean you won't help?'

'There was something that struck me about him this morning,' I said. 'It was the size of his hands. Have you looked at them? The size of his fists, I mean. His hands are like . . . I don't know, like hams or something—'

'Not terribly imaginative, darling.'

'I'm not a bleeding writer, am I? You supply the metaphor, if you like.'

'Oh, no, I wouldn't want to criticize. The world is full of enough critics as it is!' she chuckled. She had a fruity laugh that was utterly infectious, and I couldn't help but grin.

'Another bottle bites the dust,' she said contemplatively. 'I think I know what you need, old fruit – a vodka and tonic.'

'No, seriously, I don't think that would be a good—'

'Nonsense. I'll go fetch the makings. Prepare two glasses. Do you have ice?'

I can always sleep. Once, I had to sleep in a spooky house in Greenwood, South Carolina, which was being used as a collection point for dolls of all sorts. There is something strange about sleeping in a room with fifteen or more pairs of eyes watching you from the top of cupboards and chests of drawers. Have you seen Chucky? But I still slept.

On the way there, I was held up at Atlanta, because there was snow on the runways. It was not a common problem for the airport, so it was shut down, and I was forced to wait in the terminal overnight, with no food or drink, since no one could drive to the airport to run the concessions. I pulled some chairs together and slept.

Then again, I was once on a journey to Spain, and was forced to wait in Paris Nord for twelve hours. And yes, I settled on the floor by a pillar, and I slept – much to the irritation of my companion.

I can sleep on the ground, on chairs, even on rattling, ancient trains and planes. I have done. Usually, it takes a loud detonation or a hand shaking my shoulder to stir me, or – on one appalling occasion – a dog's cold, wet nose in an unguarded armpit (that was not a pleasant wakening). That night, however, I was brought to wakefulness in an instant.

There was no reason for it. I lay on my back listening to the nightly noises. An owl hooted, and there was a brief squeaking, which I assumed was some poor small creature being converted into a gourmet meal by a cat or stoat, but apart from them there was nothing that struck me as a cause for my waking up.

You know how it is. Sometimes I can roll over, close my eyes, and soon I'll drift off. Others, I just know that I'm buggered, and I may as well get up, make a cup of tea, read for a little, and perhaps in an hour or two I'll be able to sneak back into bed and get another few hours of sleep.

I glanced at my watch. The luminous dial has all but ceased to function, it's so old now, but I could just about make out the hour hand at about three, and the minute hand at five to the hour. Ugh. There was no reason for me to be awake. I closed my eyes and tried to settle myself, ignoring that rising sense of the inevitability of not getting more sleep. Instead, I found myself thinking of the previous evening.

Megan had returned, as promised, with a pair of bottles, and poured me a generous helping of vodka, adding a splash of tonic. 'Don't want to drown it, darling,' she said, before pouring a measure for herself and sitting.

It was the beginning of a raucous evening, and she had a substantial fund of rude stories with which she regaled me, every so often looking up the hill towards Jez Cooper's chalet. After she had poured a third large helping, I was feeling quite amiable and well-adjusted to the world, and when she suddenly frowned,

I was tempted to chuckle at her. 'What, seen another county lines dealer?'

'No, but there are two men accosting your friend,' she said.

I lumbered to my feet and made my way to the handrail of the decking. She was right: there were two men at the chalet's door, and one had his hand on the door handle. He opened it quietly, pushed the door open, and was about to stroll inside, when something caught my attention.

The two men were at the side of the chalet, where there was a short flight of steps leading to a small standing area outside the door itself. While the two had approached his front door, I saw Cooper slip over the rail of his decking and fall noiselessly to the ground behind them. In three steps he had covered the distance between himself and the second man, and kicked behind the man's knees. He crumpled with a gurgle of shock, and then Cooper was on the steps, grabbing the hand of the first man and yanking, hard. Unbalanced, the man was forced to tumble from the landing area, straight on top of his companion, who gave another gurgle, and then the topmost man tried to clamber to his feet, but Cooper was already there, and slapped him hard across the mouth.

'If I see you trying to break into my shed again, you'll get hurt. Now, *fuck* off!'

The two rose to their feet, exchanged a glance, and walked down the hill towards me. As they came closer, I got a reasonable look at them in the light from the posts near the house. Both had the appearance of heavies. I have seen a few like that, big men with less large brains, who are used to bullying and getting their own way. The first had a broken nose that had been badly mended some time before, and the second had cauliflower ears from rugby. I've seen men get them from playing too often in a scrum. They both glowered at me, then were past and out through the exit. A short while later I heard an engine start up, rev and hurry away.

Up the road I saw that Cooper had returned to his deck. He was standing, leaning on it, and again he was staring at me. It was a look that left me feeling distinctly uncomfortable.

'Now do you believe me?' Megan said.

That was then. Now I was suddenly wide awake. I had heard

a noise, and this was no edible morsel attacked by stoat or owl. This was a light creaking from inside the kitchen-diner room. I pulled on a pair of pants, crossed to the door and listened. From there I could hear a slight shivering of friction as a drawer was pulled open, then quietly slid shut. There was a rustle of papers, and I realized someone was going through my sketchbooks.

I was incensed. Usually I would not risk my safety in confronting someone, but I am not used to having strangers wander about my house, rootling through my belongings. I put my hand on the door handle and shoved it wide, shouting, 'Oi! What the hell do you think you're doing? Who are you?'

There was a shadowy figure in the darkness, who had a mouth of bright light. Well, all right, thinking about it later, it was someone holding a torch in the mouth, but just at the time I was perhaps not fully awake, and yes, I had drunk a significant quantity of wine and vodka that night, so perhaps my judgement was not as clear as it should have been. In any case, the sight was enough to bring to mind various horror films I have seen, and I may well have given a bit of a squeak of terror before reality and common sense kicked in. 'Get out of my . . .' I began, and that was when I found that the courage flowing through me wasn't entirely justified. I repeat, I had been drinking a quantity of wine and vodka, and now I found my foot was not as agile as I would usually expect. I tried to take a step forward, but there was a bag beside the sofa to my left, and my foot caught it. However, my body was not immediately aware of this anchor, and continued in its forward motion. My brain realized when the foot remained at some distance behind the rest of my body when it should have been ready to hit the ground in front of me, and I can recall the urgent signal sent to that limb even as my body began to obey the laws of gravity. In other words, I tripped and fell over.

By the time I had disentangled my foot and risen to my feet once more, my visitor had fled through the door to the decking, over the rail and away.

I locked the door and put on the kettle.

A drink was what I needed, and for once I wanted one without alcohol.

FOUR

I woke up late, still sitting on the sofa where I had gone to sleep. Since it was a two-seater, and not the best quality, neither was my sleep. I had a crick in my back, a stiff neck, and an arm that had gone to sleep, and I lay there a while reviewing the previous night.

After making a pot of tea, I'd hunted through my belongings to see what, if anything, had been stolen. I assumed that someone engaged in what the Americans term excitingly a *home invasion* would have the ambition of finding something useful – money, credit cards, an iPad, phone or laptop. Sadly, with my enviable lack of fame, I didn't think it was likely that I had been woken by an enlightened art collector who wanted my sketches. No, far more likely, I felt, that this was merely an enterprising opportunist who had broken in to grab anything that was potentially available. And then to sell it on to make some money for drugs, no doubt. I've often read that most break-ins are committed by addicts seeking funding for their next fix.

So, yes, the thieving scrote must have come to rob me. However, my phone was charging by my bed; my iPad was in my sketching bag; my wallet was in my coat pocket, and all the cards were in it. In short, nothing appeared to be missing.

Now, with the sun shining brightly through the heavy drapery, I stirred myself, boiled the kettle and brewed a cup of coffee, drew the curtains, opened the door to the deck and went outside to sit in the sun.

One question plagued me: should I report the break-in? Nothing had been taken, and I hadn't been injured, if you didn't count the nasty bruise on the shin I'd sustained when I went over, so was there really anything much to report?

I somehow doubted that the police would be able to achieve anything, were they to come. Would they want to look for DNA (in a chalet which had a different family every few days, that would surely be an entirely pointless exercise)? Similarly, would they really want to look for fingerprints? With the vast number of guests who had been through this place, as well as the cleaners, was it likely to be effective use of a policeman's time?

In short, no. However, there was the possibility that someone else had been robbed. Maybe I had simply managed to thwart the robber by waking up and disturbing him. Others may not have been so lucky. Unless mine was the first chalet he had tried, someone else might have already have been robbed.

I would have to tell the park's management.

When I entered the reception area, it was the same woman who had greeted me on my arrival.

Her blue eyes grew behind her spectacle lenses as I explained what had happened, and I have to admit, I thought she might soon weep. She looked appalled, and as I said that perhaps others should be warned in case things had been stolen from their chalet while they slept, her bottom lip began to wobble a bit.

'Nothing like this has ever happened here before,' she said. And yes, it was a bit of a wail.

'It's not your fault. It was just some local thief who thought he'd found an opportunity,' I said, trying to calm her.

'This is terrible! If we've had a theft, people will leave. They won't want to come here if they're going to be robbed!'

'I'm sure no one will blame you,' I said, trying to be soothing, but conscious that my best efforts seemed to be falling on deaf ears.

'I'll have to speak to the manager,' she declared, and disappeared through a door behind her. I could hear her talking, and then a second voice joining in and speaking with a distinctly more authoritarian tone.

Soon the owner of this voice appeared at the desk. She was a smart woman in her fifties, with a round face, round spectacles and rather round figure. 'I understand you have been burgled,' she said.

'Yes, I found an intruder this morning. He woke me up.'

'Was anything taken?'

'Well, not as far as I can tell.'

'Good. How did the intruder enter?'

'I think through the French windows from the deck.'

'He broke the lock?'

'No.'

'He picked the lock?'

'No.'

I could sense myself shrinking like a salted slug.

'You mean you didn't lock the door?'

'Well, no, I suppose I didn't.'

'Was there any reason why you didn't take any sensible precautions?'

'I didn't expect to be burgled.'

'This may be the Peak District, but we do have our own quota of thieves,' she said rather primly. 'Perhaps in future you should ensure that you do lock the doors before you retire for the night. Now, perhaps you could show me the chalet?'

We walked back to my rooms, and I felt the embarrassment rise in a flush as she entered and gazed about her. Her eyes fixed firmly on the empty bottles of vodka and wine. She said nothing, but then again, she didn't really need to.

'This was the French window by which they entered, you think?'

'I think so. It's the one he left by.'

She opened it and took a good look at the lock from the outside. 'There are no scratches or damage to indicate it's been tampered with. It seems likely that it was just an opportunistic break-in, someone looking for a quick reward, your wallet or a phone.'

'That's what I thought.'

She nodded as if to herself, opened the door and entered the sitting area again. Once more her eyes fell upon the empty bottles. 'I could of course call the police,' she said. 'However, they do have a lot of crimes to investigate, and I am sure that their first thought will be to wonder whether you could have dreamt the matter. I mean, perhaps you fell asleep after watching a movie about a robbery, and woke up convinced you were in that situation yourself. Some people find that they have nightmares after eating cheese late at night; I know others can grow depressed if they drink too much gin.'

'You mean, was I pissed and did I dream up the whole affair,' I said, and I have to say, my tone was not affable. It was bloody annoyed, as was I. 'I fell over and have an almighty bruise on my shin!'

She looked at the vodka bottle again. 'That can happen even without a burglary.'

'So you think I was drunk?'

'No, of course not. However, the police may. They have a—'

'I know. A lot of crimes to investigate. So you don't intend to report this.'

'I will do, happily, if you want me to. However, I do not wish to expose other guests here to the fear that there is a burglar stalking the grounds, waiting to spring upon any unsuspecting holidaymakers. If you are quite sure of this burglary, I will of course report it. But I do wish for your absolute assurance that you are quite certain that a burglary happened and it is not possible that you dreamed it. As you say, nothing has been stolen, there are no signs of a break-in, and you were drinking last night.'

'Not to excess, though,' I said defensively, thinking of the size of Megan's measures. I had drunk a fair bit. But the memory of the break-in was so precise that I could not have dreamed it up in some sort of alcohol-fuelled hallucination. I mean to say, I've drunk more than that in my time, and not had more than an occasional nightmare. Much more commonly, I've just slept very well, very quickly.

I wasn't convinced, before speaking with her, that there was really a need to involve the police, but after the third mention of how much I'd been drinking, I submitted.

No, not to her, to the irritation. 'Just call the police. If you won't, I will.'

The two were the little and large of the local police force.

'Little' was a wiry sergeant of about thirty-five or so, a man slightly shorter than me, with the build of a welterweight. He had a face that looked rather pale, along with sandy hair, but there was no doubting he was the boss. The other was taller, carried a lot more weight around his middle, and looked perpetually anxious. He was a cadet in his early twenties, I guessed.

'So you found the burglar here?' the sergeant said, gazing about him in my sitting area.

'Yes.'

'And the receptionist says you had been drinking.'

'Yes. But not enough to make me dream it all,' I said somewhat forcefully. 'I occasionally drink a little. Last night I did, but that doesn't mean I imagined a thief in here.'

'No, sir, it doesn't,' he said, his tone offhand, as though whatever I might say was not as important as his impressions. 'Was anything moved around?'

'He had been leafing through my notebooks, I think.'

'Were they rearranged?'

'I . . .' That was not something I had thought about. 'Oh, yes! The main sketchbook had been in my bag there, but when I scared him off, it was here on the table. He had been looking through it when I woke up, and must have dropped it on to the table.'

'Have you looked inside? Could he have wanted to take it?' His voice indicated a slight suspicion. After all, he seemed to imply, *who would want to steal a painting by an unknown like you?*

'I doubt he'd have taken anything,' I said, and took out my A4 sketchbook. It was a spiral-bound Seawhite paint book with hard covers, and I began looking through it, only to stop with surprise. 'That's odd!'

'What?'

'There are some fragments of paper in the spirals, as though someone's torn out pages.'

'Let me see.' He leaned over my shoulder. In the spine were three pieces of paper, little irregular shapes of watercolour paper that had been torn from the book. 'Is there a missing picture?'

I went through it page by page. The sketches of Swann's house were all there, as were two of the church and the manor house at Tissington – but there was one missing. 'Yes, there was a picture here of earthworks next to the church, and others of some youngsters and cars and things.'

Who on earth, I wondered, would want to steal a picture of the pasture and the Morgan and other cars parked in front of it? Or my sketches of the four teens while they stood talking? For whatever reason, they were definitely gone.

* * *

Sergeant Hawley was as much in the dark as me. 'You are sure? Just the hill and some cars?'

'Yes, one had a couple of figures too, but they were outline sketches, really. I wanted them in to give the impression of the relative sizes of things, distance, context, that sort of stuff. It helps the viewer make sense of things, especially when it's all black and white. But why someone would want to steal a picture like that . . .'

'Well, it doesn't look like there's much for us to do. I'm afraid I can't justify calling out scenes of crime to investigate a sketch which, as you say, is worth very little. If it was a valuable painting . . .'

I bridled. 'It may not be worth—'

'I don't mean to insult you, sir, but if it's a rough sketch preliminary to making a painting, it's hardly valuable enough to justify a large investigation. And we do have a lot of other crimes to look at. However, I would recommend that you keep your doors locked in future.'

'I will.'

'It's a good area, this. Lovely landscape, beautiful views, good people. But we have our own little crime waves too.'

At last his companion spoke up. 'We have drug problems,' he said with pride. It was clearly good for a small, pastoral police force to have big-city issues.

'Really,' I said, thinking to myself that it was unlikely they would have anything like the inner-city issues where I lived.

'I'm afraid so,' Hawley said, giving his cadet a sharp look. 'We've had drug gangs here. Some threatening violence. Knives, guns, the lot. They're even recruiting children and getting them to carry weapons. We can't just search them all willy-nilly. You can imagine the grief we'd get from parents and do-gooders if we did that. I would if I could.'

'Because you . . .' I stopped. Look, my local police are the Met, and they've had a certain reputation, carefully built up over many years, of not strictly adhering to the law. In my area, stop and search was a very hot topic, and while I didn't want to suggest he enjoyed persecuting youngsters, well, men in positions of power often rather like the thought of using that power. And no, I'm not sexist. Women in uniform were responsible for a lot of hideous crimes in Nazi Germany and Soviet Russia.

'I don't want to get in the way of people who are just trying to enjoy themselves, even rowdy kids. But the simple fact is, kids are carrying weapons and the people getting killed are other kids. I want to stop that. If that means I have to stop and search them, I don't care what their race or background is, if it saves a life.'

I rather liked this dour-looking policeman. I thanked them both for coming, and they were about to leave when the cadet saw my Morgan. 'That yours?'

'Yes. My old migmog.'

'Did it take long to build?'

I smiled thinly while his sergeant rolled his eyes. 'No. It's not a kit car, it's built by Morgan in Malvern. They haven't seen a need to radically change the design since the Thirties. Only the engines, so that they work more efficiently.'

'Yeah?'

I fetched the key and went to turn over the engine. It always impresses people new to English technology and design. Of course the tech nowadays may be German, with BMW engines, but at least the design was all British. Apart from the three-wheeler, which I think came from a Californian company. Still, most of the cars are still British. Even mine – with its Ford engine.

Yes, all right. It still looks English, anyway.

Today my migmog lived up to expectation. I turned the key, and there came a muffled whine from under the bonnet. I tried again, and the engine shook and rumbled, but didn't fire. I stared at the car, perplexed.

'I think you need a mechanic,' Hawley said.

My first task was to call Derek Swann and let him know that I would have trouble getting to him soon. He wasn't there at the moment, I was told by Adela, who made my heart sing by giving me the impression that she was glad to hear from me. I let her know that I had a problem, and that I would be along to start work the next day.

Then I started calling mechanics who had been recommended

to me by the still grumpy manager at the reception. After several abortive attempts, I tracked down a guy who promised he would be up to see me before lunch, which I felt was probably a result.

Returning to the chalet, I made a coffee, and stared at my sketchbook. It really made no sense that someone would have stolen that group of roughs. Most were little better than tonal sketches, some outlines and then shading to show where the shadows and darker patches were. They showed the lines of the earthworks quite well, the layout of the road, the church, some other buildings, but that was pretty much all. The cars in the foreground, a few figures, and that was about it. What could have tempted someone to come and steal that, compared with the far better picture of Tissington Manor, for example? I did wonder whether they intended to steal other pictures as well, but if that was the case, why not merely pocket the entire sketchbook, and run off with it? There seemed no logic to it.

I was sitting on the deck when a grimy old Sierra appeared and drew to a halt beside the Morgan. A bald-headed man climbed out and plonked a narrow-brimmed fedora on his head. It was stained dark with oil, as were the creases on his face and fingers.

'Mr Morris?'

Joel Bradshaw was methodical and painstaking. He lifted the side panels to get to the engine and listened carefully while I turned the engine over, diving inside to play with spark plugs and wiring, I imagine, but soon he reappeared with a perturbed expression on his face. 'You made it up here without problems?'

'Yes, of course.'

'Well, I don't see how. You've lost the rotor arm.'

'Lost it?'

'It's not here now.'

'Oh, bollocks!'

'Yeah. Either you had it fall off on the way here, which is just about impossible, since the car would stop immediately, or someone's nicked it.'

'Who would bother to do that?'

He shrugged and pulled an e-cigarette from his pocket. 'Dunno. If you want, I can get one and fit it for you, but it'll take a couple

of days to get it. Not till Monday, earliest, I reckon.' He blew out
a long feather of smoke. Or steam – what do those things use?

'I need to be able to get around. Do you have a car I can
borrow?'

'Sorry. I'm only a small garage. I might be able to help,
though.'

And that is how I rediscovered the joys of cycling.

There was a time, once, when I was a proficient cyclist. I used
to get to school and back every day, pedalling ten miles or more,
and I was fit. I was also several decades younger, considerably
stronger, and more used to hills.

It is a surprising thing that, no matter where you go in the
country, there are hills. You tend not to notice generally, when
you are out and about in a car, but suddenly, when you pick up
two wheels and pedals, you become a great deal more aware of
every slight incline.

The bike Joel Bradshaw dropped off later was a pleasant-
looking racer. It had three big gears at the front, and seven more
at the back, and the frame was a more or less uniform red, with
the occasional speckles where paint had been chipped off. The
gears were changed by a paddle fixed behind the brake lever and
adjusted in the other direction by pushing the brake lever itself.
It took me a while to get used to that.

Some previous owner had enjoyed several horizontal journeys,
from the look of the scratches and scrapes on the handlebar tape
and brake levers. They were, at least, evenly balanced on both
sides. There was no one-sided aspect to this rider. And I assume
the owner must have ridden this standing and pedalling because
the seat had all the ergonomic comfort of an ice-skating blade. The
first time I tried sitting on it, I just knew this thing would be
agony to ride. I wasn't wrong.

It was almost lunchtime when the bike arrived, and I was keen
to get out and try it – mainly because I wanted to get away from
the chalet and do some work. When I glanced at a map, it was
clear that getting to Derek's house would be a little challenging
for me, in my current state of inexperience. Better, probably, to
attempt a shorter journey first. From the map, it looked like there
was the perfect route for me to try. It was called the Tissington

Trail, and led straight to the village. That, I thought, was ideal. Not only because it was only a four-mile journey so, even if the saddle gave me acute haemorrhoids, it wouldn't be impossible to walk home, perhaps having thrown the bike into a patch of stinging nettles first. The additional fact that the trail was itself a modified railway line, and therefore only a very shallow gradient, was appealing too.

I packed a few brushes, a paintbox and sketchbook into my messenger bag, carefully locked all the windows and doors, and left the building. My computer and iPad I installed in the bed under the sheets. I didn't think anyone would look there, even if they did break in. I couldn't lock them in the car – the only lockable place in my Morgan was the glove box, and that was too small for either of them.

To pick up the trail I had to cross over the road to Ashbourne, and then take a lane down into a valley, before climbing a hill. There was a bridge over the road here, and a footpath sign pointed hopefully over a field which seemed to be composed largely of mud. Working on the hope that the Tissington Trail would have a second ramp leading to it, I continued up the road – pushing the cycle because I had already experienced enough of that hill – up to the bridge. Here I found a second access to the trail. Pushing the bike through the gate, I found myself at the base of a steep series of steps. Picking up the bike, I clambered up, and at the top I took a swig of water from my watercolour emergency bottle, and then with a feeling of anxious trepidation, swung my leg over the saddle again.

I might not have been the most confident cyclist on the track that day, but after the first few wobbles, I began to get the feel again. It was one thing to ride the bike down the hill on the way to the trail, and another to steer it on a dirt track with largish stones appearing every few minutes. The thin tyres were clearly designed for roads, not this surface, and it had been a long time since I had dealt with the curved handlebars of a racing bike, but the further I went, the more comfortable I grew. After a mile, I was regaining confidence in my balance and ability; after the second, I was beginning to enjoy myself; after the third, I felt like both legs were ready to drop off at a moment's notice, and it was with huge relief that I found myself at the site of the old

Tissington railway station, which had been converted into a coach and car park, with its own small café and picnic tables for weary travellers like me.

I swung, with difficulty, my leg over the bike's saddle to dismount, almost collapsing as both legs took my body's weight. The saddle had caused a significant injury – I need not go into detail – and the overall effect of my short ride had been crippling. I hobbled to the café. A selection of protein bars and sandwiches were set out, and I was tempted, but there was a man with a petrol strimmer clearing weeds at the side of the trail. The noise was hardly conducive to a restful coffee.

I watched him for a few moments, struck with the impression that he was familiar. A heavy-set man with a broken nose and narrow, suspicious eyes. And then I realized it was one of the men who had tried to get into Jez Cooper's chalet and been beaten off.

Taking the road from the car park into Tissington itself, I pushed the bike thoughtfully to the café where I had met Derek Swann. There was a convenient bike rack, and after installing the thing, I asked the staff for a coffee. Thus armed, I returned outside and sat at a bench with my legs outstretched.

It was gloriously sunny, although the wind was still chill, and I was glad of the coffee while I took in the view.

The church was there, the trees, the wall, the pasture, the strange earthworks. All exactly as I had sketched them yesterday, and I racked my brains for some reason why anyone would want that specific sketch.

It was only while I was wondering this that a sudden idea came to me. When I woke up, I had thought it was footsteps that made me stir, but what if it was something else? My sketchbook had heavy-duty watercolour paper. When you tore that from its spine, it made a lot of noise. Maybe that was why I had woken, because the sketch had been loudly ripped from its moorings? But the thief was still there, still held a torch in his mouth, so surely he was still looking for something else – something more.

There was another picture he expected to find, perhaps?

I opened my sketchbook and peered at the pictures. There was nothing else that sprang to mind as having any relevance, no matter how hard I stared. In the end, I went to the café and ordered a light lunch of Derbyshire oatcake with ham and cheese, together with a second coffee. With these promised shortly, I returned to my table and idly took up a pencil to sketch.

The hill before me was still plain as anything, and the idea that someone would have stolen those pictures was ridiculous. Why would someone want them?

And then it struck me that there were other things. Cars, the kids in front of the pickup, other vehicles parked nearby – but again, who could give a damn about those?

I had a reasonable afternoon. Yes, the legs ached, but not as badly as I had expected, and after making some more sketches of farmyards, cottages, the manor house and a few other select scenes that might work as cards, I picked up my belongings and strode down to the bike where I'd left it padlocked in a rack.

Pulling my machine out of its rest, I swung my leg over the saddle – on the second attempt. I had forgotten how high a bike saddle is, and my legs had almost given up the ability to lift that high. It felt as if I'd dislocated my hip when I finally had my backside on the razor-saddle. I nearly fell off as I started pedalling, since I'd left the damn thing in the wrong gear, but soon I had stopped my hazardous wobbling, and was back on the Tissington Trail heading to the park.

Oddly, I recall thinking that I would be able to have a little rest when I reached the chalet.

I was wrong.

Megan came to me that evening when I was in the kitchen putting a little watercolour on to some of my sketches, and it was obvious that she was unhappy about something.

'Come on in and sit down,' I said when her face appeared in the open doorway. I was trying to keep a little fresh air in the chalet – it helps to dry the paint – and she walked straight into the living area and sat on one of the dining chairs. 'Do you want a wine? Or a gin?'

I offered them reluctantly, knowing that any such acceptance would be the precursor to another potentially heavy head in the morning, but to my surprise, and relief, she shook her head. 'No, but a cup of tea would be good.'

Bustling about with the kettle and teapot (yes, the chalet had a teapot, although no tea strainer), I gave her occasional glances. 'What is it? Something has upset you.'

'No, no. Not at all,' she said, but I could tell that wasn't true. There was something about her poise that spoke to me of distress kept carefully under control.

'Cheers,' she said when I passed her a mug. 'I need this.'

'Come on, so what's happened? Something's got to you.'

'I was out for a walk. You know, I took the path up the hill, with the old house in the background up there, and I had hardly got anywhere, when these two men on motorbikes came up the road past me. That boy, the one we saw yesterday morning, was in the road, and I swear they tried to hit him as they passed. You know the two we saw the other day? It was them. I recognized the bikes and their helmets. It's not as if they were trying to keep a low profile. They could have knocked him down. I had to shout to get him to notice them, and he jumped out of the way just in time.'

It was plain enough that she was more than convinced that they had deliberately tried to knock him down. I patted her hand. 'It must have been an accident. What on earth could have tempted them to try to knock him over? Maybe they were talking to each other, and not paying attention.'

'They had their visors down. How could they hear each other?' she said with some asperity.

'A lot of motorcyclists nowadays use walkie-talkies,' I said. 'I have a friend who does. He has a microphone and headset inside his helmet, and he and his wife can hear each other perfectly. Perhaps these two did and just weren't watching the road ahead.'

'Well, if that's the case, they should be reported. What if there was a child in the road?' she demanded. 'What then, eh? They ought to stick to the speed limit of the park, anyway, and I'm sure they were going faster than they should.'

'You may be right,' I said. I eyed her doubtfully. It seemed more than a little preposterous that someone would try to run someone over for no reason, but then again I had no idea why someone would have anything against the lad. He struck me as a perfectly normal, teenage boy. Would that make him a target for some kind of biker nutcase who had a violent grudge against boys in hoodies? It didn't seem particularly likely.

If they had tried to hurt him, that was one thing. But I suspected she was imagining the danger, so going and reporting two innocent bikers who were unaware that they had given cause for concern might not be the best way to proceed.

'Look, let's finish our teas and go for a walk around the park,' I suggested. 'After all, this may have just been a mistake on their part, and the surprise of seeing him in the road would be more than enough to persuade them to be a lot more careful in future, I expect. What reason could these two have had to want to hurt him? Unless,' I chuckled, 'you were right and the lad is the son of an international arms dealer, and these two are professional hitmen sent by Putin to punish him. Not that they're successful at being professional, of course!'

I laughed again, but my laughter died when I looked at her. She was not joining me, and I was left wondering whether she did have a point.

But this was England. Better, it was bucolic England, in the peaceful Peak District. Who on earth would know how to hire a hitman – or even want to? Maybe in Manchester or Leeds, but here? No, it was nonsense.

'Come on!' I said. 'I think we both need a walk.'

The sun was going down as we left my chalet, and walking up the hill was delightful in the cool of the approaching twilight. The chalets were all turning on their inside lights, and as we walked up to the top of the hillside, the pillar-lamps that lit the roadway were flickering and starting to burst into life.

It was only a short walk to the chalet where the Hell's Angel and his Harley were staying, and it was a relief, for once, to see he was not there leaning on his rail, staring down at me. The expression of malevolence on his face that day when he had barged into my chalet and threatened me had made me really anxious, and I had no desire to see him tonight. Nor, I was sure, would Megan. The sight of his scowl might be enough to drive her screaming from the park in her present mood.

When a vehicle came into the park, I saw her shiver and stare round, alarm in her eyes. I was able to calm her and draw her from the roadway onto the grass at the side as a quiet hybrid car drove past, the tyres scrubbing at the tarmac. It had been almost impossible to hear, and I was surprised how she'd reacted. For me, her story had raised the possibility that she just hadn't heard the two bikes coming up behind her, and neither had the boy, particularly if he had been in the same mood as when I spoke to him at Tissington. I had felt that either could have missed two quiet bikes idling along within the park's speed limit – but seeing her reaction now I realized it was clearly not a valid hypothesis. If she could hear that hybrid, she would be unlikely to miss the sound of those two bikes.

Past 'Jez the felon's' place, we continued up the hill. At the top were three or four larger chalets, more properly holiday cottages for larger groups. Each would have had four bedrooms, I imagine, with decking that looked out over the whole park and beyond, towards the Tissington Trail.

'This is where the rich ones live,' I commented. 'Must be hard for the poor folk down below, like me.'

I said it with a snigger, but she threw me a look of such anxiety that my chuckling was stifled immediately. 'What is it?'

'I don't know. I just have this feeling . . . it's like a premonition . . .'

'Come on, Megan! There's nothing to be worried about here,' I said heartily. 'Just enjoy the walk. We'll soon circle all round the park and then get back to my chalet and open a bottle of half-decent red and have a laugh about it all.'

'Yes, I'm sure you're right, darling,' she said, but she still wore a haunted look.

We passed over the top of the hill and began to drop down again on the other road that led to the entrance and exit; it was then that I saw the bikes. They were parked near a small chalet just over the brow of the hill, both on side stands, as if parked deliberately, like some kind of military motorcade, where a sergeant major had measured the angle of the handlebars, the position of the front wheel, to make sure both were entirely parallel.

'There they are,' she said.

'Yes, but they need not be any concern to you now,' I said. 'They'll be inside drinking a more expensive bottle of wine than

you or me. They look like bankers on a holiday rather than our
drug dealer, don't they? Just think, they're probably discussing
the merits of a hundred-pound bottle of . . .' and there my imagination failed me. I had no idea what sort of wine would go for
that sort of price. If you haven't ever had the income to spend
that much on a bottle, you're hardly likely to look up the various
brands. In much the same way, I can recognize a Bentley from
the badge, but I've never had a need or desire to look up the
price of one, and whether it's fifty, a hundred, or two hundred
thousand is, to me as a man who'll never own one (or even sit
behind the wheel of one), supremely irrelevant.

'I expect you are right,' she said.

'Of course I am,' I said.

That was when I saw the rabbit bounding over the road ahead
of me. It seemed to be in a hurry, and must have been disturbed
by us.

'I wonder how big the rabbit warrens are here,' I said.

Megan shrugged, and since we were close to the treeline, we
turned to follow the rabbit without any further discussion. It was
a quieter part of the park, with a thick wood of some forty to fifty
yards depth, huddled in the darkness under the trees. We were
drawn there, as a friend would have said – but she's more than a
little 'fey', as some people say. The less kind say she's barking
mad, and will always warn of disasters to come because of the
alignment of the stars, or the spirits telling her of risks to life and
limb or something similar. She can see spirits and auras, she has
told me. Bully for her, I think. I'm happy to see the colours of
trees, grasses and bushes, without seeing a whole different spectrum
around every human being. Or rock, as she claims she can.

The grass was overwhelmed by little bushes, brambles and inva-
sive plants taking advantage of their position in no man's land. I
could smell wild garlic, a little pine resin, and a little gust of wind
startled some leaves. We were almost past it, when Megan stopped.

That was when she pointed and said, 'What's that?'

Sometimes, when I have been bored, one of my many work
displacement activities has involved wandering the streets
collecting empty beer and Coke cans, McDonald's cups, takeaway
cartons, crisp and chocolate bar wrappers, placing them into a

rubbish bag, and then searching for a convenient wheelie bin where I can shove them. Occasionally I've found almost entire wardrobes of clothing lying at the kerbside, and usually been quite grateful. After all, such a find will fill my moderate-sized bin liner and leave me with a feeling of satisfaction at a job well done, even if it does mean I have to return to work.

This wasn't the same. Partly, I think, because I recognized his clothes almost immediately. He hadn't changed since I saw him at Tissington, when he told me he wanted to know how to commit suicide. A light blue hoodie with that strange symbol on the back, like stylized wings that stretched out to either side. Yes, I recognized his clothes. I was just relieved that he lay face down. I didn't want to see his face. I should have realized he was serious when he mentioned suicide, and that hurt. I should have done something . . . spoken to him for longer, not just assumed he was speaking with teenage angst. At least whatever he had done to himself had not been destructive in the way that other suicides were. There was no shotgun to the mouth, no pistol to the brain, no . . . but I didn't want to think of that either. The main thing was, it looked like he had taken an overdose or something. There were no gushes of blood, no signs of violence that I could see. Just a body lying as though sleeping.

But his body was not composed in the way I'd have expected. After all, if someone takes a drug to commit suicide – and they're serious, and not just attempting a cry for help or something similar – I sort of assumed they would find a comfortable place to sit. Perhaps with a back to a tree, overlooking a pleasant view, say, or in a bed so that the last moments could be as relaxed as possible.

This lad was lying face down in brambles and weeds. Admittedly, he may well have taken the drug somewhere nearby, decided to walk in among the trees one last time, and collapsed as he went – but that looked odd. Surely if he had suddenly been taken with the pain of his heart stopping, you'd expect him to fall and thrash around a bit? And even in pain, he'd try to avoid stinging nettles? Or maybe I was just overthinking the scene as a means of distracting myself from the reality of the boy lying dead in front of me.

I dialled the emergency services.

* * *

'So you have seen him around here before, sir?'

My last experience of a police officer investigating a dead body, and a missing person, had involved a man who looked more like a skinheaded football hooligan from the 1970s than a representative of law and order. This was very different. No, this was no avuncular Morse. Instead this was a slim, fair-haired woman of perhaps thirty-two, with a serious but slightly fretful appearance to her, but she said she was a detective sergeant, so I guess she was pretty important.

She had appeared in an unmarked Ford Focus with a pale plain-clothes officer of about twenty-five, who looked like he could have been a mate of the trio at Tissington. I doubt he'd ever had to shave.

They climbed out of the car and gazed about them, while lights from three other police cars flashed and strobe-lit the park. Officers in uniform ambled about, apparently aimlessly, peering at the chalets and into the trees, like so many cadets out on the training course of 'How to Look Busy at a Crime Scene'. While they did so, people milled about, parents holding their children to them, gazing fearfully, while others stared with frank interest, like drivers rubber-necking on a motorway. One couple in particular I noticed stood a little apart. They were both men, both the right sort of build to fit inside leather riding gear, and both looking distinctly interested, while attempting to look completely uninterested at the same time. They failed in that endeavour.

'Yes, I told you. I saw him here at the park a couple of times, and I saw hin a couple of days ago as well, over at Tissington. He seemed deep in thought. Worried about something,' I said, somewhat incoherently. It has to be said, I was feeling more than a little frazzled by things. Yes, I know I've found another dead body or two in my time, but this was somehow different. The boy, whose name I now discovered was Richard Parrow, was too young, and in any case, it was deeply sad to know that he had announced his intention of committing suicide. I had refused to believe his assertion at the time, but now I could only assume that he had been in deadly earnest and had actually succeeded in his attempt. I should have remained with him and dissuaded him.

I said as much.

'So you believe he committed suicide?'

'That was what he said to me,' I admitted. I wasn't thinking too clearly still, but I saw little need to change my first impression, based on his words about suicide. Would you?

'I see.'

No offer of sympathy or anything, you'll notice. Only the cold, officious recognition of my statement as she scribbled in her notebook.

The other officers in uniform seemed more interested than her, and they kept glancing over at me curiously. I think it's fair to say that this was the first death they had encountered for some time, from the way that they all kept eagerly walking about and telling spectators to disperse, or at least to move back behind a notional line that might have spread along the line of the grass. Someone had been sent to get some tape to seal off the area, but it seemed that no one had thought to bring it with the first cars.

Yes, from the look of the officers, this was all far more excitement than they had enjoyed in a long time.

'Sorry?' I said.

'I asked whether you knew him to talk to before?'

'No, not at all. I've seen him here, and I spoke to him a couple of days ago, only because he looked so miserable. I thought I was being . . .'

'And did you see him with anyone at other times?'

I had a flashback to the hall of my chalet and those fists. 'Um . . . well, yes. Tuesday I saw him with a girl and two boys in Tissington – that's when I spoke to him – but they didn't look like they were giving him any sort of trouble. Rather the opposite, really. He looked downcast when he met them, and perhaps they were giving him support,' I said, my voice trailing off as I recalled the scene. I would have grabbed my sketchbook to show her, had it been closer to hand.

'And?'

'Here,' looking up at the next chalet above mine on the opposite side of the road. 'A man called Jez Cooper, who rides a Harley-Davidson, seems to know the boy. Richard Parrow, I mean. The boy came here a couple of times. He looked really troubled and reluctant to go inside, but then he did, and . . .

well, that's about it, really. Except the other day I saw them talk at Tissington, too.' I explained about seeing them while I was talking to Derek.

'So you got the feeling Mr Cooper knew Parrow?'

'It certainly looked like it,' I said. 'Look, I'm really worn out after all this. Can I go now? I'm just really . . . well, it feels like I let the boy down badly, not staying with him when he told me he wanted to die. It's so . . . I feel guilty.'

She tilted her head just a little and gave me a long, considering look as though assessing my actual vulnerability. 'Yes, I suppose so,' she said at last. 'But don't knock yourself down. It's not your fault the lad's dead. If he did kill himself, it's likely a mental illness you couldn't have spotted, or something he'd done, or someone else had done to him, that tipped him over the edge.'

'You've seen this sort of thing before?'

She nodded, glancing over to the covered body. 'Yes. Young men and farmers. They're the two I normally find like this. It's sad.'

I spent that evening on my deck looking up through the trees at the scene. Blue lights still flashed, occasionally red ones too, and a tent had been erected over the corpse. A black van arrived, and I saw people climbing out, and then I saw the small figure of the detective sergeant walking through the trees to the Harley chalet. I wondered whether Cooper was there and, if he was, whether she would be safe with him. Perhaps I ought to go with her as protection, I wondered, briefly. If a police officer couldn't protect herself, I very much doubted that I would be any help to her.

Megan had already returned to her chalet. She had looked like a soldier after enduring a two-day bombardment: completely shattered and traumatized. It was as though every worst nightmare of hers had come at once, and I suspected that her vodka would get a hammering tonight.

As for me, I couldn't concentrate on anything. I just hoped that the Morgan would soon be back. I felt trapped. Ridiculous, I know, but once my migmog was back, parked outside the chalet, I would feel a great deal more comfortable.

It was a while later that the detective appeared at the railing to my deck. She peered up at me thoughtfully. I gestured towards the kitchen. 'Would you like a tea or coffee? I suppose it's been a long night for you already.'

She accepted, and soon she was sitting outside with me, her notepad on the table, a biro on top.

'He was so young,' I said. 'It's such a waste.'

'Yes,' she said. 'I never have got used to seeing young men like him dead. It's the same with any death, but somehow a man who was bright, who had only just become an adult, to see him come a cropper like this is very sad. His mother will be in a dreadful state.'

'Single parent?' I guessed.

'Yes. One brother and him. It'll be horribly hard for her to lose him.'

'I can't imagine.'

'You have children?'

'Yes. They're with their mother,' I said. I didn't want to go into details. Emily thirteen, Sam at ten, and both left a desert in my heart that I saw no need to share.

'I can't imagine what it must be like to lose a child,' she said, staring back at the scene.

For a moment it was easy to forget that she was a policewoman. At that moment, she was just a young woman; perhaps she was considering her future in the police and whether she could bear to witness more violence against others – or self-harm. She looked young and vulnerable. Although the idea of giving her a hug was appealing, it was also a real no-no. A man doesn't willingly try to comfort a police officer. Still, she did look introspective and somewhat dejected.

'I know I shouldn't offer an officer at work . . . but would you like a whisky?' I said.

She gave me one of those very straight looks. You know the sort – the type that makes a man think, *This time I have gone too far – here comes the slap.* But then she shook her head and opened up her notebook again, peering down at the page.

'You are sure about him saying he was contemplating suicide?'

'Yes. Not precisely which words he used, but it was to the effect of, if I wanted to help him, the best way was to help him die. Or the only way to help him was if I knew the best way to commit suicide. I suppose he meant he wanted to know which was the least painful method, or something.'

'Perhaps. But not necessarily for him.'

'What do you mean?'

She snapped the notebook shut and took a gulp of tea. 'It is like this . . . he didn't commit suicide.'

'Eh? I thought he'd taken an overdose or . . .'

I didn't want to add that I'd assumed it was the Harley-Davidson rider who had sold him the drugs.

'No, it doesn't look like a drug death. The forensic pathologist has already given an initial diagnosis.'

'Yes?'

She looked at me with those serious eyes of hers. 'He thinks Rick Parrow died because of a very fine-bladed weapon that stabbed him through the heart.'

I couldn't think of anything to say to that.

FIVE

The next morning flew by in a bit of a fog, I have to admit. I suppose I was in a bit of a state of shock. It's not every day you stumble over a dead boy in a stretch of woodland, after all, and to be convinced that I was in part responsible, if only by negligence, was horrible. Then again, after my discussions with the police detective, whose name was Ruth Daventry, I discovered, there was little comfort in learning that the poor lad had been stabbed. However, no one seemed to have seen him at the park that afternoon. I hesitated, and then had to tell the detective. I couldn't let it go. 'Have you spoken to Megan Lamplighter?'

'Not yet.'

I told her about the two bikers who allegedly tried to run him down, according to Megan. However, I did say I still favoured the thought that they were simply not paying attention – if Megan was right and they came close to him. In any case, I had not seen anything. However, it was in her hands now. And I added that Cooper had had an argument with Rick on Wednesday morning.

She had some rather pointed questions for me, based on that, but as I said, until I heard that he had been murdered, none of it seemed relevant. Basically, I was a bit shell-shocked by it all – it just didn't occur to me to mention the bikers or Jez while I was still processing his (as I thought) suicide.

Now all I could think of was the look on Rick's face as he walked away from me at Tissington, the hangdog look he had about him, the childish petulance and resentment as he stood talking to the other three kids. He had looked so young, so vulnerable, the more I thought about him.

Megan remained in her chalet all that morning, I imagine. I certainly didn't see her myself – not that I was expecting to. Rick Parrow's death had affected me, and I thought it was bound to affect her still more. Well, I am a bloke, and whether you believe in feminism or not (and yes, I do), I still believe that most women find encountering death more traumatic than the average bloke. Certainly a woman like Megan who, for all her loudness and the impression of invulnerability she tried to give off, was still a kind woman. Finding a corpse was definitely not something she would be used to.

I tried to keep myself busy, brewing coffee, making an effort to distract myself by reading the news on my phone, checking my emails, all the little things that usually keep the world at bay, but nothing would work. It was like having an ear worm that could not be shifted. No matter what I attempted to take my mind off things, the picture kept returning of that young boy. It was horrible to think of him dying there.

My phone rang. It was Adela Grzenda.

'Mr Morris? Are you on your way?'

In my shock of the previous day, I had completely forgotten that I was due at Derek Swann's that morning.

'I am so sorry,' I said, 'but I had no . . . I forgot, because I was, well, there was a body found here last night, and it's thrown me, I'm afraid. I will get over as soon as I can, if that's still all right.'

'A body? You mean you found a dead person?'

I nearly snapped something along the lines of, *I wouldn't give a toss if it was a dead fox or rabbit*, but managed to curb my tongue before I could give offence. 'Yes. A young lad. Someone stabbed him, it seems.'

'That is terrible. I will tell Mr Swann and say that you aren't comfortable coming today.'

'No, no. I'll still come and do my work. I need to, just to stop myself thinking about it too much,' I said hurriedly. And then I realized. 'But I'll have to find a taxi or something. I have a pushbike, as my car has had to go in for a service.'

'Oh . . . that is difficult. I would send a car for you, but Mr Swann is out with the car himself, and will not be returning until later today. But if you have a cycle, you could perhaps find your way here on the Tissington Trail? The house is very close to the old station at Parsley Hay. It is not too far, I think?'

'I'll have a look on the map, and get to you as soon as I can,' I promised.

When I closed the call, I checked on my phone. The Ordnance Survey app provided me with a map, and when I pinched the picture to find Parsley Hay, I saw that Adela was quite right. Derek's house was only a short distance from the old railway line. A quick study of the map also showed me that although the route to Parsley Hay was a good twelve or more miles from the chalet, the entire route, pretty much, was along the Tissington Trail again. Nice, flat and easy.

Or so I thought.

When I'm out sketching, I rarely take more than an A4 or A5 hardback book with 150 gsm paper, a palette full of paint, a bottle of water and selection of brushes – only three or four. I don't need more than that. Today, with a painting that would become at least A2 (about two feet by one and a half), I needed a plywood board larger than that, as well as my easel, in addition to the other items.

I stood staring at them sombrely. My rucksack would hold most things, and I could even bind the easel to it, but the board was a real problem. It wouldn't fit on the frame without getting in the way of the front wheel's turning, I thought. If I were to tie it to my back it would become a massive drag – it would act like a giant braking parachute – and I could hardly stick it under one arm while cycling. Eventually I decided I had no option but the first. Luckily I had plenty of paper-based masking tape, and succeeded in rigging it to the rear of the bike on the left, away from the cogs and chain, and hanging from the top bar of the cycle. I would have to ride with my left foot carefully held away from the board so it didn't get too scuffed. I looped masking tape over the bike's frame and down and under the board twice, just to make sure that it would hold, then more tape to hold it to the saddle's post. And on this ungainly looking contraption, I set off on my cautious way.

The ride was surprisingly easy, bearing in mind that I hadn't really used a bike in years, and this was going to be three times the distance I had managed the day before. Tissington was easy, and from there the landscape opened out into rolling hills and stone walls that reminded me of Dartmoor from last year. The sun shone, there were larks and other cheerful bird calls, and I was utterly content until I swallowed a maybug and, choking, had to pause to try to spit it out. Having a crash on a bike as overloaded as this would be embarrassing. However, soon I was on my way again, my water bottle somewhat diminished as a result of the accident.

Just beyond Parsley Hay, there was a strip of rough track that led down to the left of the cycle path, through a little copse of trees which was deliciously cool and smelled of pine needles. I checked the map on my phone, and reckoned this was the right place. At the end of this track should be Derek's house. When I expanded the view I could see the road which I had taken in the migmog the other day, which had a lane that looped around to the south of the building, giving way to the driveway. This track would join up with the drive itself.

I freewheeled down through the trees, enjoying the chance to ride without pedalling, and as I came out the other side of the trees, the track met with the driveway, and I dismounted, rather than pedal up the driveway to Derek's house.

'Good morning,' Adela called and gave me a smile to melt an ice cap.

You know, a lot of people are fascinated by artists and how we do our work. People aspire to doing similar work, which they assume is easy because there's no formal training.

In the case of painting, many people feel that they could pick up a pencil or brush and do a similar job, if only they could be bothered. Not many confess to an absolute inability to draw. One guy seriously told me once that, as soon as he had retired, he thought he might take up painting as a way of making a little pin-money.

That's the sort of sneering attitude I really hate. The *Oh, if I had a little spare time, I'd easily be better than you. But I won't give up my vastly better-paid job quite yet* sort of attitude. After several gins and wine, Megan told me that it's exactly the same for authors. People know they can talk, therefore they can write, and it's obviously easy to get ideas for a book. You only have to sit down and think for a bit – probably during the adverts from a favourite programme. It's that straightforward. No one ever stops to think about the years spent learning a trade, how to mix paints, how to get the correct consistency, how to mix the right proportions to make the colour you want, and then to know how dry the paper should be, how different paints will mix and shade, how . . .

No, I won't go into one. Let's just say that in reality, the work of an artist *is* pretty simple – once you have years of practice under your belt. You set up the easel, clamp the board to it, and stick the paper down with masking tape. Then fill your pot full of water (mine is a delightful, collapsible dog-water bowl that folds flat), and stand back, staring at the subject of choice.

I already had the preliminary sketch and a second that gave me the outline tones I wanted. That one was ideal, because it was later in the day, so today I would make the main sketch based on my initial planned composition, with the trees behind to bring the house forward, but looking at the house from the front left side. That way the driveway leads in from the bottom right of the picture, drawing the eye naturally towards the house. And with the judicious alteration of the drive itself, that would work still more strongly.

Changing the scene? You bet. If someone wants a precise replica of the actual view, they can go buy a camera.

So, standing, I started sketching in the outlines. Always best to start with big shapes, focusing on detail as the overall image works. Soon I had the house set out, and was moving on to the background, the trees behind, the lighter, smaller shrubs to the left, a hedge and stone wall on the right. It was all going brilliantly, until Adela materialized behind me and said, 'Very nice. I brought you a cup of tea.'

I jumped, the pencil lead snapped and dug in, and I was left staring glumly at the sort of scar that would be impossible to conceal. This sheet was ruined.

'Can't you erase that?' she asked.

'No. The paper is too damaged. It won't take the watercolour as I need it to,' I said. I didn't feel the need to point out that the score marked a section of an inch and a half of blue sky. I had been outlining some conifers when she startled me. If it had happened while I was sketching a building, I could have concealed it, possibly – but I doubt it. It was too deep.

'Oh, I am silly,' she said, apologizing profusely and very nicely.

I couldn't remain angry. Certainly, I would have to return to the chalet to fetch more paper. That would entail a round trip of twenty-five miles, and later another twelve and a half to get back for the night. Although the ride here had been not bad, riding that same distance another three times in one day was really impractical.

'I think I will have to return tomorrow,' I said, hoping that by then my Morgan would be back in my hands again.

'My stupidity has caused this extra trouble. I am sorry,' she said.

'It's all right. The proportions weren't perfect. Starting again will be good,' I lied.

'You are sure you can't just rub it out and paint over it?'

There was no point going over that again. Sometimes an accident could be a 'happy accident', which either became a benefit to the artist or at the least didn't harm the overall effect. A deep scar in the paper was different. With lighting above or below, this would cast its own shadow. Rather than explain, I asked, 'Where is Derek today? You said he was away till later.'

'He had to go to London. There was some kind of business there he had to deal with.'

'I suppose he often has to do that – drop everything and run back to London for meetings.'

'No, not often. Most of his business he can conduct from here over the phone or by computer. Much of the time he will hold long conversations on his phone while he walks over the grounds. He loves to walk.'

'I can see why, when he owns such a lovely place. The walks about here must be glorious.'

'For people who enjoy walking, this is a wonderful area.'

'You don't, then?'

She smiled. 'I have much to occupy me here. Although I would like to walk around the old ruins.'

I got her agreement to store the board and easel in the house, threw out my water, packed up my palette and brushes, and wobbled down the driveway on the bike.

It took little time to reach Parsley Hay, after pushing it all the way up the hill down which I had freewheeled so enthusiastically only a couple of hours before, from where I could look down over the copse that concealed the house from the railway line. I assumed that was why the trees were planted in the first place – to prevent ignorant tourists and travellers from peering down into the house from the railway line.

I mounted the cycle again, and set off on the rough surface towards Tissington. It was a bit of a scramble, and after some eight or so miles, I paused. Tissington's little café should be open. I gladly dismounted and pushed the bike up the little slope to the high street, intending to leave it in the bike racks outside the café again. Before I could, I was accosted by a friendly woman offering me a booklet describing the 'Tissington Well Dressing', and I bought a copy out of mild interest. After all, I had heard a little about it.

The little village was busy. People were wandering the main street, then up to the pond and up another road. Each held a well which had been decorated with scenes from the Bible, or similarly recognizable pictures. They were well done, and it was tempting to pause and look at all six, but I contented myself with the four in the main road and one just beyond.

It was while I was standing at the Hall Well and gazing at the depiction of a group of evil-looking monsters which was, so the legend declared, *The Fall of the Rebel Angels* – and very effective it was, too – when I saw two of the three friends of Richard Parrow's. The girl and the first boy. Seeing them, I wandered over, and was about to speak when the girl turned to exhale a long stream of smoke and saw me. 'Oh, you're back.'

Hardly the most welcoming comment I've ever heard, but at least it meant the ice was broken. 'Hallo again,' I said, trying to give a smile. 'How are you two?'

Her companion had a square jaw under reddish-brown hair and serious eyes nodded to me. He would one day be a good-looking man, if he kept off the sugary drinks. As it was, he was polite enough. 'We're doin' OK.'

'I was so sorry to hear about your friend,' I said. I didn't see the need to explain that I had been there when their friend's body was found.

'What friend?' she said.

'Rick Parrow. He was the lad found dead yesterday, wasn't he?'

'Yeah,' the lad said before she could deny knowing him, as I suspected she might. 'Poor bastard. They said he was found in a holiday park.'

'Yes,' I agreed. 'He wasn't happy, was he?'

'No,' the boy said.

'Come on, Al, shouldn't talk about things like that,' she said, and inhaled again. Steam streamed as she continued, 'Not when we don't know . . .'

She hesitated and looked at me, slyly, so I thought.

'You don't know who I am, you mean?' I said. 'Don't mind me. I'm not a cop or anything. But I spoke to Rick that day. He was sitting over there on a bench, and I happened to sit next to him, and we spoke a little. But when he got up to go, he was really upset about something, obviously, and I said could I help him, and he said something like, "Only if you know the best way to kill myself", and wandered off. I just wish I had spent a little more time with him to try to help, but he didn't seem the sort who'd appreciate me sticking my nose into his problems. And anyway, it never really occurred to me he might be serious.'

'Even when he said that to you?' The girl curled her lip – but whether that was the thought of my incompetence or the taste of the bubblegum smoke she kept inhaling, I wasn't sure.

'I wouldn't blame yourself,' the boy said. He had shoved both hands into his pockets, and now stood staring up the road, rather, so I fancied, in the direction of the place where they had met Rick that day.

'What was upsetting him so much, do you know? Was it family problems, or something at school, or—'

'Why? What is it to you?' the girl snapped, and now she rounded on me.

I have to admit, with her long hair and fair complexion, she was a very appealing sight, and anger gave her features a deliciously rosy flush. Standing in front of me with her shoulders parallel to mine, her anger was all too plain. I almost took a step back.

'He's dead, and even now on social, people are like getting at his family, putting up snarky, bitchy comments to upset his mum, and all the nosy wankers from miles around are like sitting outside her door, just to get a sight of her and his brother so they can laugh at them, right? And you're just like them, like some bleeding newspaper dick who wants to know all about him, well you can just *fuck off!* He wasn't a friend of yours, he was nothing to you, so leave us in peace!'

She turned and strode away up the road, leaving me somewhat deflated. After all, in books, when someone expresses interest in some poor fellow's death, generally everyone rallies round to explain every detail of the victim's life. I wasn't used to the idea of being berated for my interest in Rick.

'Al' did not hurry after her as I had expected, but remained at my side for a few moments. 'He was Penny's boyfriend for a while,' he said apologetically. 'She knows his mum and brother, and well, this has all come as a real shock to everyone who knew him.'

'He seemed a pleasant enough guy. I've seen him around a few times.'

'Yeah? Rick was a good bloke, I think. Nothing mean about him.'

'He had problems, though.'

'Who hasn't? His old man left his mum to it when he realized she had one up the spout, and Rick never knew him. He felt really bad, especially at school when people started calling him *bastard* and the like. Who wouldn't? He never really fitted in. It's only the last few months he's seemed at ease with himself.'

'People started accepting him?'

'No, I think he started accepting himself. He just grew up, you know?'

'I see. So what happened?'

'His dad came back.'

'His father?'

'Yeah. Suddenly arrived a few days ago, and wanted to get to know Rick again. Not that Rick wanted anything to do with him. Not really. But then . . . well, you can imagine, can't you? It was still his dad. He wanted to know about the family he came from.'

'Yes. I see,' I said. In my mind's eye, I was seeing the reluctant, resentful, bitter young man in front of my chalet, staring up at the biker's rooms, making as if to go to it, then turning to return home, before biting the bullet and striding off to the Harley-Davidson's rider. Megan and I had theorized he was a criminal of some sort, but what if he was just a remorseful father trying to get to know the boy he had sired twenty years before?

'Poor Rick. He never had a chance,' Al added.

'How do you mean?'

'You know: he was just getting his life together, realized he was as valuable as anyone else, and then here comes his old man and throws everything up in the air.'

'By wanting to meet him?'

'No, he told Rick he wanted to take him away. He said he had money, and he wanted to give Rick a future. All Rick had to do was leave his mother and never go back to her. I don't think he was very polite about Rick's mum. But she was the one who looked after Rick all his life when his dad pissed off before Rick was born – I mean, which one would you want to keep in touch with?'

'It's pretty clear cut, really,' I said.

'Yeah. But it unsettled Rick, you know? Like, this could be the one chance he had to go away and make something of his life, rather than staying here and serving behind a bar or working a farm or something. His dad said he had money, and he'd leave it to Rick if Rick went with him. But not if he kept in touch with his mum. Bleeding mad!'

'Yes.' And all the while the ideas were bubbling. A man who was rich, but dressed like an extra from *Easy Rider*. A man with no care for social niceties and behaved like a rebel – it did sound very much like Megan's initial assessment of him. A criminal from the underworld, perhaps, who had made a fortune from smuggling or dealing in drugs, and who was now desperate to catch up with his only son . . .

Except that didn't sound like any film I'd ever seen. In those, the drug dealers tended to be psychological types, sociopaths who really weren't bothered by anyone else. Still, someone brought up as a Brit must have some remnants of British culture left, I supposed. And what could be a stronger driver than the need for companionship, the need for seeing future generations take over what a man had built up? It did sound entirely logical.

'I'd better go,' Al said. 'Look, sorry about that. Don't mind Pen. She doesn't mean it. She's just sore at the world now.' He looked up after her, and there was an ineffable sadness in his eyes as he did so. When he spoke, his voice was quiet, hushed. 'You see, I think she only came to me to make him jealous. I think she always loved him, really. I was just second best.'

I dumped my bags on the floor and went to the bathroom. My legs were almost converted to jelly, but there was just a small amount of energy left in them, about enough to send me tottering into the kitchen for a coffee. I stood a moment staring at the kettle, debating between tea and coffee, and which would be the most refreshing just now, and in the absence of any decision, I instead grabbed the bottle of Famous Old Grouse and a small jug of water and took them with a glass to the table outside. Later, I would have a bath.

Pouring a largish measure – I was reminded of a friend who, when asked how much, responded 'Just two fingers,' and held up his index and little fingers with the large gap between – I heard a loud knock on my door. I walked to the side of the deck, which allowed me to peer over the railing at my door. There I saw an enraged-looking Jez Cooper glaring at my door.

I pulled my head back in quickly. Memories of our last conversation returned, along with the consideration that his fists had not apparently shrunk in the intervening days. I could, of course, go and let him in; that might involve a certain amount of risk to my personal health, which was unappealing. On the other hand, if I didn't, he might well walk round to the deck and see me here. If I went indoors, he would be bound to see me through the windows, and pulling curtains would only draw his attention to the fact I was inside.

Of course, there was also the minor, but relevant, detail that I had not locked the door. That is why, while I remained in the chair wondering what to do for the best, I was suddenly aware that the sun was being blocked by something.

It turned out to be a bear-like figure in old army fatigues and leather waistcoat.

I looked up at him with what I imagine was a rather sickly smile.

'Oh! Er . . . hello, Jez.'

'You bastard.'

There have been more congenial meetings and introductions, I imagine. As things stood, if you can believe it, he was standing in the double French windows, looming over me, his moustache quivering. I was quivering too, sitting back in my cheap, aluminium-framed chair. Both of us were rather too full of emotion to begin a sensible chat, it's fair to say.

However, as it became apparent that the first order of the day was not to pull my head off, I developed a certain – perhaps irrational – confidence that I might survive this engagement. That was only enhanced by the lack of venom in his voice. If he'd said, 'You *bastard*,' or shouted 'YOU BASTARD,' I would have been more alarmed. However, as it was, I pushed a chair in his direction and said, 'Jez, do you want a Scotch?'

He glanced at the table when I gestured towards the bottle and gave a curt nod.

'So,' I said once he was sitting down and had a fresh glass before him, his without water or ice, mine with fifty-fifty whisky and water, 'what can I do for you?'

'You couldn't stop getting in the way, could you? You kept on staring at Rick when he visited me. He saw you.'

'I'm sorry, but I could hardly miss him. He looked really anxious, and I was concerned for him,' I said. 'It was the same when I saw him Tuesday.'

'You saw him Tuesday?'

'Not here. I was in Tissington, and he was there with a few friends. I know – you were there too. Afterwards I had a brief chat with him while we were sitting on a bench.'

'What did you talk about?'

'I thought he looked unhappy about something, and I asked if there was something I could do to help. You know how boys are. Sometimes a stranger can get through to them more easily than someone they know really well. Like a parent.'

He shot me a look. 'You heard, then?'

'I saw a couple of his friends this morning, and they told me.'

'It shouldn't have happened. I only ever wanted a son, and I was so happy when he was born, but then *she* ran away and took him with her . . .'

'Eh? I was told that you left Rick's mother when she got pregnant.'

'What? No! We had used a surrogate. My wife Sue had cancer when she was young, and couldn't conceive, so when we married, it was always in our minds to adopt or something, but . . . well, I suppose I was selfish. I wanted to have a child with at least my genes in him, even if Sue's weren't. So we advertised and got through to an agency. The agent seemed really dedicated to her job – a young, blonde thing, eager to help couples in our situation. And she put us in touch with Helen. She seemed perfect.'

'She was willing to bear your child for you?'

'Yes. She made no bones about it. She was enthusiastic about helping childless couples, so she said. She was happy to work with us and bring Rick into the world. Although I'd planned to call him Charlie, after my dad. Helen didn't want that, apparently. All through her pregnancy, she kept calling him Rick. "My bump, Rick," she kept saying. Sue got quite upset about it, and whenever she met with Helen, she tried to tell her that the boy was going to be Charlie, but Helen didn't care. She made it clear that it was just for herself, and it would make it easier for her to give away the baby after it was born. We didn't think much of it at the time.'

'But then she decided to keep the baby.'

'She decided early on. We didn't realize she had no partner. She'd lied about a boyfriend who was keen to support her – in reality she didn't have anyone. She wanted a baby for herself, and we were just a useful couple who could provide her with the necessary sperm, and money.'

'I thought paying for a surrogate was illegal?'

'Of course it is. But we were desperate, and we wanted to make sure our boy had a good start in life, so we gave Helen four thousand for the pregnancy. But as soon as the baby was born, we learned Helen had changed her mind. She took our boy from us. Oh, I tried everything I could, spoke daily with the agent, who seemed genuinely upset for us. She tried everything she could to find Helen, but it was no use. We lost all contact from the day Rick was born. I've only now been able to get in touch properly. It's taken this long to find where they were living.'

'What of your wife? How was she?'

'She died. Another cancer six years ago. It was horrible, an aggressive one that took her away in a couple of weeks. You can't imagine . . .' He broke off and stared across the park with tears in his eyes. He dashed them away angrily. 'You can't imagine how hurt we both were to have lost all contact with our son. We had hoped to be able to enjoy our child, see him grow, watch as he went through all the usual milestones of a young life. Instead, all our dreams were snatched from us.'

'How was Rick when you spoke to him about all this?'

'He was confused. His mother had told him that I was some kind of monster, and he believed her, of course. Who wouldn't? It was his mother, and she'd been lying to him all his life. And then I appear and start telling him the truth, and he didn't know who was being honest with him, who was lying. Poor devil was confused. But yesterday he had been going to come here and tell me his decision. He hadn't told Helen I was in touch with him, I got him to promise to keep that quiet, but I went through the whole thing with him, showed him photos of Sue, told him I wanted him to be called Charles . . . not that he agreed, and I can see why. He's been Rick all his life, and changing that for my comfort was a step too far. And now it hardly matters. He's gone.'

His face folded like a sheet of crumpled paper, and his head bent as the misery overwhelmed him, his hands over his face. 'All this time, searching for him, and just as I find him, this happens! Poor Rick! Poor boy!'

I poured him another whisky and considered patting him on the back, but it would have been too intrusive. Instead I sat back and gazed out over the other chalets, towards where blue lights still flashed. When he had recovered himself, and taken a hefty belt of Scotch, I asked hesitantly whether he had gone to the police to explain all this.

'No. Not yet. I . . . I don't think I can face them. I only heard this morning that Rick was dead. I saw the lights and everything last night, but it didn't occur to me that it was him. I just thought it was some kid who'd had an accident or something.'

'I'm really sorry.'

'All those years wasted, then to find him and *this* to happen!'

This time I did pat him on the back. He seemed grateful.

He sobbed for a bit, and then stared over towards the woods, blinking hard, trying to regain his self-control.

'I have to ask,' I said hesitantly. 'I mean, feel free to tell me to . . . but the other day, I saw two guys trying to get into your chalet, and you dissuaded them somewhat, er . . .'

'Forcefully, eh? Yeah, well, while I was in Thailand, I learned the basics of Muay Thai, their own martial art. It was really useful, and I had a real knack for it.'

'Who were they?'

'I think they were messengers from Derek Swann, to try to persuade me to bugger off. He learned I was here. I have to admit, I'd no idea he was in this area. Ironic, eh? I come up here to reunite with my son, only to find that my old mate, Derek, who took me for more or less everything I had, was also up here.'

'How did you learn?'

'When I saw him with you. I had no idea before that. That was why I thought you could be watching me for him. Then, well, when the two thugs turned up, I couldn't see how you could have been involved.'

'You don't know the two who turned up?'

'No, but I know the sort. Dim, but eager for a few quid to get some beer or steroids. Mindless fools with muscle.'

'And you think Derek hired them to scare you off?'

'Yeah. It's the way he'd work. Try to put the frighteners on me to get me out of the way. But I was here to win Ricky back, and I wasn't going to let the git scare me off. Poor Rick! My poor boy!'

'You had a bit of a shouting match with him the other day.'

'Yeah, it was when I was trying to get him to agree to come with me. He said he didn't want to desert his mum and brother, and we . . . well, I said some things I really wish I hadn't.'

'Did he agree to go with you?'

'No. I gave him until yesterday, and he promised he would come talk to me. Oh, God! If he hadn't, he might still be alive!'

SIX

Megan's cabin was close by, and I was growing a little concerned for her next morning. After all, I had not seen her all the previous day, and it seemed out of character for her to hide away. Even after the shock of finding a corpse, she struck me as the sort of woman who would want to get out and about as soon as possible, to celebrate life and the fact that she was herself still alive and kicking. A woman who has been widowed twice and remained larger-than-life is not someone who will hide away when a relative stranger has died.

She wasn't on her chalet's deck area. There was no sign of her. Her car was still in the paved driveway, but the building's doors were shut. I knocked, but there was no answer. In the end I came to the conclusion that I could do little better than make my way to the police taped-off area, in case she was loitering in the hope of gleaning some sort of detail for a future book – I was pretty certain that she would be more likely to see the lad's death as an opportunity, rather than solely a terrible incident.

There were two officers manning the tent and taped barrier, one an officious-looking sergeant with a clipboard in his hand, the other an appallingly young-looking woman who reminded me more of my daughter Emily, now approaching fourteen, than a woman in her twenties

'Hallo, I'm looking for a friend: Megan Lamplighter,' I said to the sergeant. 'I don't suppose she's been here? A woman with dark hair and a lot of bangles and necklaces.'

'She's not been here so far as I know, sir.' He glanced over me, as if reassuring himself that I was not an immediate threat. 'But I have been busy with keeping the record here.'

'I saw someone rather like that,' said the young officer 'A long face, lots of jewellery. She was here for a while when the forensic team were getting ready, and I think she wandered off that way, towards the reception area.'

I thanked her and followed the path she had indicated. The reception area had a café with simple snacks that overlooked the swimming pool, so that bored parents could be occupied while their youngsters disported themselves. Among the eagerly nattering parents was a solitary figure with a blank face.

'Can I join you?'

'Thank God you're here, darling. I've been in need of company, but didn't want to disturb you in case you had had enough of the poor boy's death. It's all these ghouls can talk about,' she added, a hand waving to encompass the entire room. Since her voice was never particularly quiet, and she had an ability to project like an actress with a megaphone, several heads turned to stare, all of them with anger or frank consternation written on their faces. It was of no concern to Megan, who continued to speak in the same loud tone that could be easily heard six miles away in Ashbourne.

I fetched a coffee for myself, and sat opposite her with some trepidation, but luckily she had used up the invective aimed at the others in the room – or her mind had simply flitted off in another direction.

'You know, the police came to my chalet yesterday, first thing in the morning, as if I could have forgotten to mention something about finding the fellow. Poor devil! I wonder how he died. It didn't look like suicide to me. I saw a couple of them when I worked in A and E.'

I kept my voice low. 'They questioned me again that evening, too. The police detective came to my chalet to check on some details, and she told me that the boy had been stabbed to death with some sort of very thin weapon.'

'Really?' Her face went blank as she absorbed this, and then she nodded to herself and said musingly, 'I have heard of gangs who use bicycle spokes, sharpened, to stab their victims. Apparently, it's very difficult for the average forensic pathologist to see the wound. Sometimes they might miss the wound entirely and assume it's a natural death, I suppose. And a slim wire like that would be easy to conceal.'

'Perhaps,' I said.

'Which ties in with the idea of him being a crook, darling. Perhaps he was a county lines supplier? His gang disliked him, found out he was keeping back some of the profits, and made an example of him? Or maybe it was a rival gang that discovered he was edging in on their turf. I'll have to think about this.'

'I think it's more likely he was killed for some other reason. There is nothing to suggest he was involved in the drug trade,' I said sternly. 'You could be spreading complete nonsense.'

'Yes, I know. But I write crime: it's how my mind works,' she said, and this was almost apologetic. 'I do feel sorry for the boy, but it's like when I hear of someone killed on the radio or TV. Yes, I am appalled by the vicious brutality, but a little part of me will be thinking about it as a subject for a book as well. I can't help it.'

I nodded, and we finished our drinks quietly, listening to the hubbub all around us. It was comforting, to hear the normal, everyday sounds of parents and children, but all the while I couldn't help but recall Jez Cooper's face. To have found his son after so many years, only to lose him again in a matter of days, must have been devastating. Surely the last thing he would want to hear was that his son was some kind of underworld kingpin and had died for that.

And that was when I decided, I think. Until that moment I had been moved along with the tide of the event, but now I had a focus: I would see if I could find out more about Rick, and who could have wanted to have him killed.

The first thing I would expect the police to do would be to look close to home for a killer. When a spouse was found murdered, invariably the first suspect would be the surviving spouse. Perhaps in Rick's case it could be his brother, or someone else who decided to kill him? His friend who was jealous of his girlfriend's continued lust for Rick, perhaps? But the poor devil didn't seem the murdering type. Yes: an artist making a quick assessment like that. OK, just call me a fool and be done with it. I still say he didn't seem like a murderer.

If Rick had been going to leave his mother and go to stay in touch, or live with, Jez, might she have become so incensed that she decided if she couldn't keep Rick, she wouldn't let Jez have him? There were some twisted, weird people in the world, and this was a classic form of abusive relationship – but a mother killing her own child? She only raised him because she wanted him, and wasn't prepared to give him up. It didn't seem logical that she'd plan to kill him, no matter what the incentive – but then again, I was looking at it from a nice, safe, liberal-minded background. I had no way of telling what sort of woman she was, nor what she was capable of.

It was hard to see Jez suffering as he obviously was. If possible, I wanted to help Jez and find out what I could, if only to put his mind at rest regarding his boy. Not that I'd be particularly competent, of course. I'm a painter, not a detective.

However, as an artist I did have some advantages. With that thought, I made my way back to the chalet and took out my paints.

It was ridiculously easy to find out where Rick had lived. Facebook gave me a bunch of photos of him, one of which had his house in the background of a photo. It had the house's number visible, and it was a short and rather easy task to find it on Google Maps. So far, so easy.

I packed my new painting into my bag, and went down to the pushbike. Soon I was on my way back to the Tissington Trail, where I turned left towards Ashbourne. It was a nice, easy, downhill ride the whole way, and apart from one horrendous down-and-up section, which once would have been covered by a railway bridge that had collapsed or been removed, it was pleasant.

At the far end there was a lengthy tunnel and, emerging at the far side, I found myself near the supermarket. I decided to return there later for more food, but there was little point in carrying it around with me while I was speaking to Rick's mother.

Hers was a plain terraced house in a bland row that could have done with a fresh coat of paint. It was interesting in the way that such rows are: each with different replacement windows, a variety of doors, some with tiled roofs, others with slates, and most with paved-over gardens to give some off-road parking. Almost all had weeds growing through. If I was generous I would say that the houses all had that appearance of genteel dilapidation, like a once-valuable car that had given up to rust.

It was easy to see which house was Helen's. A small crowd

of reptiles was huddled at the gate, watched by a stern police officer who stood with his hands thrust into the armholes of his stab vest. When I approached the entrance to the house, he suddenly held out a hand in the familiar, 'Oi! Stop there!' display of a palm out towards me, as though directing traffic.

'I'm here to see Helen,' I said.

'She doesn't want visitors. Are you a friend or family?'

'I was a friend of Rick's. I've a painting of him, and thought it might be something she'd like,' I said, and pulled out the painting I had quickly made. If I say so myself, it was a very good likeness. I am, generally, a better landscape artist than portrait painter, but I was quite proud of this. I think I'd caught his rebelliousness, but also the glimmer of humour too (it was from a couple of his selfies on Facebook).

He looked at me – then the picture – doubtfully. 'You certainly have him there,' he said with grudging respect. 'All right. You can knock, but if she tells you to sod off, just go. I don't want her harassed.'

'Fair enough,' I said, and went to the door, with him escorting me a pace or two behind.

There was a bell, and I pressed it. It had a camera fitted into it, and I leered at it in what I hoped was a reassuring smile. A crackly voice that was clearly male said, 'Who are you?'

I moved slightly to one side in the hope that the policeman would be in the frame. 'My name is Nick. I'm an artist, and I met Rick a few times this week and painted him. I don't know, but I hoped it might be a little memento for you. I don't want any money,' I said, and held up the painting to the camera.

There was a click, and then I saw through the frosted glass of the door that a figure was approaching. Soon a young lad of probably fourteen or fifteen opened the door. He glanced at the reporters and curled his lip. 'Come on in.'

'Who're you?' he said, as soon as he'd closed the door behind me.

'Nick Morris. I'm an artist. I'm painting a place just up the road, and I was in Tissington and met Rick a couple of times,' I said with, I think it's fair to say, a certain lack of candour. 'But because I thought he wasn't very happy, I made this picture of him. I thought it might be good for you or his mum to have . . .'

'Why'd you think we'd want some crap like that?' he snapped dismissively, and I guessed immediately that coming here was a bad idea.

'I see. Well, I wanted to just try to . . . Look, I'll leave you in peace. Really sorry about your loss,' I said, backing towards the door. But before I could reach it, a waft of Helen's favourite scent flowed towards me, and then she was there in the doorway to the kitchen. Her favourite scent? Marlboro. She stood in a pink, fluffy dressing gown, smoking like a First World War soldier waiting for the whistle, sucking hard until the hot coals were almost at the filter.

'Come here,' she said in a voice husky from tobacco and vodka. 'Let me see.'

I carefully stepped around her son and made my way after her into a kitchen that was dingy. A small window gave out on to a small concreted yard with not a single plant. There was nothing green out there, apart from a plastic bag moving gently with the breeze.

She sat at a small, square table, stubbed out her cigarette and gazed up at me with eyes that were filled with unshed tears. Somehow those wet eyes affected me more than Jez's tears the evening before.

'Look, I'm terribly sorry for your loss.'

'It's OK. Just got to get used to it,' she said, pulling another cigarette from a pack on the table. The cover depicted something very grey and dark, and I didn't want to look too closely. I'm a bit squeamish about what might be going on internally, and the thought that her organs were that colour was . . . well, pretty unappealing. 'You said to Jon you had something you wanted to give us?'

I put my hand to my bag reluctantly. My use of a fabrication to gain entry to her house just when she was at her most vulnerable made me feel guilty as hell. Still, I couldn't stop now. I handed it over silently.

She said nothing, but put her cigarette down in the ashtray and held it in both hands, staring. Her face was greyish, with a slight yellow tint, as if she was anaemic. Pale mousy hair hung in rat-tails about her face, which was thin and worn. She must have been nearer fifty than forty, I guessed, but from her appearance she could have been even older.

'It's very good,' she whispered, caressing the picture with her fingertips as though stroking his face. She went quiet then, and I saw her bottom lip tremble, before she suddenly lost all restraint and gave herself up to floods of tears.

Jon rushed in to her, and threw his arms around her. She patted his arm, eyes squeezed tight shut, while he glared at me. If there had been a kitchen knife available in that moment, I'd not have lasted long.

'Look, this was a mistake,' I said, rising. 'I don't want to bring you any more misery. I'll see myself out.'

'Sit down. Jon, put the kettle on, will you? You'll have a cup of tea, eh? Or coffee?'

I had a sudden vision of these options. A cup of grey liquid, no matter which I chose, but of all the abominations created by a food industry desperate to force processed muck down people's throats, the worst must be instant coffee. 'A cup of tea would be good,' I said quickly, and sat before I could show cowardice in the face of a mug.

'He was my first, poor Ricky.'

'Yes.'

She was still staring at my picture. 'You've got his naughty grin, there. He always looked cheeky. He knew when he was being bad, and he could be right wicked when he wanted. Always flew close to the wind, he did, but he never meant any harm. And he cared about people. Especially those he loved – family, friends, the like. He wouldn't hurt anyone.'

'He seemed a lovely guy,' I said.

'He was . . . he *was*!' she wept again.

'Why don't you go and leave us alone!' Jon said, his arms about her again.

'Don't be rude, Jon. Make the tea,' she said, snuffling with a paper handkerchief over her nose.

'I just don't understand why this sort of thing happens,' I said. 'How can someone decide to take a weapon to a lad like Rick?'

'You hear about this happening, but it's always other families. I never thought it would happen to Ricky,' she said, touching the painting again.

Jon deposited a cup of dark brown liquid that looked like it could strip the enamel from my teeth. I smiled up at him, trying to conceal my horror. 'Thanks!'

'He never did the things other boys did,' she continued. 'He didn't do drugs. I know most of his friends did, but he didn't touch them. Just a bit of a drink when he had time, that's all.' She reached into the pocket of her dressing gown and pulled out a half-bottle of vodka, pouring a good slug into her tea. She hesitated, then offered it to me. When I shook my head, she restored it to her hiding place. 'The police, they just want to make out he was some sort of drug dealer, or gang member who got into a fight with boys from another gang. What, my Ricky? He was a bit naughty, like he'd maybe siphon petrol from someone's car, or something, but a gang? He wasn't in any gang, was he, Jon? He wouldn't do that.'

'Did he have any special people who had reason to want to hurt him?'

'Who'd want to hurt my Ricky?' she said, and then the misery hit her again and she started sobbing into the crook of her elbow. 'Why'd anyone want to hurt him?' she wailed.

'I'm terribly sorry, I really am,' I said.

'Everyone's *sorry*,' she said scornfully. 'That police detective, she said she's sorry. The WPC with her, she did too. They offered me some shrink to help me get over Ricky. What, some psychowhatsit is going to make me feel better? I told them to fuck off. Oh, sorry.'

'That's fine, Helen. I can only imagine what you're going through.'

'You really got his look there,' she said again, touching the picture. 'Oh, Ricky, Ricky . . .'

'Is his father around? I mean, he ought to know,' I said disingenuously.

'That bastard?' Jon spat.

'He's got a right to know, I suppose,' I said.

'No he hasn't,' Helen said. She cast a sharp look at Jon, I saw, and then peered down at the picture again. 'He deserted me when he knew I was pregnant. Jon's dad was different. He was a good man, but Ricky's, he was no good.'

'In what way?'

'He never had an interest in Ricky or me. He was one of those who take advantage and then run,' she spat. 'He didn't even accept paternity or help with the upkeep. Nothing.'

'He was a complete bastard,' Jon said with real venom.

'I'm really sorry to hear that. So you haven't heard from him in years, I suppose?'

'No. Not since Ricky was born. He never came back or kept in touch. Soon as he heard I was pregnant, he was off like a scalded cat.'

Soon afterwards I left.

If there was one thing I was absolutely convinced of, it was that Helen was truly distraught at the loss of her son. But equally high on my list of firm beliefs was that she was lying through her teeth about Jez. He was infinitely more convincing.

After retrieving my bike I made my way up the road into Ashbourne's town centre. A small coffee shop called The Tunnel stood at the far end of the main street and, judging by the elderly folk sitting on chairs in the sun outside, it served reasonably priced drinks. From the dog bowls, bedding and treats, the owners were keen on dogs, too. Since, as I've mentioned before, I have a growing aversion to cats, owing to the number of vicious monsters which have scarred me for life since I started painting moggies for their besotted owners, I have a liking for dogs that is growing.

There was one standoffish dog here, a large golden-coloured type with an intelligent, if supercilious, expression on his face. That changed to a look of mingled contempt and amusement when it took in the sight of me. He sat next to a couple who were nattering away about things in the town. I entered the café, ordered a flat white and a slice of carrot cake. I looked at the Bakewell tart, but the idea of all that sugar was not attractive.

Told to go and wait outside, I took my seat near the aloof dog, who gave me a condescending once-over, before returning to study the view. I did not rate as a threat or object of interest, clearly.

While I waited, I did what I usually do, and began to sketch the road. There was a lovely wooden bar over the road ahead, which proclaimed the Green Man and Black's Head Hotel, and all the buildings seemed to be ancient, probably Georgian, with little in the way of modernization. It made for an interesting study, with all the various rooflines and the uneven road surface.

'You an artist?' the man said. He was small, spry, with alert eyes that twinkled. His wife was a birdlike little creature with white hair and bright, intelligent eyes behind wire glasses. She was one of those people who seemed congenitally incapable of unhappiness. Her face wore a smile all the time I spoke to them.

'Yes. I'm down here to do a couple of landscapes,' I said, with a flash of guilt. I'd have to get back to Derek Swann's and start again. Ah, well, it was the weekend. Even painters need an occasional weekend off. 'Handsome dog. Some sort of Labrador?'

The dog turned to stare at me again. He had quite light-coloured eyes. They were still brown, but tending towards amber. And just now they registered disgust.

'No, he's a Ridgeback,' the man said with a laugh. 'Except he has no ridge. So he's a Ridgeless. The breeder was going to have him put down at birth, so we rescued him.'

My coffee arrived, along with the cake, and both were as good as I had hoped.

'You live here?' I asked.

'Yes. Man and boy, although Ethel here is a foreigner. She came from Derby.'

'I had to struggle to get all the way here,' she said.

'It's a pretty town,' I said. 'It seems so peaceful.'

'Ah, there are undercurrents even in a lovely place like this,' my new friends told me. He, 'Harry', was a retired plumber, and Ethel had been a nurse. Harry went on to tell me of a series of appalling crimes, from wing mirrors smashed, windscreen wipers snapped off, and even worse, soda syphon cartridges left lying in the road and at beauty spots.

'Terrible,' I said, thinking of the area where I lived in south London. I doubted that these two would be able to cope with the sight of the graffiti, rubbish, and rough sleepers. I forbore to mention that the soda syphon cartridges were more likely canisters of laughing gas. Since I used a soda syphon myself, I knew that the cartridges looked exactly the same.

'I suppose all towns have the same problems now,' I said. 'It doesn't matter where you live, the kids all have access to the internet and that gives them all sorts of ideas that aren't very good.'

'Especially the last kids through school. Covid has given us a lost generation.'

'How do you mean?'

'Many of them got out of the habit of school and learning. They started gaming and playing on computers all night. When I was in Derby Royal Infirmary back in the Eighties, we used to get some people turn up in A and E reeling drunk after too much cider or beer, and some could be very aggressive. Now it's less alcohol. When I see boys reeling in the streets, I am pretty sure it's not from booze.'

'They can get hold of drugs even here?'

'The sort of people selling them don't care who they sell to, do they? And they make a lot of money, so they can afford cars. I expect they just fill up their car's boot with whatever they have to sell and drive around. It's a bit like a courier company, isn't it? They have contract drivers, and I expect the drug dealers do too. It makes it easier for them to pay someone to drive here from London once a week and supply their local distributors. It's really very worrying.'

'Yes, it must be.' I thought about the trio I had seen at Tissington. At the time I had been sure the girl wanted to get away and find a hedge to drink a cider, but that was my guess as an old fart. More likely they were going to take a couple of pills, or perhaps puff on a nitrous oxide balloon.

Was it possible Rick was involved in that? The police told his mother that he might have been involved in drugs or in a gang, which was probably itself involved in drugs. Ricky, his mother said, was not, but what would she really know about such matters? Which mother knew what her young son got up to when he was away from the house? Boys will, as they say, be boys. And one aspect of growing up is to want to spend time with other boys of the same age, to test boundaries, to risk life and limb, and hang the consequences. After all, boys of Rick's age think they're going to live for ever.

I had a sudden thought. 'Where do you find these metal cylinders usually?'

Their dog gave me a long, hard stare. It was more effective than a police interrogation, but I wasn't going to crack.

I think Harry and Ethel were glad of the interruption to their daily routine of sitting and watching the world go by. After finishing

our drinks (the coffee was superb), they took me along Church
Street, then St John Street where the hotel stood, and beyond, to
the park. There was a memorial to the lost of two world wars at
the entrance, and then we were into a large recreation ground.

Harry and Ethel led the way along a pleasant pathway lined
with trees and shrubs to a bandstand, an octagonal building in
the middle of the park. It had been renovated not long ago, and
the timbers were all painted, although already graffiti was
covering every larger surface. I propped the bike against the wall
and walked inside, gazing about me. Harry pointed beneath the
bench seats to where there were a couple of metal canisters.

His wife called us back outside.

The dog was sniffing with a form of regal disdain at a bush,
and then turned to look at us as if disbelieving we had not already
realized what he had found. When I lifted the leaves of the bush,
underneath I saw a couple of flimsy cardboard boxes, with *Cream
Chargers* printed on the side. Beside them were twenty or more
canisters, and two balloons.

'I see,' I said.

'Yes, we've found them here quite often. The park is very good,
and the keeper tries to clean up every time, but it's every single
evening. These things just reappear daily. What can you do?'

Not much, obviously. I kicked at the pile, hearing their tinny
little clinking. Looking up, I saw a dark-haired boy, who I was
sure was Stan, the third of the trio I had met at Tissington, but
he looked quickly away from me and disappeared.

I left my friends there. I did think about patting the dog on
his head, but I got the distinct impression that he'd consider that
an intolerable intrusion, and kept my hand away.

Pushing my cycle, I wondered about that little collection of
cylinders. There was something, too, that struck me about Stan.
He looked furtive and more than a little desperate. It would be
really stupid, and I mean utterly moronic, for a drug dealer to
go somewhere that the police and all the locals knew was a place
where drugs were used.

At the road, I stopped. Then I very slowly and deliberately
turned the bike round.

I had seen a map at the entrance to the park, which showed a
car park at the other side of the gardens. If I cycled around the top

on Cockayne Avenue, I would soon come to it. I could leave the bike chained up there, somewhere, and return to the bandstand.

That's what I did. I had a suspicion that Stan was waiting there for someone to supply him with a fresh little canister. I left the bike carefully chained to a swing-gate, and made my way along the paths to the bandstand. There were several trees to hide me, and thank God I hadn't succumbed to the lure of Lycra with day-glo colours. In my, for me perfectly trendy, shorts in olive green, and somewhat worn (and paint-spattered) faded navy T-shirt, I could conceal myself without too much trouble. Not that I needed to worry.

The dealer was one of those who clearly assumed there was no risk of being observed, as he walked down the path from the town, nonchalantly turning as though to check he wasn't being followed. And then he walked up into the bandstand and stood there, hands in pockets, his face set in the usual teenage scowl that I had seen already that day.

Yup. It was Rick's brother, Jon.

I watched the transaction take place. Stan looking as guilty as only a boy raised on *Narcos* and *Breaking Bad* could. He was as subtle as a shark in a swimming pool. Honestly, if I was in central casting and looking for the obvious drug addict looking for a fix, I'd have rejected him on the basis he was so obvious.

Stan wandered up to the bandstand, and Jon went down the steps to meet him. The two exchanged money in folding plastic notes (yes, I hate the damn things), for a rattling box that chinked and clinked as the two walked away, Stan in considerably more of a hurry than Jon.

On a whim, I decided to follow Jon to see where he was going. He led me up to the main road again by the entrance to the park, where two other youngsters more his own age were waiting. He took some cash from them too, and they received a handful each of, I assume, cylinders. I couldn't really see from a distance.

From there, Jon continued back along Cockayne Avenue and, a short way along there, he stopped and walked to a large pickup truck with aubergine paintwork. It was rather a nice colour, I have to say, and it seemed familiar. I tried to get a good look at it, but the angle was all wrong for me to see inside since I was approaching from the back, annoyingly. I say annoyingly, because

Jon went up to the driver's window and leaned in. I saw him hand over something – money? – and in return he received a couple of boxes like the one Stan had taken.

There were cars parked between me and the truck, and I trotted forward to try to get the licence number, but as I approached, the truck pulled out and drew away. Parked cars blocked my view, and when there was a gap in the traffic, the truck was already too far away for me to see the plate.

However, I wasn't so far away that I couldn't grab Jon's shoulder.

'I think you want a cup of tea or coffee, Jon.'

'Get off me!'

'It's chat to me now, or I tell the police you're dealing drugs to the local kids and Stan,' I said conversationally.

His eyes retained the stubborn, bitter look. 'You try that and I'll be out in an hour. You think they give a shit? I'm too much paperwork for 'em.'

'But when I tell them about the pickup truck,' I said, and held up my phone, 'and give them these photos with the registration and everything and give them my evidence that I just saw you buying Nox from there, your supplier will be in shit. I don't think they'll like that, will they?'

There was a pleasant little coffee bar just along from the pub, and we walked there in a less than convivial silence. I ordered at the bar – he wanted an iced latte that stank of caramel and made my belly lurch in disgust, but I ordered it anyway – and sat with him.

'What's going on, Jon?'

'Nothing.'

'What did Ricky think of your drug dealing?'

He threw a harassed glance around to make sure that no one could overhear us. 'Don't!'

'What?'

'Don't talk about it in here, shithead!' he hissed.

'About your dealing? But you seemed so happy to be arrested just now.'

'Stop it! It wouldn't do Mum any good to have me nicked – not now,' he said, and at last there was an indication of remorse. His eyes seemed to film over slightly, and he started blinking profusely.

'Who was in the pickup, Jon?'

'I'm not telling,' he said resolutely. He held his chin higher as though emphasizing his determination.

'Why not?'

He shook his head.

'Tell me about it, Jon. How did you get into this? What did Ricky say?'

'He didn't like it. He said, like it was daft, that I'd get into trouble.' His eyes filled with tears. 'And then he gets killed!'

'Do you have any idea who'd do that to him?'

'Course not! Who'd want to hurt Ricky?'

'I don't know, but someone stabbed him with a sharp weapon. Someone really hated him, or feared him, perhaps.'

'No. Not Ricky. Why would anyone be scared of him?'

'That's what the police need to find out. So, tell me all you know, Jon. I don't like to think that a good guy like your brother can be murdered and the killers get away with it.'

'He didn't care about us. He was going to leave us.'

I shook my head. 'He told his dad he wouldn't leave home because he wanted to look after your mum. And you.'

'He never.'

'Yes, he did. So come on. He was loyal to you, Jon. And your mum.'

He looked away, past me, chewing at his lip. 'I don't know . . .'

'He was staying to look after you both. Don't you owe him something? *Anything* you know that could be useful. Anything at all.'

'Look, Mum used to be a druggie, and we had to help ourselves to get by when she went on a bender. We needed money for food when she was out of it. What else could we do? Sure, Ricky wanted out, but we had no choice. We started selling a few things, some vapes and then whiffies, but nothing bad.'

'Those things are bad enough. What happened, then?'

'Rick's dad – he turned up and tried to tell him to go away with him,' Jon said, and his eyes filled. 'He was going to leave us, I thought. He told me his dad said he'd give him a new life, with money, everything he wanted, and I didn't think there was any chance he'd want to stay here with us. He told me everything, but he didn't tell me he was going to say "no".'

'He maybe didn't know himself until the last minute,' I guessed.

'Do you know what he was supposed to be doing that last night, when he died?'

'I don't know. He was going out to see someone, but he never said who. Someone about his father, he said, that's all.'

As I walked back along St John Street to Cockayne Avenue and my bike, I could not help but wonder about what Jon had said. He was convincing when he said he didn't know who Rick was seeing that day, but what if Rick had seen something? Perhaps he saw a drug deal happen, or a drug gang member thought he had? Could he have been killed just because he saw something of that sort?

Later, back on the bike and near the Tissington Trail, another thought came to me, and this time I had to stop, gripping the handlebars while my mind flew over the possibilities.

Because if there was something of that nature going on, could it mean that Rick saw something at the holiday park itself? If he had seen something here in the town, it was hardly likely that he would have been chased for miles all the way to the wood at the edge of the park near his father's chalet. Surely, if he was going to be killed for seeing something, he died very soon after seeing it – whatever it was. The murderer wouldn't hang around and give him time to think about whether or not to tell the police. I had a belief that murder, when it was a matter of drug dealers falling out, was a crime committed in the heat of the moment. I had a vision of a badly inebriated drug dealer wobbling down a street demanding, 'You lookin' at me? You lookin' at *me*?' with a knife in his hand. Shades of *Taxi Driver*, I know, but it's the sort of thing that comes to my over-inflated mind every so often.

But I kept coming back to the main point: when Rick was killed, that must have been shortly after he witnessed something. Either that was in the park, or somewhere else, as I suspected, and then his body was dragged to that field and over the fence to be dumped.

Carrying a lad his size wouldn't be terribly easy. Maybe two men would be needed. The two who tried to warn Jez off? Or the bikers? Megan had seen them try to run him down, she said. It was enough to make me stop in the street and think really hard. I'd have to tell the detective. It wasn't much, but it might help.

Luckily I remembered that I had to visit the supermarket for some essentials, and soon I was back on the pushbike and at the

entrance of the long tunnel to the Tissington Trail, and gingerly
swung my leg over the saddle, wobbling alarmingly before I
caught the pedals and gained the necessary momentum to ride
in a straight line.

All the way back, I was thinking about the boy's body, how it
didn't look like a suicide. Because now I was pretty sure that
it didn't look like he'd been murdered there either.

I don't know, I'm a painter, not a forensic pathologist or CSI
expert – I've never even seen the programme – but I have studied
bodies. I've painted athletes, cricketers, cyclists, old people,
youngsters, and I've studied how they move and walk and so on.
I'm not certain, but if someone's heart is stabbed, I think they
die very quickly. Without blood pumping, a man can't stay alive,
stand or do anything much. As far as it goes, I would doubt he
would step three or four paces in amongst a bunch of weeds. It
just didn't seem *right*, if you know what I mean.

I dismounted at the collapsed bridge section, and continued
thinking furiously as I climbed the hill at the far side, remounting
and pedalling.

What if Rick wasn't killed there at the park? I had assumed
he had been killed there since Megan saw him. That led to some
interesting ideas, such as, why dump him in an area where he
was barely concealed, in a holiday park? To leave a message?
To warn someone? Who could be warned, though? The only
person I could think of was Jez. After all, everyone else in the
park was a stranger to the area, presumably, just like me. They
were holidaymakers, for the most part. That was the entire purpose
of the park.

Except for the two other bike riders, of course.

And with that my thoughts took a bit of a dive. Were they the
dealers who brought cylinders of gas for sale in the town? It
seemed unlikely, because surely they would have arrived, sold
their gas or drugs and immediately left. At least, that's what I
would have done. I wouldn't hang around in case of another
interested client. I'd dump the goods, take the money, and be
off. Besides, would the panniers on their bikes hold enough to
make the trip worthwhile? Surely they'd want a car, like the
pickup Jon had been to. Who had been driving that?

Who were those guys?

But before wondering about them, I wanted another look at the site where the body had been found.

And that was when I recalled the pickup outside Jez's chalet on the evening Megan came round with her bottle of wine. That had been aubergine, too, like the one Jon had got his cylinders from. There were surely not many pickups of that colour around here.

Whose was it?

OK, look, I know I'm not a police detective, forensic expert or even a scientist of any sort, but I do reckon that sometimes it can help to have a second pair of eyes on a problem.

I parked the bike at my chalet, but kept my messenger bag with me as I walked around the park to the blue and white police tape. There was still a young, rather nervous and spotty youth in uniform standing near the tape, clearly petrified that someone might approach too closely or ask him a difficult question. Apart from that, there were all the signs that an investigation had taken place. The tent was removed, I could see, and when I looked under the trees, it was clear that the weeds and shrubs were severely affected. Many had been cut back, and the soil underneath removed. I assumed it was in case they might find the weapon, or something that could offer a clue.

I don't know about you, but when I have seen TV programmes or films about crime scenes, I'm always fascinated by how the investigators can glean so much. I mean, knowing my luck, if I was to try to look into a crime, I'd probably fall at the first hurdle. 'Oh, it's the ring pull from a beer bottle,' and throw it away, whereas an experienced detective would pick it up, ideally by a pencil through the ring, and pronounce that, because this was from a tin of Harp Lager from the 1970s, the murderer was a collector of crap beer from the past.

Then again, maybe I'd be right, too.

The grass and shrubs were so devastated that any signs that the killer could have left behind would be long gone. However, there was one thing that immediately struck me: this was a quieter part of the park, admittedly, but even so, there were a lot of people around. Surely someone would have seen two men walking around the track here? And still more, if the two went in under the trees here, surely someone would have noticed if only one came out again? Had the police heard anything from witnesses about seeing Rick with someone else up here on the day he died?

Glancing about me, I realized not many of the chalets were full at this side of the park. Those that were had been arranged artfully to conceal each deck area from the next, so people weren't overlooked, but most decks looked away from these woods. It really was pretty secluded. A good place to commit murder or hide a body.

Someone could well have come from the entrance to the park and committed murder here, it was true. But why someone would want to do so was a different matter.

And why would Rick have come this way, in any case? It was the long way round for him. His father's chalet, if he was going there to visit Jez, was lower down the hill, and the route there would be a lot easier from reception going past me. This was taking more than three sides of a rectangle when he could have taken the shorter side. It made no sense.

The officer was watching me with increasing alarm. I smiled and nodded to him and walked back up the hill again. One thing about the park was that it was bounded on all sides by fields. I had a vague thought: was Rick walking about the park on that day? Perhaps he had been dumped here. Entering under the great trees at the top of the hill, I pushed my way through the thick undergrowth for some forty yards or so, and through to a fence. It was plain wire, no barbs included, and I grabbed a tree's limb and swung a leg over. It wasn't easy. The fence was higher than the saddle on my bike, but I eventually managed to retrieve my remaining leg and could look about me.

I was in a pasture, which had no cattle or sheep in it just now. It was a bright mass of buttercups, and it was glorious to stand there and feel the sun on my head. Thoughts of bodies and death melted away just a little. I walked down the edge of the field until I came level with the crime scene. The police tape had been wrapped around the fence here, and there was plenty of torn-up ground. I was gazing at it glumly, thinking no one would be able to make any sense of what might have happened, when I forced myself to be a little more positive.

My provisional hypothesis was that Rick had not died in the park. That meant he had been killed somewhere else, carried here, thrown over the fence, perhaps picked up again and placed where his body was later discovered. That meant someone would have been here in this field. I assumed at least two, because he may have been scrawny, but he was still tall, and I've heard that bodies make for an ungainly weight.

I hunkered down like a golfer eyeing his putt, and viewed the grasses. There was nothing much to see, at first, but I reckoned there was a kind of line, vague and indistinct, but possibly a series of footsteps. And then I felt a rising excitement. After all, a line could indicate where a flock of sheep had been wont to wander. It's what they're good at. But this led like a slightly wobbly arrow to a gate at the road. I carefully avoided standing on the mark, but walked a couple of yards to the right of it, following the route towards the gate, and it was there that I found it.

A bright metal tube, blue, with a lid that screwed on to the base, and which had a lip about it, and four puncture marks. I recognized this. I'd seen folks use them near the Bedford in Balham: this was a delivery system for nitrous oxide.

I suppose 'Thank you, Mr Morris' would have been a little much to hope for. After all, my finding the little delivery system meant the police had missed it. Oddly enough they didn't seem delighted by the discovery. Perhaps it was merely the fact that I had found something that they had missed, but I got the distinct impression from Detective Sergeant Ruth Daventry, when she crouched at the side of the little metal cylinder, that she was not best pleased.

'Have you touched it?'

'No, of course not! I've seen the TV,' I said.

'Did you walk near this line?' she said, pointing to the path I had seen trodden in the grass.

'No, you can see where I walked. It's at least two yards away,' I said.

'What made you come over here?'

'Well, it just occurred to me that it was odd the boy would have walked this side of the park. His father's cabin is over the other side. And I thought you'd have been searching for someone, if anyone had seen him with someone else around here. I just wondered whether he could have got there by a different route. And as soon as I saw this field, I thought "Bingo".'

'You do realize that interfering in a police investigation is a serious offence?'

'Come on! I'm not, am I? I'm helping you with your enquiries.'

'If you want to go down that road, I'll be happy to arrest you and take you back to the station,' she snapped.

'No! I mean it, I'm trying to help. I had an idea, checked it out, and this is the result.'

'Hmm.' She did not look or sound convinced. Beckoning her sidekick, and indicating he should avoid the route which could have been taken by the murderer, she waited until he was with us before telling me to repeat what I had told her.

I started again, with a sigh, and related the thoughts of how the body could have arrived there, and then my reasoning about this field, and stumbling across the nitrous oxide tube.

'It's possible that this was something to do with a drug deal that went wrong,' the detective sergeant said.

'That's what I thought,' I said. 'There are a lot of laughing gas users in Ashbourne, I guess.'

'No. Not yet. If I can stop it, there never will be,' she said firmly.

Her voice had a ring of determination that I rather liked.

'Right. Thank you for your help.' She stood.

'That's fine. What now?'

'Now? You go back to whatever you should be painting and you leave the investigation to the professionals. You don't want to come and help us with our enquiries in the station, do you?'

I would like to say that this was spoken with a twinkle in her eye, or that there was a tone of humour in her voice, but there wasn't. I was left with the very definite impression that this was no joke.

'Oh. Er, yes. Yes, I see,' I mumbled.

'And if you have any other ideas like this – tell me first. Don't go off half-cocked and try to look into it yourself. Remember, Mr Morris, this is a *murder* enquiry. One boy has been killed already. I don't want to have to come looking for your body as well. Do we understand each other?'

'Yes, of course.'

'Go back to your painting and forget about all this. At least, until you're called by the coroner for the inquest.'

'Yes.' Oh, hell. I'd forgotten that I'd be called to the coroner's court. I began to make my way to the gate.

'And Mr Morris?'

'Yes?'

This time she actually smiled. 'When I said thanks, well, I meant it. We had missed this.'

I left her there. And no, I didn't mention Jon's sideline in supplying Stan's needs. His mother already had enough to deal with, as he said.

I returned to the chalet and took up my sketchbook, but put it down again some minutes later without making a mark. The TV in the corner of the room took my interest for all of three minutes. That was how long it took to pick up the remote and realize I had not the faintest idea how to get a channel. I got the list of channels up, but whether I typed in the number or pressed 'OK' to change to a different programme, nothing happened. In the end I turned it off and thought, 'Sod it.' I poured a whisky and went out to the deck.

It was nearly seven o'clock when I went inside and stared at the little store of provisions I had bought in the supermarket. Nothing too complicated, I thought. I put butter in a frying pan with some olive oil, threw in a couple of rashers of bacon diced small, chopped an onion and threw that in, then added a tin of tomatoes and salt and pepper before setting a pot of water on to boil. Just as it was bubbling nicely, I chucked in a handful of pasta and stirred it.

I would like to say that I came to some radical conclusions about the murder and who was responsible but, to be quite frank, I was much more interested in the food than the murder. I was sorry for Rick and his family, of course, but just now I was more concerned that my belly thought my throat had been cut. I had eaten nothing since the slice of cake at the Tunnel Café, and I really needed some food. And there is little to beat a good, warming pasta dish when you feel like that. Unless, of course, someone interrupts you just as you're going to eat.

I had just got to the stage where the pasta had to be drained. Getting a colander, I set it over the sink, and poured the pasta into it. Hopefully I could refresh it later, I thought.

It was obviously Megan. I hadn't spoken to her since that morning at the café beside the swimming pool, and she was probably keen on getting outside a bottle of wine again. I hurried to the door and pulled it open. 'Hi, Megan. Oh.'

There was no Megan. Only two men wearing leathers, who pushed past me and into the sitting room.

'So, sir, let's start with the easy stuff, shall we?' said the first one.

When he had been wearing his helmet, I had not been able to see his face behind the reflective visor. He was a good-looking guy, I suppose. He had the high cheekbones of an East African, with calm, gentle brown eyes that were somehow reassuring.

His colleague was not. He was a shaven-headed thug, in my terms. If I came across him in a dark alleyway, I would run as a matter of course. He had a heavy, prognathous jaw, beetling brows and the sort of expression that made me think of a human Rottweiler. And I have to add there, that I have known several lovely Rottweilers – apart from Kylie. She wasn't so nice, but that could have been an automatic and natural response to being named after a diminutive antipodean.

'Who are you two?' I demanded.

'The first question is, how well do you know Jeremy Cooper?'

'I said, who are you?'

Skinhead bared his teeth. 'You really don't want to know, sir.'

This, I have to admit, gave me pause for thought. I was quite prepared to believe that these two were villains of some sort. Perhaps they were competitors of Jez's, and wanted to make his life difficult. And as soon as I had that thought, the picture of Jez's son flashed into my mind, along with the shiny little metal cylinder in the field. Was it possible Jez was actually involved in crime? Perhaps these two were challengers to his business? They had killed his son as a means of getting to him, perhaps, and now wanted . . . I don't know what.

One of my 'guests' was sitting on my sofa; the other was standing in front of me. Behind him were the open French windows leading to my deck. However, behind me was the door to the passageway that led to my front door.

I looked from one to the other. And then bolted.

In the annals of great chases of all time, that one won't score highly. Generally for a chase to be exciting, there's a need for a degree of challenge, for some derring-do, perhaps, or a longish period of adventure before the prey (me) manages to escape.

As it was, I pulled the door to the sitting room shut behind me, delaying skinhead for at least a quarter-second, reached the front door, yanked it wide, squeaked as I felt a hand brush my back, and then I was outside, leaping down the short flight of stairs, past my pushbike (it was padlocked, and I really didn't think I had time to unlock it), and down towards the reception area. Perhaps at the back of my mind was the idea that I could go there and ask for help or the police but, even as I drew nearer, it occurred to me that it was past seven o'clock, when the reception closed for the night.

Instead, I had the brilliant idea of running to the police officer out by the murder scene. I bolted up there, flying along like a hare before the hounds, and I would have easily made it to safety, were it not for two things.

I was unfit, and it was uphill.

Perhaps halfway to the blue-and-white-taped area, my legs went jelly-like, my eyes began to bulge, and I ran out of air. It felt as though my lungs had suddenly taken on forty years of a sixty-a-day habit. In short, I was knackered.

'Help!' I cried. I would have shouted, but I refer you to the last couple of sentences. Then I bent over, hands on knees, and tried not to vomit.

'Right, Mr Morris. If you've got that out of your system, we have some questions for you,' the skinhead said. He hadn't even broken into a sweat.

I really disliked him.

'Sit!' his colleague said, pointing at the sofa opposite him. His expression had gone from moderately benign to rather suspicious.

I sat.

'What was that about?' he asked.

'Are you serious? Two thugs barge into my chalet, start questioning me, and you want to know why I try to get away? Who are you?'

'My name is Pearce, and this is Edwards. We are working for the government.'

'Which?'

'His Majesty's.'

'You're police?'

He gave an apologetic little clearing of his throat. 'Not quite, no. But that doesn't matter.'

'What do you want with me?'

'We are investigating some business transactions. How well do you know Jeremy Cooper – and please don't run away again. It makes Edwards get tetchy.'

I looked up at the shaven-headed brute. He reminded me of films of the Vietnam War. You know the sort, the kind where the brutal bully has all his hair shaved off, as if to symbolize his violence, and goes on to show that actually, yes, he really was a psychopath.

'I won't.'

'Good. Well?'

'I don't know him at all. He's here, his son has just been murdered, and he wanted a little compassion and sympathy, I suppose.'

'From a stranger?'

I shrugged. 'Maybe he thought I had an understanding face.'

The skinhead bent down to my level. 'You think this is funny?'

I considered his face dispassionately. It really wasn't pleasant. However, if these two were government officers, I felt considerably more confident. 'If you're with the government, let's see some ID.'

'Why?' Pearce said with amusement.

'I want to make sure you're bona fide.'

He smiled broadly. 'And how will you be able to tell? I could have the best-looking ID card in the world, if I wanted. It could be a perfect replica of any card I wanted to show you. And even if it were genuine, you would have not the faintest idea, would you? After all, how many government warrant cards have you actually seen?'

That was a rather perceptive point. So while I tried to think how to confirm who these two were, Pearce eyed me with a more or less genial expression. In the end, I shrugged. 'You have me there. OK, so what do you want from me?'

'You had not met Cooper before coming here?'

'No, not at all.'

'So, what are you doing here?'

'I'm painting a house up the road. Derek Swann's.'

'Really?'

Now, although I am better with landscapes than portraits, I could read his expression. I'll tell you now, Pearce was interested. It did not show in his face; he didn't lean forward intently or anything like that, but there was a sudden stillness to him, as though he dared not move even a finger in case it distracted me.

'How did you get to know Derek Swann?'

'He's a friend of a friend. A banker friend of mine put me on to him,' I said, baffled. 'He's leaving the country soon, and wanted a memento of his house, so I'm painting it for him. Why?'

'And he commissioned you to paint his house for him?'

'Yes. Why?'

'Did Cooper have anything to do with this commission?' Edwards said.

'No, it was just my friend and Derek. Why, what's this all about?'

Pearce and Edwards exchanged a glance. I could see that the skinhead was reluctant, but Pearce's dark eyes passed over me, as if forming a judgement. 'Very well, sir. But first I have to warn you that this is entirely confidential and you must not discuss anything I'm about to tell you with anyone at all. Is that quite clear?'

'Yes, all right.'

'We are part of the investigative branch of Border Force. We are looking into businesses which have broken trade sanctions. Some firms have smuggled electronics from the West into Iran. As you can imagine, this is a huge business, with vast profits for those who are prepared to take the risk of getting caught. Jeremy Cooper's business is the leader in this trade.'

After they had reminded me of my promise not to discuss any of their suspicions with anyone, the two left me, Edwards with a meaningful glower, Pearce with a more or less gracious leave-taking, shaking my hand and leaving me standing in my sitting room with a sense of utter bemusement.

I sat on the sofa, then went to look at my pasta. It was interesting, if you like solid sculptures, but didn't look edible. I boiled the kettle to run hot water over it in the hope it might recover, put the tomato sauce over a low heat, and wandered out to the deck to recover my glass of whisky. I stood there sipping, wondering what on earth Jez could have got himself into. If he was really an international electronics smuggler, he was little better than an arms dealer, and I wanted nothing to do with someone like that . . . but he still gave me the impression of vulnerability.

Then I had a second thought, which was, anyone providing serious aid to the Iranians would have a lot of enemies. There would be other smugglers keen to make money from that business, while there would also be plenty of people with the desire to see such a business closed down. I had grown up knowing that Mossad had earned an enviable reputation for their very earnest determination to catch Nazis, Black September terrorists, and others who were thought to pose a specific threat to Israel or Israelis. It was said that the Israelis were about the most ruthless of all foreign intelligence services – and considerably more competent than the muddled Russian secret services. Not that it would be terribly difficult.

If a man had managed to make enemies of a group like Mossad, it was likely that he would find his life potentially much shorter.

And then I had to wonder about his son's death. I didn't think Mossad would murder a boy just to get to the father, but then again I wasn't in the secret services. It was quite likely that they played by different rules. Could someone have been trying to get to Jez to persuade him to stop supplying the Iranians? Was he supplying them? It didn't sound likely.

Even so, I would have to be careful. I mustn't let on that I had heard of his business dealings, and I was keen not to confront Edwards or Pearce again. I didn't want to have to get into difficulties with them.

Yes, that was when I realized that there was a burning smell. My sauce had burned down to a black coating on the saucepan, and the pasta had miraculously converted from spaghetti to a stodgy mass of carbohydrate that might have appealed to the local rat population, but for me was unattractive.

I tipped it into the bin, filled the saucepan with hot water in the hope the burned mess might dissolve a little. It didn't.

I poured another whisky.

SEVEN

The next morning I woke with a mild hangover to the sound of my phone ringing. It was Derek Swann.

'Hi, Nick, hope all's well. I understand there was a bit of a problem on Friday, that right?'

I didn't want to get Adela into trouble by mentioning the scar across the drawing. 'Only a minor difficulty. It just means I'll be a day behind, nothing more,' I said lightly.

'How long have you got the chalet for?'

Shit! That was one thing I had not considered. My changeover day was today.

'Look, Nick, it'll be a good idea for you maybe to extend, but if there's a problem and they need the chalet, why don't you come up to the house and stay with me? It'll make your commute a lot easier, after all, and you'd be very welcome.'

That took a moment to consider. Away from this park, away from Jez Cooper, and from the two investigating bikers. It was a very appealing offer.

'Thanks. I'll be over as soon as . . .'

'What?'

'Oh, I forgot, I don't have a car.'

'How long do you need to pack?'

'An hour or two.'

'I'll come and get you at half past ten. That be long enough?'

'That'll be perfect, thanks.'

I put the phone down just as Megan appeared at the side of my deck. 'Are you free for a quick coffee?'

'Yeah, but it's got to be a quick one. I'm off today.'

'You're leaving?' She looked quite upset at the news.

'Yes, I need more time to actually get on with my work. Derek Swann has offered to put me up. I was due to leave the chalet today anyway. I was only ever going to be here for a few days. How are you – are you all right?'

'Oh, I'm fine. I've seen worse in my time.'

'The park will need the chalet for the next guests. Hopefully they won't be put off by news of the murder.'

'Oh, they won't be,' she said confidently. She came round to the door and walked through my sitting room to the deck, casting an eye over my bags. 'If there's one thing I've learned over years, it is that people are very keen to go and visit sites of special sickening interest. Doesn't matter whether it's somewhere like Ten Rillington Place, or Fred and Rose West's home, the gruesome gangs will always turn up, like they're places deserving worship or something. The same frightful fellows will go to any murder scene for the cheap thrill it gives. Same thing used to happen over the centuries with public executions. And now it's rubber-neckers on motorways, desperate to see the wounded or injured after a car crash, often causing their own crash as a result. Or it's the horrendous films you see on YouTube and other places, dedicated to horrible scenes from war zones or foul abuses inflicted on people. I hate it.'

'You sound like you've been involved in such things, rather than just writing about them,' I said.

'Yes, well, when I was in hospital – you remember I said I was a nurse for a while? – I ended up as a staff nurse in A and E, and we used to have a few nasty cases there, and you know, it was terrible to have victims of knife attacks or shootings, and as soon as we did, the vultures would turn up at the doors, hoping to catch a glimpse of someone in agony. And the next day it would be all over the paper, if they succeeded.'

I had made a coffee and set it before her. She barely noticed, her eyes clouded with the memories.

'It was partly because of that that I became an author. You know, to exorcize the demons. I just found I couldn't spend all my time with people who were suffering. When my husband died, it was obvious to me that I ought to get out of that kind of environment, but what else could I do? I was trained as a carer, so at least I could look after Peter and Ron and make them comfortable, but then, well, afterwards it didn't seem to me like I had any more to give. Besides, I'd dabbled in writing for years already. I realized I loved reading, so what could be more natural than to see whether I could write?'

'Was it always that bad – nursing, I mean?'

'Oh, God, no!' She snapped out of her reverie as quickly as she had entered it. 'I had a hoot for a lot of the time! I loved working with geriatrics and the youngsters. The old and the children were the most rewarding, without a doubt. I'll never forget giving an elderly man a bed bath. He must have been in his eighties, and I was only in my early twenties, and while I was washing him, well . . . I have to admit, I was slim and tall in those days, with a lot of fair hair from a bottle, and he got an erection, and I was, well, you know, embarrassed, and tried not to notice, but he just grinned at me and said, "I may be old, but I still have lead in me pencil!" and that had me almost wetting myself. I used to enjoy work in those days. I suppose it was the others, the ones who were dying, the ones with horrible injuries or the victims of dreadful crimes – those were the ones who made me want to get out. I just couldn't face it any more.'

She was pensive again, and I didn't want to push her. She was a loud, brash woman, but she was also kind and caring.

When I saw the car appear, it was a relief. I had spent my time since the phone call staring variously up towards Jez Cooper's chalet, or in the direction of the two bikers, or at the blue-and-white police line. I honestly hadn't the faintest idea which of the three was most alarming to me – all I knew was that I definitely didn't want to be here any longer.

However I have to admit to a certain amount of doubt when I took a look at his Porsche. A soft-top car is always a joy, obviously – I wouldn't own a Morgan otherwise – but it has to be acknowledged that the cabin space and boot space (that's trunk space to you foreigners) is limited. I looked at my small case, my messenger bag, the second bag with food and the collection of additional items – iPad, spare paints, brushes and so on, and began to have my doubts.

By the judicious use of my footwell for some bags, the trunk under the bonnet for others, and the little gap behind the seat for a few more, we finally managed to get everything in. Then, of course, there was only the bike.

'I'll send Adela over for that later. She can bring her truck for it,' he said. It would do. I went to reception, checked out, and soon we were on the way.

He was a fast but cautious driver. Every left-hand bend he would take wide, every right-hander he almost scraped the kerb, giving himself the best view of the road ahead. While he did take corners rather too quickly for my taste, the car felt like a go-kart. It was so exhilarating I almost felt myself regretting not owning a Porsche. But then I reminded myself that the migmog had a nice, easily maintained Ford engine with cheap spare parts, whereas a Porsche had a beautifully engineered German engine whose air filter would be out of my financial reach as an artist.

I'd stick with the moggie.

The wide tyres made a glorious noise as we rolled down his driveway on the gravel. Soon we were in front of his house, and I climbed out reluctantly.

'Leave your stuff. I'll get Adela to take it up to your room. Unless you want to get cracking? I'm assuming it would be good to take a day off. It must have been terrible finding that boy's body. I read about it online.'

'It was a horrible shock, yeah,' I said. 'I knew him a little, from seeing him around, and I wasn't expecting to find him dead. Or anyone else, for that matter. We aren't used to the sight of death nowadays, are we? I guess the Victorians got quite blasé about it, since they would have older relatives living with them, and one day, they'd be dead. For us, it's all clinical and remote. Someone gets old or unwell, and they're sent to a hospital, and sometimes we may see them close to the end, but all too often we don't. They pass away and we get a call later. Mind you, even Victorians must have been upset to lose someone as young as the boy.'

'Yes, it was Rick Parrow, wasn't it? I vaguely remember him around town. He was one of those boys who always looked a bit . . . well, grumpy, I suppose.'

'I think that is the banner of youth. Resentment, anger, grumpiness, call it what you want,' I said lightly. After all, we were both of an age to remember Harry Enfield and his constantly aggrieved teenage character, Kevin. Anyone who had ever seen his 'You're *so* unfair!' rages would recognize the look on Rick's face, the poor devil.

'Strange that he should be there,' Derek said.

We had reached his kitchen. It was a part of the house that had clearly been extensively modernized, and was bright and cheery, with tiles that reminded me of Madrid and Seville. He had a coffee machine that made superb espresso, and he asked whether I would like a shot or a long coffee. I was happy to accept a mug with milk while I glanced around the kitchen. I could appreciate it.

Counters ran around the majority of the room, with windows down the side where the sink was set into the dark marble counter-top. It was, of course, a Belfast type, large, white porcelain, with ancient-looking taps and spout made from bronze. In the middle of the room was a huge island for extra preparation space, with a glass panel that I assumed was an induction hob. Everything was clean and sparkling where it should be.

'There?' I repeated.

'Yes, I mean he was a local boy to Ashbourne, but why would he be there at the park? It seems a little peculiar. Maybe he had a part-time job there. Cutting grass or taking deliveries or something.' He had his back to me as he spoke.

'Yes.' I wasn't going to commit myself. After all, Rick and his father were really none of my business. I felt sorry for both of them, and for Rick's mother, but the fact was that they were nothing to do with me, and it didn't seem right to spread any guesses with the man who had helped destroy Jez Cooper, from what he had said. It was reinforced by the visit from Edwards and Pearce the day before. They had succeeded in getting the wind up me somewhat, and just now I wanted nothing to do with them or their 'investigation', whatever that might involve. I was happier out of it.

The coffee was good. Derek took me out into the back of the house. There was a long sunroom along the back, with a games area – table football and a bar billiards machine that made me stop and gaze wistfully – and then out to the paved terrace overlooking a large rose garden.

'I always loved roses,' he said somewhat wistfully. 'Give it a couple of months and this will be a riot of colour.'

There was a massive red ceramic barbecue under a slate-roofed shelter, a pizza oven nearby. A large table with seating for twelve and two folded parasols showed that he took his outdoor cooking seriously – or that he had dedicated cooks who would come in to prepare food for him and his guests. Somehow I didn't see him wielding the fork, tongs and turner over the burgers and chicken wings. An apron with 'I'm the Daddy' or 'BBQ King' didn't seem his style.

He sat at the head of the table and I took my place on his right. A little presumptive, you might think, but it meant I had my back to the house and face to the view. And it was stunning.

Over the top of the roses, the hills rolled away into the distance. It was rather a hobbit-like landscape, with small hills all merging, and in the distance, perhaps a mile away, the only other habitation, which looked like a farm set in a little group of trees, presumably as defence against the winter's gales. I imagine the wind would blast like a sirocco over this landscape. It was a wonder any trees survived.

'You'll miss this,' I said, waving a hand vaguely at the view.

'Yes, but I won't miss the rain,' he said, with just a touch of smugness.

Adela appeared. 'Telephone for you, Mr Swann,' she said, and held out a mobile.

'Excuse me,' he said. 'Adela, could you take your pickup to collect Nick's cycle? It's at the park.'

And then he was gone, and I was left with Adela.

Adela seemed to consider it her responsibility to occupy me while the master was away. She had her hair down now. Rather than the plaits, it hung in glorious swirls about her face.

'I'll have to paint you,' I said.

'Me? No! I don't want to be in a painting.'

'Just to add a little proportion to the picture of the house. You would be perfect, and then Derek will have a means of remembering you, too.'

'I am sure he would not want me in the painting, no.'

She was absolutely determined, that was certain. 'If you're sure,' I said. 'But then I could make a study of your face. I would like that. Only for the pleasure of your features.'

'No, I do not think so.'

'Why not?'

'It is not . . . hmm . . . *seemly* for a man to paint me. I do not know you well enough,' she said primly.

I was about to quickly point out that I had meant I wanted to paint her clothed – which wasn't entirely true – but, in any case, I would have been happy with a picture of her smiling face, just head and shoulders. Before I could, Derek reappeared. He glanced at Adela and nodded. She rose and left. 'I will fetch your bicycle,' she said to me as she glided away.

'Sorry about that,' Derek said. He sat again, toying with his coffee. Suddenly he looked over at me. 'I hadn't realized that the dead boy was Jez Cooper's son.'

'Oh?'

'Apparently Jez has just been arrested. That was a friend of mine who works for the local paper. Jez was taken into custody this morning, and it seems that the police are questioning him at Derby. I have to say, I find it incredible, but apparently the boy was Jez's son. Quite incredible.'

'What's incredible is that they'd think Jez would kill his son! Why would he want to kill the lad?'

'According to the police, it's because Rick didn't want to live with him, and told his father he was going to stay with his mother. I suppose it's the old story. If Jez couldn't have his son, no one else would. So he murdered the boy.'

I shook my head. 'From all I've seen, I don't think Jez could have killed him. He's not that sort of guy.'

'And you know such men? You have experience of murderers?' Derek said, gently enough to be teasing, but with a hint of sarcasm too.

Yes, I rose to it. 'I've known several murderers,' I said, thinking of the previous year in Dartmoor and the Russians.

'We can't really tell what will drive someone to murder, though,' Derek continued as if I had not spoken. 'I have met a couple of men who were capable of killing, and neither looked any different to you or me. The thing was, the situation in which they found themselves. One was a mild, calm accountant. He had been embezzling smallish amounts from his company to keep his rather younger wife happy, and then one day he realized she was having an affair. That wasn't enough, quite, to tip him over the edge, but the discovery that she was taking his money to pay her boyfriend, that was. He didn't kill her, mind. He adored her. No, he went after the lover and beat his head in with a club hammer. And then didn't know what else to do, so he went to the police and gave himself up. Which sort of begs the question, why bother, if all you're going to do is ensure that you're going to spend the rest of your life in prison anyway? He couldn't sleep with her again after that, so why bother? Better to divorce her and give her a lousy settlement, but be free, I'd have thought.'

'And the other one?'

'Ah, he was different. He was a security guard, and I think he had a screw loose. At work he seemed perfectly well adjusted, but when he was outside the company, he was a totally different man. He used to work in his spare time at a little club in London's East End, working as a bouncer. Hah! We used to joke with him that his job there was to see how far he could make unwanted visitors bounce off the road surface, but then he was arrested. It seems he had been selling advanced services to other clients – basically taking contracts to murder people. Which was a lucrative sideline, apparently. But again, at work he seemed perfectly well adjusted. You'd never have guessed what was going on behind his eyes. You wouldn't have been able to tell he was a murderer for hire.'

I felt a little frisson at his words. I was thinking again of Jez and that evening when he came round to threaten me. It was all too easy to imagine him clenching a fist and pummelling me to death in my hallway. When I glanced at Derek, he was watching me.

He nodded a little sadly. 'Yes, it's like I said. I cannot imagine it either, but when you say Jez doesn't seem the type, it means nothing. Until you see the way that someone is wired, and how they react to things in their private lives, it's hard to see how they might respond to specific events. Perhaps this was just enough to tip him over the edge. And Rick paid the price.'

'If that was the case, surely losing his business would have been as strong a spur to him? Why didn't he attack you when he lost his business? You said he blamed you for that.'

'Ah, well, maybe there was a core of rationality in him still. He knew full well that it wasn't really me, so there was no justification attacking me. When it came to his son, though, that was simple jealousy.'

'Jez told me the boy was his, that he paid Rick's mother as a surrogate, but she changed her mind, kept the money and the boy, and deprived Rick of any contact.'

'Yes?'

'But I spoke to her, and she said that she got pregnant with Rick and Jez deserted her, and that was certainly the story she told Rick and his brother.'

'I wonder. Jez had a lot of bad luck, and I know he and Sue never had children of their own. I think she had a form of cancer when she was young, and because of that, and the radiotherapy they gave her, she had to have a hysterectomy, so obviously couldn't have children. Then, when they married . . . well, he was desperate for a son, I know. Whether he decided to have an affair, or to pay for a surrogate – either would be in keeping.'

'But murdering the boy wouldn't be,' I reflected. It wasn't the way Jez was 'wired', to use Derek's phrase.

'Like I said. You can't tell. If his mother had fed the lie to Rick well enough, perhaps the lad became convinced that Jez was lying to him, trying to break up his family, attempting to steal him away – who can tell? If he went to Jez and just said he was a liar, a coward for deserting his son and family, who's to say Jez wouldn't respond heavily? He might go completely over the top.'

I was not convinced. We both finished our coffees, and when Derek said he had a couple of phone calls and emails to deal with, I said I'd go for a walk, and maybe a cycle ride. The land-scape was so appealing it cried out for a paintbrush.

The fact that the police had arrested Jez was a real surprise. It made little sense after finding the gas canister in the field, I thought. After all, that indicated that someone was walking over the field, surely. But then again, perhaps there was no real proof that anyone had been there carrying a body. Maybe someone else had seen Rick walking up the road, and I was mistaken to assume that the nitrous oxide had any significance. The police might have other incriminating evidence against Jez. It was possible.

Of course, it was also possible that Jez had been taken in for questioning because of his smuggling, as Edwards and Pearce had said. And it would make sense for them to arrest Jez, since once they told me about it, they could not be certain that I would keep it all quiet. People sometimes could not help letting something out when they had a secret.

I was bemused by Derek's words about Jez's surrogacy. I was absolutely convinced that he was telling the truth about that. There was too much detail in his story for him to have made it all up on the spot – likewise, Helen had been spilling the same tale for years. She didn't need to make anything up on the spot with me, it was a story she had rehearsed with both her sons. And I was sure that she had not been entirely frank. There was something about the way she cast a sidelong glance at Jon when she spoke of Jez's betrayal of the family that didn't ring true.

When it all boiled down to it, I was convinced that Jez had told the truth about his surrogacy contract with Helen, the result being Rick. And I could not help but believe him when he said Derek had ripped him off somehow. Someone was lying, but I didn't think it was Jez. He seemed too transparent.

And then Jon himself – a local dealer in drugs himself, so hardly honest. So many people, so many distortions. How could the police ever sort out the truth from the exaggerations and outright lies? I was glad I had never joined the police.

The gas cylinder wouldn't leave me. It was a shiny little tube at the back of my head as I walked, as were the little cardboard boxes and empty gas reservoirs lying down by the bandstand.

I had no idea how, but I was absolutely convinced that they had something to do with Rick's murder.

Adela was in the kitchen when I returned from my meanderings. My bike, she told me, was out at the side of the house in a small shed, which was left open so I could use it whenever I wanted. She was tied up with household chores, and Derek was busy, she told me, and would probably be tied up all afternoon. Accordingly, I decided to go out for a cycle ride. The weather was fantastic, and I didn't want to stay cooped up in the house, and although I could have started on the house and getting my preliminary sketch redone, I really didn't feel like it. I didn't have the concentration for work. Some simple landscapes were more appealing.

It was easy to find the bike. It was in a small garage designed to fit a gleaming red quad bike. However, more interesting for me was the vehicle parked outside the garage. A pickup truck in dark aubergine which I recognized. And it was Adela's, according to Derek. I couldn't check the number plate – I'd never got a good sight of the plate at the park – but I was as sure as I could be that this was the same one. I peered into the back of the cab, and there I could see a box. It had *Cream Chargers* printed on the side.

I hopped on to the bike and cycled back to Parsley Hay, deep in thought. There I bought a sandwich and bottle of water, and sat at a picnic bench in the sun.

Adela must have been the driver of the truck at the park. It was she who had supplied the gas cylinders to Ricky's brother. Suddenly her comments about visiting festivals came back to me – it would be perfect for a supplier of drugs to meet people. Festival-goers would have a fair proportion of E, Ketamine and Nox users among them. It would be the perfect location for a woman to make a quick profit.

To distract myself, I took out my sketchbook and made a couple of simple sketches which I coloured with washes of ultramarine blue and pale greens, adding red to make a light grey which perfectly complemented the stone walls, especially when I went over some of them with a black fine-liner to bring out the outline.

A man wandered over to look, and within fifteen minutes, I had lost one sketch and gained fifty pounds in cash. It seemed a fair exchange to me!

However, my mind was fixed like a train on rails, on Adela. She was subsidizing her income by flogging drugs to kids. *That* was a real shock.

Getting back on the bike, I took the trail back towards Tissington from the north. There were several appealing views from the old railway line, and I paused to take a few photos on the phone, but nothing grabbed me particularly while my mind was churning about Adela, and I ended up at the village again and decided not to pause there. In preference I continued all the way to Ashbourne. I had to occupy myself.

I won't go into the various areas where I sat and sketched and painted. Such aspects are about as exciting to readers of crime stories as a detailed history of a football match would be to me, I know. There really is very little more guaranteed to send me to sleep as the appearance of a bunch of football pundits on television. So I'll save you that. Instead, let me just say that Ashbourne has some stunning Georgian houses, and it was worthwhile sitting in the sun with my sketchpad and just recording my impressions. Apart from anything else, it cleared my mind a little, concentrating on pencil and brush strokes, adding small dabs of colour to bring out the scenes. And there was no police station that I could see. The nearest was in Derby.

It was while I was sitting there that I became aware of two figures behind me. Mainly, because there was a waft of horribly sweet-smelling smoke that floated past me. When I glanced round, I saw it was Al and Penny.

The two youngsters were interested in my painting of the town's marketplace. It was a pretty, triangular space with views of an ethnic clothing shop and several old buildings, and I have to say that the overall effect of my sketch was pleasing.

I opened my palette and began to put water into the bigger wells. 'How's life, Al?'

'You know,' he said, with a shrug of boredom. 'Be better in somewhere with a bit of life to it.'

'We want to go to London,' Penny said, exhaling another thick cloud. She seemed desperate to compete in the 'cumulonimbus of the year' awards. I coughed gently, in a subtle-ish hint, but she didn't do subtlety.

'What would you do there?'

'Like, get jobs?' she said with the irreverent contempt of the young for the ancient. Since she was about half my age, I guess she looked on me as one half-shuffle from the grave.

'Doing what?'

'Whatever!'

'Pen wants to get into advertising,' Al said. He spoke in a mildly apologetic tone, as if recognizing that such a career was considerably out of her reach.

'A fun job, but not easy to get into.'

'Yeah, like you know?' she said, and this time there was a hint of genuine interest.

'I have friends in it. What do you want to do, account management, creative, planning?'

'I dunno. Just advertising.'

I pursed my lips as I added a touch of ultramarine blue, light red and some yellow to the water, mixing well to get a pale grey for the clouds. 'It's best to have an idea of the type of role you're looking for,' I explained gently. 'And ideally a degree.'

'What, from university?' She appeared appalled at the concept.

'Yes. Advertising firms only take on graduates generally. What about you, Al? What do you want to do?'

'I don't know. I want to travel, really. But I don't know what I'd fancy.'

'I had a friend at school who wanted to travel. He got into a degree course where they taught business management, and he became a travel organizer for companies, arranging their incentive trips. He got to go to Africa, Thailand, Malaysia, Australia – and all paid for by the firms he worked with. Had a great time.'

I tried to keep the jealousy out of my voice. I'd always wanted to see the world. As it was, I tended only to see aspects of London and England, mostly on expenses generated by paintings of cats. Ah, well: the things we plan when we are young!

'I like that,' Penny said suddenly. She pointed at the picture as I added clouds, using a dry brush to remove some areas which were too dark. I carried on painting with more colour as I covered the buildings, then trees, and on down.

'Thanks.'

'You're not bad,' she considered, as if surprised. Apparently I'm better at buildings than grassy hummocks.

'Thanks,' I said, a little less heartily. Then an idea occurred to me. 'You two want a drink?'

Judging by the eagerness with which the two accepted my proposal, they were desperate for some form of refreshment. And as Al brought my bike, Penny walked at my side, apparently more interested in me as I explained I had several friends in advertising agencies in London.

The two took me to a pub called Smith's Tavern, a gorgeous little bar with windows either side of the door. Al leaned my bike against the window, where we could keep an eye on it, and we walked into a welcoming front room which had a bar perpendicular to the door. A range of oblong and circular tables with chairs from the last century were scattered about, and I found myself presented with a range of ales I had never heard of. I tried one of the local dark beers, while Al asked for a lager. Penny? As I had first thought as soon as I met her, she wanted a cider. Not, of course, a real cider. She wanted one flavoured with elderflowers. It seemed to go with the vape machine. Elderflower and bubblegum. My stomach rebelled at the thought. Only a good dark beer could settle that, I thought.

'Where's your friend Stan?'

'He's around. He didn't feel too good this morning,' Al said. 'I reckon he overdid things yesterday. He likes a drink, does Stan.'

I caught a warning glance from Penny, and so did Al. He shrugged. 'He wanted to stay in today.'

I got the distinct feeling they knew it wasn't only drinks he enjoyed. 'How are you two keeping?'

'You know.'

'Not really. It's never easy to lose a friend. And you both liked Rick.'

'Yeah,' Al said.

Penny was a little slower to respond. Ever straightforward to read, I saw her quick look at Al before saying with casual lack of interest, 'He was a good mate, I s'pose.'

'It's always hard to lose someone you've grown up with.'

'Yeah,' Al said. His eyes were fixed on his drink. 'Pen and him went out for a while, but we were still mates. He never gave you crap, you know? He'd always see the better side of you.'

'How do you mean?'

'Oh, if someone got into trouble, it was always Rick would make them see sense. Like, if someone was getting a bit too drunk, Rick was the one who'd walk them home. If someone was misbehaving and could get themselves into trouble, it was Rick who'd try to talk sense into them.'

'That's not easy when it's people your own age.'

'It's easier than talking to folks who're younger,' Al said, and Penny nodded her head vigorously.

'Yeah, like talking to Annie the other day, I had to tell her, like, she was being a bitch, and she took that from me, but if it were someone older, she'd have given 'em shit.'

'Yes,' Al said. He looked up at me, his eyes troubled. 'I mean, Rick found it hard at home. His kid brother made it difficult for him. Jon was always getting into trouble, and if Rick told him not to be a dick, he'd just tell him what to do. Jon never had any time for Rick, just said he was a bastard.'

'Wasn't Jon too?'

'I s'pose. But Jon's dad died, didn't run off and leave their mum. So Jon felt more legit, I suppose. Rick never got nothing but stick from him.'

'So when his father turned up, that made trouble?'

Penny's drink was already empty and she was tapping the glass hopefully. I ignored her.

'Christ, no! He reckoned no matter what, his dad had left them, and he wasn't going to go with someone who could do that to him. No, he was staying with his mum, where he knew he was wanted.'

'Even if his younger half-brother wasn't keen.'

'Yeah. Right. And, I mean, Jon's been in trouble of all sorts before, too, so probs Rick wanted to look after his mum in case of anything else happening.'

'What sort of trouble?'

Now Al hung his head. 'The sort of trouble only a dickhead like him would get into. He was selling cigarettes at school, and reckoned he had a supplier of other things too.'

'Drugs?'

Al suddenly snatched a glance at Penny. I got the impression a particularly sharp elbow had caught his rib. Struck with a quick intuition, I glanced at my drink, then their two. 'Penny, you're empty. Do you want another?'

When she nodded, I passed her a note to get herself another foul concoction. Meanwhile I leaned forward. 'Al, was it drugs?'

'Why'd you want to know? You a cop?'

For a moment I was flummoxed. Then I grinned. 'You think a cop could paint like me?'

He gave a twisted little smile. 'Yeah. Right. So, it was drugs. But nothing serious, right? It was just some laughing gas, and that's not even illegal. Everyone's tried it. It's like a tab of E or something. Nothing in it. Safer than aspirin, they reckon. So Jon got a stash, and he was selling the metal things, you know, that hold the gas, and it was good money for him. Then Rick found out . . .'

'He wasn't best pleased,' Penny said as she returned with a fresh bottle of sickly imitation cider. 'Don't think Rick would be any more pleased to know you was talking about it to someone you don't know.'

'I'm only an interested artist,' I protested. 'I met Rick and spoke to him a couple of times. It's just such a tragic thing – especially since I found him.'

'The police said it was a woman what found him,' Penny said shrewdly.

'It was. It was Megan Lamplighter, who was walking round the park with me that evening,' I said. 'She actually saw the body first, but we were together.'

'Was there lots of blood?' she asked.

I suddenly really disliked her. She seemed like the archetypical modern person, self-absorbed, selfish, uninterested in anything other than social media and the cost of a boob-job. A rather cutting remark was on the tip of my tongue, when I realized that her eyes were glistening not with self-interest, but with remorse and regret for a lost lover.

'No. And for what it's worth, I think he died really quickly. The police mentioned a thin weapon, and I assume it struck his heart. Perhaps it was an accident, and he was carried there afterwards, but I am as sure as I can be that it was quick. If his heart was punctured, it would have been very fast.'

She nodded, shot a look at Al, and subsided.

'Al, was Rick's brother caught by the police?'

'No. Rick found his stash and told him he'd tell their mum if Jon didn't lose it, and quick. He told me all about it. Rick was really worried. You see their mum had used. She's been clean for years now, ever since Jon's dad died. It was an overdose, you see. Rick felt Jon was doing to other people what the dealer did to Jon's dad.'

'Did Jon listen, do you think?'

Al looked over at me and lifted an eyebrow. 'What do you think? Jon's more of a dickhead than most, and he was making good money. What would you do if you didn't have a brain, but were making two hundred a week easy money? He's only young.'

'Yes,' I said, but I was also thinking about Jon's antagonism towards me, and the way that so often murders seemed to be committed by youngsters with weapons they shouldn't have had in the first place. They were more likely to reach for them than older people.

Could Rick have discovered Jon was carrying on with his dealing, and made some sort of threat to expose him, so Jon reacted as so many kids might, pulled out a weapon and stabbed his half-brother?

It was a thought.

Supper was a pleasant affair. A fillet of mackerel each, with a large slab of beef to follow.

'The joint will be in the fridge, if you fancy a beef sandwich tomorrow,' Derek said, swirling red wine in his glass with a contented smile.

I doubt my own smile was any less cheery. The effect of red wine, good food, followed by an extraordinary cheese selection including something he called Gorgonzola pudding, which looked like a sort of cream cheese with large lumps in it and some blue bits materializing at random as the spoon went in. Yes, spoon. When I say it was like cream cheese, I mean a wet, creamy cottage cheese, only the lumps were much larger. And it was delicious.

Drinks followed the meal, outside. The weather had been warm all day, and now it was balmy, with the grey stone of the house radiating some of the warmth it had absorbed during the day. Instead of more red wine, Derek suggested a pleasant, fairly sharp white from New Zealand. It was perfect for the evening. Refreshing and good on the palate, without stripping all the enamel from my teeth like my usual cheap French plonk. I could settle back in the chair and enjoy the weather as the sun sank behind the trees.

'I'm going to have to leave in a couple of days to sort out some business in town,' Derek said. 'Will you be OK here?'

'I'll be done by then, I expect,' I said. I was contentedly wriggling back into my seat. 'I reckon a couple of hours of careful

sketching, and then . . .' I performed a very quick mental calcu-
lation, mostly involving what I was charging him, and how much
time he would anticipate my spending for that fee. I didn't want
a demand for a discount, after all. 'About a day and a half of
actual painting here, then another half-day or more in my studio
adding the final touches.'

'You can do that away from here?'

We discussed the finer points of completing a painting, the
detail, the highlights, the shadows, for some little while. I won't
bother to repeat it all, and after another pause, during which he
gazed at his mobile phone, I asked whether he had heard any
more about Jez Cooper's arrest.

'Nothing, no. I believe he's still with the police, but as to what
they're questioning him about, or whether they seriously believe
he has anything to do with poor Rick's death, I don't know. It'll
make things sticky for Helen and her other boy. It's just such a
tragic case. I can't imagine what she is going through.'

'No. Tell me, in Ashbourne, do you hear much about drugs?'

He peered at me slightly owlishly. By now we had drunk more
than a bottle of wine each, so I suppose it wasn't entirely
surprising. 'Drugs? No, not really. It's not as if we're in London.
Derby has some dodgy areas, and Chesterfield, but Ashbourne?
No, I don't think so. The police aren't particularly bothered by
the threat here, anyway, from what I've heard.'

'From the press?'

'No. I speak to the deputy chief of police regularly. I help
sponsor Victim Support, the charity looking after those who get
attacked or robbed. As far as I'm aware there's nothing much
about drugs or dealers in the regular reports. Why do you ask?'

'I was watching some kids in the town today,' I lied, 'and they
looked a bit stoned. In London we're always hearing that things
in the country are really bad because of these county lines gangs.
You know, young kids plonked on trains with bags full of drugs,
and sent off to distribution centres all over the country, where
other kids will take the drugs to the school's gates and try to sell
them.'

'I'm sure we have nothing like that here,' Derek said comfort-
ably. 'It's much more the usual problems of drink, vandalism
and casual silliness. I'm sure that there are areas with other

problems, but Ashbourne is not one of them. It's one of the ten safest towns in Derbyshire, you know. From memory, there was only one drug offence registered last year. It's one reason why I decided to move here when I did. There were over twenty assaults and sexual assaults last year in Ashburton, by comparison. No, this is a really safe area.'

'That's good.'

'But you thought some of the children in the town were on drugs?'

'They looked a bit wobbly. It could be that they were tipsy, I suppose.'

'Yes, well, it was probably only the usual things: cheap vodka, extra-strength lager or cider. I remember drinking myself stupid with that kind of thing in my day. Still, make sure you do report anything suspicious,' he said seriously, his finger wagging. 'We don't want youngsters getting into trouble over things like that. Better to nip it in the bud.'

'Especially after Rick's death,' I said.

'Yes, of course. Especially after that.'

Adela had materialized with a tray of coffees. She deposited it between us on a low table, and I thanked her, smiling, but all the while I was wondering whether she offered other drugs to go with the nitrous.

There are some women who, I can flatter myself, like me and enjoy my company. It could be my devil-may-care approach to things, or the way that I can sketch them, but some women find me attractive – usually to my astonishment. I grew up in an age when feminism meant never showing respect to a woman – never offering a seat, never complimenting their dress sense, never opening a door for them, never suggesting anything improper. It did rather stultify relations. And then there were the problems for anyone who happened to work in the same company. Any suggestion of fraternizing outside office hours was distinctly dangerous, with the potential for allegations of unwanted attention all the way through to rape. Luckily, some delightful women took pity on me, and decided to make it quite obvious even to my mean intelligence that they would not be opposed to a little horizontal hula, to make my life more enjoyable.

Adela was certainly not one of those. Her lovely eyes did meet mine, but it was not like those across a crowded room full of boring people. In her case it was more a matter of alertness, as though she was concerned that she might be the victim of my unwanted attention. Or maybe it was just the reticence of a drug dealer to get involved with other people.

She retreated, and Derek continued.

'You know, I blame myself. I mean, I should have supported Jez more. I should have realized he was in a bad way. I just didn't see how much of a blow he'd taken. Oh, no. That's not right. I'm being disingenuous. I knew, all right. I knew that he was really upset, and I could put myself in his shoes, but at the end of the day, some business is a zero-sum game: one guy wins, another guy loses. That's just how it is. It's not like you artists, where you can all make paintings, and because of the different styles and approaches you all take, each painting is equally desirable. Know what I mean? It's like books. Authors aren't all in competition with each other. There are enough readers for several authors in the same field to make money. But in a business like mine, there's sometimes a need for a company to stage a takeover, like I did with Jez, so that the business can grow and develop in ways it couldn't otherwise. Like a computer company buying a firm that has specialist software, stuff that will complement its own offerings. Or a car company buying up a lighting manufacturer to use the lights in their cars because of some kind of innovation. Complementary, you see. Creating some kind of symbiosis or synergy. Something like that.'

As he rambled, I was reminded of past managers in companies I had worked for. Endless gushes of words which were only vaguely understood, their meaning dissipated by endless management-speak.

'With Jez, I really should have taken more care,' he said at last. 'I knew him, I knew Sue, and I could tell how badly it hit him when she died. Those last months for him . . . they must have been terrible.'

'You were still in contact with him then?'

'Oh, yes. He was still a director of his division then – five, six years ago – and in the process of handing over to the new team, but still involved, still *invested*, if you know what I mean. He was the sort of anchor for the firm, the rock on which the company was built. But I was away, striking deals, it's my main skill, you know, and while I was away the rock started sinking, and the anchor lost its grip . . .' he frowned as if recognizing that he was rambling badly '. . . and, anyway, we had to let him go, since he was doing nobody any good at that stage. If I'd only thought about it, I'd have realized it was because Sue was dying. I should have been more understanding. Still, no use crying over spilt milk.'

He poured more of the wine into our glasses.

'Yes, it was a real shame.'

Especially, I thought, since he had managed to not only dispose of Jez, but had also ripped away the one remaining thing Jez cared about: his company.

My room was a delightful chamber overlooking the rear garden. I could gaze out over the top of the terrace at the buildings in the distance, and I stood in the bay window for a while, just staring, my elbows on the heavy oak windowsills.

The more I was learning about Jez Cooper and his involvement with Derek, the more I was convinced that the merger of the two firms had not been in Jez's interests. What was it Derek had said? Something about some business not being fair – that was it: he said some deals were a zero-sum game. That means someone had to lose so that someone else could make a fortune. Derek had been the winner and, therefore, Jez had lost. Except he had lost so much more.

And here, last week, he had thought he had recovered one little thing: the son he had thought he'd lost for ever. But then, according to Al, that had been a foolish dream. Rick said he wasn't going to leave his mother and brother to go away with the man who had left him behind. The man who, according to his mother, had deserted the family.

It seemed off, to me. It was a hill in the distance painted with too much contrast. It sort of looked all right, but when you really stood back and considered the picture, it was too detailed and spoiled the overall effect. Does that make sense?

So, in this case, Jez had said that he had tried to contact the surrogate and keep in contact with his son. Helen, on the other hand, said that she had been deserted by him; he got her pregnant

and ran a mile. But as she said that, her eyes moved away in
what I could only think was a tell – she was lying.

What, specifically, was she lying about?

And was Jez merely a more accomplished liar than her?

There was a rattle from below me, and when I looked down,
I saw Adela was picking up the bottle, glasses and coffee cups,
gathering them on a tray, and then standing still in the
darkness.

It was bizarre. She was a real contradiction: beauty and yet
selling drugs. I guess there's no reason why drug sellers should
all be ugly, spotty monsters, but Adela just didn't look like one.
Not to me, anyway.

There was a flare which lit her face and the fringe of her hair
– remember, I was right overhead – and then a spark showed
where she had lit a cigarette. She stood there for some little
while, smoking and gazing at the view, a figure of wonderful
soft curves and beauty, and I really wished that she might come
up to my room and let me run my hands over those same curves.

Fat chance!

I stepped away from the window. It was time to get to bed,
clearly. My mind was racing ahead of my libido, and that was
always a dangerous thing.

EIGHT

I would like to say that I am always professional when out working on a commission, so yes, I was awake and out of bed before seven in the morning. This is not a time of day which is instantly familiar to me, but I wanted to be demonstrably keen and enthusiastic.

Showered, clad in fresh clothes and ready for a day's work, I went downstairs to the large kitchen, hoping to find a plate already being warmed, and a warmly welcoming Adela ready to serve me eggs, bacon and . . . well, you know the routine.

Instead I found the kitchen empty, as were the sitting room, dining room, garden room and all the others. I wandered out to the garden, and looked about me, but there was no sign of anyone there, either.

In the end I went and looked at the coffee machine, which seemed to boast more buttons than the console panel on an Apollo mission. Seven thirty was too early to seek out an instruction manual, and fearing that my technological skills must break the damn thing, I went back to my room and fetched the Aeropress and some coffee.

The kettle boiled, I ladled three good teaspoons of coffee into the Aeropress, and poured in the boiling water. With a good, strong cup of coffee in my hand, I went outside.

It was a lovely morning. The air was crisp and cool, but already warming. I sipped coffee while staring at the house in the distance, surrounded by its fortification of trees. It must be a farm – I could see a quad bike on the track on the way to it. No doubt heading to check on his lambs or something, I guessed. A farmer's work was never done.

This was a perfect place for sitting quietly and mulling over things, and I'd like to say that I was engaged in some deep reflections about Rick's death, Jez, Derek, Jon, Helen and others, but I'd be lying. Yes, I tried to think about all the implications of business, nitrous oxide and the investigators looking into Jez's affairs, but all that kept creeping into my mind was Adela and the way her hair moved as she walked, the curve of her back when she held up my sketches, the way that her eyes crinkled when she smiled, although leaving her eyes strangely untouched. She was a true enigma, that woman. What someone with her qualifications was doing up here in Derbyshire, keeping house for someone who was about to leave the country, I could only imagine. They didn't appear to be having an affair, Derek was distinctly hands-off when it came to her, and she had a distinct barrier between her and any bloke who approached her. Well, she did between herself and me, anyway, which I reckoned was about the same. As I've said, some women find me moderately appealing.

I finished my coffee and – in the absence of anything else to hand – I went on the scrounge.

The kitchen was large enough to serve Buckingham Palace, and had enough cupboards and drawers to efficiently store all the crockery and cutlery from the Ritz and the Savoy. I began with the doors nearest the sink, and went around the room in a clockwise fashion. The fridge was a huge one, hidden behind what I had taken to be a large broom cupboard, and had enough food for Derek for a week or so. There were three chicken breasts, a slab of ham, some eggs, tomatoes and assorted salad vegetables. And a lot of cold white wine, which rather surprised me. I had assumed that the house would have a large cellar filled with red wines, and a cooler to keep the whites at the perfect temperature. But what do I know? My own tastes run to cheaper wine than Derek's. Perhaps his tasted perfectly fine when cooled to absolute zero.

There was a loaf of bread in a cupboard pretty much as far from the fridge as it could be, and I grabbed four slices. A wooden board rested on the counter of the island, near to the hob, and I slapped the bread down on it. I smeared mustard over all four slices, added some chutney I found in a separate cupboard, and sought a sharp knife to cut some ham. I carved four good slices, found a bottle of pickled gherkins, sliced one thinly and set that over the top of the ham, added thinly sliced tomatoes, and hey presto! A quartet of half-sandwiches that would keep me going for the morning.

I found plates in the island itself, as I should have guessed, on the side farthest from the hob and sink, where they would be easily accessible to people at the table. And as I pulled a plate from the rack, I noticed something behind them. It rolled, and when I managed to get my fingers on it, I was forced to stand stock still, considering it while my brain fogged.

It was a bright, shiny cylinder. Much like a soda syphon's gas canister, but from the labels on the side, this was identical to the ones in the Memorial Park in Ashbourne, a Cream Charger.

This really wasn't any sort of a smoking gun. The fact that someone had used a nitrous oxide canister at some point was nothing in the greater scheme of things. I mean, plenty of people have bought these things and had a giggly evening as a result. And here I have to declare an interest: although I have never used it, I did try once. We had discussions about nitrous oxide when I was at school, listening to teachers talking about it and how it was a fabulously useful way to get people relaxed and calmed before they went for an operation. A few dodgy students and I considered making some, but we hit on the classic issues experienced by teenage boys: dedication and working through problems.

For example, it required the use of the chemistry block and various chemicals which were, by and large, locked away. And if we had succeeded, how would we collect our precious gas? Nowadays I would imagine a retort with a long tube leading to a bucket, with a beaker filled with water up-ended over the tube so that the gas could be collected. And then what? Turn the beaker right-side-up? And immediately lose all the gas. Hardly effective.

The new approach, as the blue cylinder in the field demonstrated, was to insert a cartridge of gas, fit a balloon over the mouth of the device, and then screw the cap down, releasing the gas from the cylinder into the balloon. Then pinching the balloon tight at the neck so that it could be passed from one user to the next. Far more hygienic than sharing a needle, and a lot easier than retorts and inverted beakers.

Not that such experiments appeal to me as an adult. Oh, like almost everyone of my generation, the generation before and every succeeding generation, I have tried weed. In fact I've tried it precisely three times. Twice it had no impact whatsoever, the third I had laid on a barbecue for friends, and tried a strong spliff. I woke up the next morning on my sofa. Apparently I had been an object of amusement for the whole of the previous evening. My friends and wife had taken great pleasure in eating the food laid on, drinking all the booze, and laughing at the sight of me (the beached whale, I think they called me), sprawled on my comfortable chair and giggling to myself.

But that's by-the-by. I've never had dealings with a drug dealer in my life, have never bought drugs, and apart from occasional sharing of other people's illegal smoking substances, I've never really had much to do with that culture. However, I know that almost everyone else has. Legal and banking professionals tend to prefer the white, sniffable powders, mixed with an occasional hash cookie now that smoking is frowned upon. Those in advertising can be more adventurous, going for periodic bursts of LSD or, occasionally, especially the creatives, something more potent. In the greater scheme of things, a gas cylinder was not important.

Apart from the fact of that blue cylinder in a field, and the dead body of Rick in the bushes. Those two made the discovery of this cartridge more . . . *interesting*. Especially having seen Adela in the truck selling drugs to Jon. That added to the intriguing nature of things.

However, I was not going to raise the matter immediately. Instead I carefully returned the little canister to its hiding place behind the plates, then picked it up, and carefully wiped any trace of a fingerprint off it, replacing it this time by holding it in a pair of paper tissues. If the police found it, I didn't want my prints on it. Satisfied, I took my plate of sandwiches out to the garden, and began to eat, thoughtfully.

The little gas cylinders surely wouldn't bring in all that much money. If that was all Adela was involved in, that would explain why she still lived here as a housemaid, rather than having her own palatial property nearby. Drugs like the hard stuff could keep dealers in plenty of money.

That was when I began to think about Derek himself. He kept Adela here, but the two seemed not to have any sort of relationship. Was he bringing in drugs and using her to sell them? That was a possibility.

When I had finished eating, I picked up my phone and put a call through to Geoff. 'Matey, things have got a little complicated up here,' I said when we were through the preliminary greetings. 'I need you to check on a couple of things for me. Two businesses.'

After all, it was easier to check on Derek's and Jez's stories using someone who had access to the best researchers into businesses – and Geoff's bank did have some of the best. They could earn their money for once.

'Sure. But it may take a day or two.'

After the last couple days, it was a relief to get out into the open air with an easel, paper, brushes and paints and concentrate purely on the picture.

I had decided that this was going to be a two-day job, and I set to carefully with a ruler and pencil to make sure I got the proportions right, making the perspective work and outlining the shadows from my previous attempt, giving the scar across the sky a disgruntled grimace. If only the blasted woman had not appeared when she did, that sketch would have been perfect.

Adela was now fixed in my mind as 'that blasted woman'. I was quite sure that the gas cylinder was nothing to do with Derek. Oh, sure, a man with a Porsche as new as his, with a house as perfect as his, and with clothes as spotless and – what? – trendy, I suppose, sounds like the archetypical drug dealer straight out of *Miami Vice*. Yeah, but this was a man whose fortune was accounted for by the money he was making selling up successful businesses. He was like a hedge fund manager – they made fortunes without selling drugs. They were much more likely to use them than deal in them. And Geoff could check on his business for me.

Besides, nitrous oxide was way below the level of a bond dealer or a man like Derek. Cocaine would be their favoured recreational diversion. I could see Derek involved in that, maybe. Perhaps, I reflected, there was a distinct demographic for users of laughing gas, as there was for glue-sniffers. Both struck me as being the lower end of the drug-user community.

Logically, older users would naturally migrate towards the more expensive, better recognized drugs. Hippier types would want grass or hash, the more professional would go for the powders. Only the poorest would go for laughing gas. As proof, I thought the location of the stash of used cylinders was indicative. A bandstand was the sort of place a group of teenagers would go to experiment.

Somehow I didn't see Derek as the kind of man to go for that. He would consider glue or nitrous oxide beneath a man of his calibre; he was definitely more a cocaine client. Adela, on the other hand, looked quite likely to experiment with nitrous. I suppose she occurred to me as the more likely simply because she had the look of someone without the disposable income to justify more expensive drugs. Not that she couldn't have got a better job and afforded them, but as a housekeeper, it was unlikely.

I finished the outline of the house and moved on to the surrounding landscape, looking at the trees and the driveway. On a whim, I started putting in a larger series of trees behind the house than I had originally planned, and rather liked the effect on the composition. I built up the oak on the left of centre, and then had the driveway moved a little to the right, as if pointing towards that tree, but in fact it meant that the eye was drawn straight to the house itself. Looking at it critically, I was content with that alteration. It did work better.

Mixing paints, putting down a series of washes, I soon had a base to work from, and could set the picture aside for a while. I'd brought an apple and a slice of flan which I'd found in the fridge, and I sat and munched them while the paint dried ready for the next level.

'I thought you would like coffee,' Adela said, walking towards me from the house – this time all the way in plain view. She was carrying a thermos and mug. 'I didn't want to make you jump again,' she smiled as she placed the Thermos on the ground and immediately stood back. 'I made it how you liked it yesterday, with milk and no sugar.'

She had a way about her that reminded me of someone, and when I thought back, I realized it was my daughter, Sam, who would have a similar manner about her when she knew she had done something that would get her into trouble. She would stand rather like Adela now, with her hands before her, her back very straight, and mouth just slightly pursed while her eyes met mine very firmly, as if to convince me of her total innocence.

'I saw you made yourself some breakfast,' she said. 'I am sorry I was not there to make it for you.'

'It's no problem,' I said. 'I found some bread and makings of a sandwich or two.'

'Yes, but I failed. My apologies.'

I wasn't sure what she was apologizing for. 'I'm sure you had other duties to attend to.'

'Yes. I am afraid so.'

I gave her a quizzical look. 'What do you mean?'

She looked over at the house, and for the first time I saw that she was anxious about something. It was not fear of discovery, as it had been with Sam, but something more concrete.

'I do not know what is happening. Derek, he is worried, and I can feel his concern. There are men asking about him in the town, and he is afraid, and that makes me scared.'

'Why?'

'He has fears about his business. It is being sold, and he is anxious. Troubled. He says any business deal can go south – that is right? "South"? Meaning go wrong?'

'Yes. Why should it go south, though? He is just selling his business as a going concern, isn't he?'

'Yes, but he is selling to foreign investors. Perhaps that is it. I don't know. These men worry him, I know.'

'Which men?'

'Men on motorbikes. There are two, and they seem to think Derek has done something wrong.'

My mind turned to Edwards and Pearce. 'Like policemen, you mean?'

'Yes. Have you seen them?'

'I think so, yes. But they showed no interest in Derek, only in other people.'

'What do they want?'

I remembered mention of the Official Secrets Act and shrugged as convincingly as I could. 'Oh, I don't know. They were just asking me about another guy at the park, not Derek.'

'It was Mr Cooper? I know he makes Derek very worried.'

'No, I don't think so,' I said. 'I've spoken to him, and Derek reckons he should have helped the man more, that's all. They used to know each other well, but in recent years they've not kept in touch, and that makes Derek feel guilty, because he knew that Jez Cooper had lost his wife. And I think he wasn't entirely kind when he took over Jez's business. Beyond that, I don't think there's anything there. The two bikers are more interested in Jez, anyway, rather than Derek.'

'Perhaps that is why Derek is afraid,' she said quietly, staring back at the house with her enormous, luminous eyes.

'What do you mean?'

'I don't know. Forgive me, you must excuse. My worries are not yours. Please, say nothing to Derek about this talk. Don't let him know I am concerned, yes?'

'Of course not,' I said. 'But tell me one thing.'

'Yes?'

'I saw your pickup at Jez Cooper's chalet some days ago. How did you know him?'

'I don't think I have ever met him,' she said firmly.

That was when she left me. I watched her make her way down to the track that wound down through the trees towards the footpath that would take her back to the house. It was a concealed route for much of the way, which was why she had startled me that first day of painting here, and now I could see her head moving down and through the foliage. Recalling the quad bike earlier, I saw it was the same track that led from the house to the farm in the distance.

I watched her thoughtfully, because no matter what else I was sure of, I was absolutely certain that Adela had just lied. Perhaps she expected me to think Derek had taken her truck, but there was no love lost between Derek and Jez. I couldn't believe that. And the only other person it could have been who met Jez that evening was Adela. It was her truck.

And she didn't want Derek to know she'd seen Jez. That was interesting. Very interesting.

She was plainly worried about her employer, although what could be so worrying was beyond me. Perhaps because my mind was too tied up with other matters to see what was right in front of me.

The furthest I managed to think was to wonder whether Derek and she were having an affair. He had money; she was delectable. It would hardly be surprising. Perhaps she would join him in his island retreat, once this house was sold. Both had denied it – but those enjoying emotional entanglements would often deny it. A man of his position, because he felt he had some status to keep up; a young woman like her because she wouldn't want people to think she was a gold-digger or worse. So the denials rang slightly off to me. Perhaps she would join him.

That thought made me rather sad. Still, the coffee was good. I drank a couple of cups and went back to work.

I was exhausted by three thirty. Don't ask me how it is that staring at a lovely scene and representing it on paper can be exhausting, but take it from me, it is. The constant attention to detail, to shades of colour, to the amount of water to add, to the constant review of the overall impression – yes, it gets tiring.

When I had packed up all my bits and pieces, I trudged back to the house, taking the route Adela had used. The other times I had made my way to the viewpoint by crossing the field before the house, but she was right. This route was much faster and easier. It only took about five minutes to return to the kitchen, where I rinsed out the Thermos and cup, and left them to drain. I glanced at the coffee machine with its rows of bright, shiny buttons, and reached for my Aeropress instead. With a good mugful, I wandered out to the terrace and sat staring over the view.

There was no sound apart from birdsong. A robin came and settled on the terrace's wall, staring at me with a beady eye, as if questioning my right to be there, or perhaps trying to persuade me to engage in some manual work, digging up the flower bed to expose some worms. I ignored him.

It was while I was out there that I received a phone call saying that my Morgan was fixed, 'Although you do need to get the frame seen to. There's a fair bit of worm in it, if you ask me.'

Yes, I knew that. I thanked him, and agreed to meet him back at the park where he'd collected it, and returned inside to find Adela. There was the sound of a vacuum cleaner upstairs, and I did call to her, but there was no answer. It was cracking on for four already, and I had a twelve-mile ride back to the chalet park. I dithered for a few moments, but then went out to the bike.

It took little time to get back aboard, and then I was riding back along the track to Parsley Hay, and on to the trail. The weather was kind again, and it took little time to make it back to Tissington, and then on the next few miles to the steps where I left the old rail bed, and down to the road. I freewheeled down that hill, and was soon at the reception area, where I dismounted without regret for what I hoped was the last time, and waited for the car to return.

I was just glancing about me when something caught my attention. Peering in at the windows to the café by the swimming pool, I saw Megan waving frantically.

It has to be admitted that I was inclined to pretend I hadn't seen her, and turn away, pretending that reflections on the windows obscured the view, but it was already too late. She must have seen my gaze fix on her, and now she beckoned. I could not refuse the summons without being rude, so I sighed to myself and went to join her.

'Darling, where *have* you been? It's been so thrilling down here, what with the police, that awful man Cooper, and then the robbery! You've missed all the excitement!'

'Why, what's happened?'

'I told you! Cooper was released from prison, and then came back here, where he was going to get packed, but before he could, someone broke into his chalet and knocked him out, leaving him for dead, and took a lot of papers or something. He was concussed, apparently, and quite distraught, and the police couldn't make head nor tail of it all, from what I saw. Poor man, I suppose, but it's hard to feel much sympathy for someone who deserts his family, isn't it? In any case, I think it was probably someone else who thought they'd teach him a lesson who broke into the chalet and attacked him. They probably just took papers to make it look like a robbery, don't you think? If there *were* any papers, that is!'

For a while I gaped. This was so soon after my own assailant, and the thought that I could have been beaten and battered and left hospitalized was enough to make me feel a little queasy. Then it occurred to me that Jez would not have had a bunch of sketches to be stolen: 'What sort of papers?'

'Oh, who knows? He's in hospital, I heard, but no doubt he'll have told the police all about them.'

'I wonder,' I said. I was thinking of his tale of Derek stealing his company. Perhaps, if the papers were evidence of that, then someone working on Derek's behalf could have decided to come in and steal them, with the aim of destroying any case Jez might have been trying to build against his one-time colleague. That would make sense. And then another thought struck me: it might explain where Derek was today. 'When was he attacked?'

'Middle of last night, I think. The police all turned up before breakfast,' she said, her tone disgruntled at the thought, I guessed, of being woken at such an ungodly hour. 'The ambulance had him away before nine thirty, I think. There's still a police officer there keeping an eye on the chalet. I don't think the owners of the park will be happy. He was supposed to be leaving tomorrow, I think, and this will muck up their rentals.'

I nodded absently, wondering whether this was the explanation of Derek's non-appearance at breakfast that morning. It would certainly make sense, if he decided to liberate any papers Jez had with him. Perhaps Jez had spoken to him and threatened something, or intimated that he had proof that Derek had diddled him out of his business. It seemed barely credible, and I was about to thank Megan and change the subject, when another thought struck me.

'The two bikers who arrived the same day, are they still here?'

'They're somewhere around here, yes, but not staying here at the park any more. They left yesterday, like you, but I've seen them riding between here and Ashbourne twice today, so they're obviously staying somewhere locally. Why?'

'Oh, nothing. I just wondered,' I said.

'Come on, spill the beans, young Morris. I won't name you as my source in the next thrilling story from my word processor.'

'Oh, don't even joke about it,' I groaned. 'All right, all I'll say is, those two struck me as fishy from the start. The way they nearly rode into Rick, the way they . . .'

'What?'

I hadn't been going to mention their visit, but now I'd started, I could hardly keep it secret. Only what they'd actually said.

'They barged into my chalet a couple of days ago, demanding to know what I knew about Jez Cooper.'

'And you told them about our suspicions of his being a crook?'

'That was *your* suspicion, not mine,' I protested. 'And no, I didn't give them that sort of wild speculation. I just explained I hardly knew the guy.'

'You're quite sure you didn't give them reason to break in? If they had a suspicion that there could be something in his chalet, that would make sense. Perhaps they heard late Saturday that he had been arrested, and decided to break in on Sunday. They didn't know he'd been released by the police.'

Her face cleared as she gazed past me into the middle distance. 'Good God! That's it! They didn't realize he was freed, so they booked out, coming back when they knew the coast would be clear in the middle of the night. But when they broke in, they found him alive and well, and asking them what the hell they thought they were doing, dropping in at such a horrible hour of the night, so they slugged him, snatched what they could, and had it away on their toes like any good villain!'

'Why? What sort of papers would they be after?' I asked dubiously.

'Don't be such a cold fish, Morris my darling. It's as plain as the nose on your face that the two bikers were up to no good, any more than Cooper himself. Perhaps it's more simple: they were both from a competing gang seeking to persuade a business competitor to remove himself from the fray before he began to acquire injuries? But I rather like the idea that he had incriminating papers on him. Who can tell, perhaps he was actually on the side of the angels after all? What if he had a job with the police, and he was there to investigate crime in the area, and the two bikers are with a local gang of thugs who are responsible for a local crime wave? They supply all the drugs to the children of the area, perhaps, and sought to find out what the detective had discovered about them?'

As was usual with Megan, while her fertile imagination blossomed, so did the volume of her voice. By the end of that sentence, almost every head in the café was turned towards her, and unsurprisingly all other conversation had ceased. Equally unsurprisingly, she was gloriously unaware.

'Megan—' I tried, but it was no good. She was in full flow, necklace and bangles rattling with her excitement.

'Yes, I can see it now! The two noted local vagabonds and bullies entered his chalet, probably using lock-picks – they'll be proficient house-breakers, obviously – and wandered about using pen torches, sifting through all the papers in his sitting room, and then go through to the bedrooms, where they wake him. Startled, he springs out of bed, determined to wrestle them to the floor, but one has a sap . . .'

'A what?'

'A sap. Dear me, don't you know anything? A leather cosh, filled with lead shot or similar. Anyway, yes, he has a sap, and thumps our hero over the head. He collapses, and they fear he's dead, so the two grab all the things they can, and hurry from the door, down to the road, where they had left their bikes, no doubt, so the noise of them wouldn't disturb people here like me, and soon they're away and over the horizon.'

She sighed happily with the contentment of a craftsperson whose job had been difficult, but was now complete. 'And to think that I was going to portray him as a master criminal and drug dealer.'

'Which would have been monstrously unfair,' I commented.

'Hardly "monstrously",' she reprimanded. 'It was a fair assumption. Now, if I can work that into my story as well,' she added musingly, 'I'll have to leave him for the first third, then explain his apparent guilt in the second, and come back to expose his innocence in the final third. That would work as a novel.'

'If you say so,' I said, but just then her eyes lit up. 'Your car is back. I've missed the sight of her. It brought back memories of mine.'

'While you were a nurse you could afford a Morgan? How was that?'

'Ah, well, when my first husband died, he left me some money, so I bought the car, but when the second passed away, poor Peter, I had nothing. I had to sell the car to repay the mortgage, because I couldn't afford it on my nurse's salary. I replaced it with a Mini. A boring little box, it has to be said. Morgans have such a lot of character, don't they?'

'Yes. And expense,' I added, thinking about the frame's woodworm.

'You ought to learn to maintain her yourself,' she said reprovingly. 'It's not as if they're difficult. You don't need a degree in computers to keep a moggie on the road, only a couple of ounces of common sense. And the ability to afford plenty of oil, I recall.'

'Yes, true enough,' I said. And I did know a fair amount. After all, I knew how to remove the rocker box cover and adjust the tappets. It was only when something was missing that I got a bit confused.

I took my leave of her and went to talk to the mechanic, who spent the next fifteen minutes describing in the minutest detail exactly how he had been forced to contact Ford Europe, and probably had to arrange for a chartered plane to fly the relevant item over, no expense spared, from the look of his bill.

However, he still held the keys to my car in an oily, hairy fist, so I had little choice other than to agree to his extortion and, before long, for the price of only three paintings of cats, I had the keys back in my hand and was ready to leave the park for good.

I climbed into the car while he was loading the pushbike into the back of a pickup driven by a friend or employee, turned the key, and found that foolish smile once more as the entire car shook herself, like a dog leaving a river, and then I could hear the burble of the engine in front of me again, and as I let the racing handbrake slip free, and felt the car surge forward, the foolish smile became a broad grin of pure joy. Pulling out from the entrance to the park, I hoofed it, and felt that push in the back once more.

Woodworm or no woodworm, I didn't care. I loved that car.

'I was growing worried,' Adela said when I drew up outside the house, pulled the tonneau cover over, and nimbly sprang up the stairs.

She was in the kitchen, and I could smell something delicious in the making.

'Ah, sorry for that. I did try to call to you, but I think you were hoovering or something upstairs,' I said. 'The garage called to say my car was ready, so I had to go and collect it.'

There was no reason to add the fifteen-mile round trip I had taken after leaving the park. The simple fact was, I had to go for a drive just to get rid of the exhilaration of retrieving my car. Yes, childish, I know, but it's how I am.

'What are you cooking?'

'We have a little grilled Mediterranean salad to start, and then a fish pie with haddock, cod, scallops and prawns. I hope you enjoy seafood?'

'It sounds excellent. Where's Derek?'

'He had to leave first thing today. I think his business in London is taking up more of his time than he had expected. He is trying to wind things down, but . . . but there are always complications, you understand?'

'Yes, of course,' I said, in reality wondering what on earth such complications could be. I have no idea how to run a large business, of course, but the idea that the business owner would have to keep taking the train into town seemed odd. Surely he would have lawyers, accountants, company secretaries to take command of that kind of thing. And at the same time, no, it didn't escape my attention that the man happened to be away just as Jez was knocked down and had things stolen. Was he preparing an alibi for himself? What if they were papers to do with the business, perhaps showing that Derek didn't have such a good claim to ownership as he had said, meaning that the sale might fall through?

'Can I fetch you anything?' I asked.

She brushed the hair away from her brow. It was entirely unmarked by creases, like a woman of only nineteen, but she must have been in her mid-twenties at the very least. In fact, looking at her, observing her confidence, I would have put her nearer thirty. She had that sort of quiet assurance that spoke of experience. As I was thinking that, she shot me a look from the corner of her eye. Her brow lifted, just a little, and she said, 'It is terrible, but for a good fish pie, it is necessary to use a little white wine. If you could open a bottle, perhaps it would be permissible for us to stop the wine going sour by drinking it?'

I grinned. 'But of course!' And went to the fridge to fetch a bottle. It was the same as the one Derek and I had drunk outside the previous night, and I unscrewed the cap and sniffed the neck appreciatively.

'You can pour,' she said sternly, and I hastened to comply. She directed me to a glasses cabinet, and I took out two large glasses, tipping a portion into each. When I held one out to her, she looked at the quantity in the glass with solemn disapproval. 'It is better to pour less, to keep the wine cool,' she said. 'Otherwise you must drink too quickly before the wine warms in the glass.'

'I can do that,' I said.

'You want me to get drunk?'

'No, no,' I lied.

She shook her head and began telling me about growing up in Poland, where the children in her village were brought up on illicit vodka. She had, so she told me, been to pubs in Oxford where the other students tried to get her drunk. They had failed, and she had often had to help them home to their own beds.

'I'll be careful, then,' I said, and sipped some more while trying to put from my mind the vision of Adela helping me into my bed.

It was another hour before Adela brought the dishes outside to the table, and we sat down companionably to enjoy the meal. I poured more wine, and we ate in silence, although every so often our eyes would meet in what I can only describe as a friendly manner.

She came from a town near a city called something like Chestahova, with the emphasis on a heavy 'h' like the sound of 'ch' in 'loch'. Apparently it was a town with a distinct past, because when the Germans wanted to evict Jews before the Second World War, many were pushed over the borders into Poland and they were held in the city. Later, when the Germans and USSR implemented the Molotov–Ribbentrop Pact and divided Poland between them, this city was already full of deported Jews. Now they were displaced again, forced to go to German concentration camps. The memory of those years was still with the Polish of the area, apparently. Oh, and when I asked her about the city, I was told that it was spelled Częstochowa – so you can thank me for setting it out phonetically.

Her parents brought her to the UK when Tony Blair opened the borders, although her mother didn't like the country, the food, the weather, and her parents returned to Poland after the Brexit vote, fearing rampant xenophobia as threatened in the press. 'But there was nothing,' she said with a shrug. 'The same people liked me, the same people who before didn't like me, still didn't. It made no difference.'

'Will you go back to Poland?'

'No! Of course not! I have work, I have a life here. I like England. It is a good country to live. And it is farther from the Russian border.'

After Russia's 2022 invasion of Ukraine, that seemed a perfectly logical motivation for remaining in the UK.

We finished our meal, and while I didn't get the impression that she was any more enthusiastic about me generally, she was definitely less condemnatory than I had sensed earlier.

I offered to make coffee, and she laughed when I admitted I didn't know how to use the machine in the kitchen. However she was gracious enough to agree to trying my own coffee, and I cleared the bulk of the dishes as I went indoors. Soon we were sipping coffee as the sun began to go down in the west and the hills took on a silvery, ghostly appearance in the twilight. It was all very Tolkienesque still, and I just drank it all in. Which was helped by having Adela at the other side of the table. She was a very tranquil companion, and while I was suspicious of her, since her truck was used to supply little nitrous cylinders, and I could not consider her as a potential partner, it was obvious enough that she didn't consider me entirely loathsome.

All in all, it was a very pleasant evening, and I was sorry when she indicated that she was feeling chilly. It was not an offer to move indoors, but rather a suggestion that it was time for her to catch up on some sleep. She rose, took up the remaining dishes, and made her way inside. She didn't need or want company while she dealt with the dishwasher, so I remained outside, wistfully thinking of what might have been. Well, all right then, you can swap 'lustfully' for 'wistfully' if you must. All I knew was, she was beautiful, and I doubt many men would have turned her down, were she to make them an offer.

I followed her a little later with my coffee cup, and thanked her when she took it and bent low to place it in the dishwasher. She had already loaded it with saucepans, spoons and all the other tools she had used to create our meal, but while I was watching her I saw that her hair was paler towards the scalp. I realized that her glorious auburn curls probably came from a bottle. Not that it was entirely surprising. Many women self-modified with hair colouring. You could hardly miss it, with the number of attractive women who had blue, pink or (bizarrely to my mind) grey dyes. Odd to see a blonde change to auburn, but it did suit her and her complexion.

Still, it was a little clue that my idol might have clay feet. No, not that I'd have cared if she had invited herself to my room, or indicated that I was welcome to join her in her own room.

No, there was no such offer. I walked slowly upstairs to my bed and lay on it with my hands behind my head, staring at the ceiling, thinking of her and very little else, oddly enough. And I was still there in the middle of the night when I opened my eyes again.

NINE

Yes, it's honestly not something I do terribly often, but just that once I fell asleep fully clothed. I guess it was the effect of hours of fresh air on someone who is based in the south of London, accustomed to the fumes and choking diesel smoke of the city's car community. My lungs just aren't used to the abundance of clean air.

At the same time, I had been busy for several days, what with finding corpses, being robbed in my chalet, having some bastard nick the rotor arm from my car, and then seeking more information about Rick and his family. All in all, I was pretty knackered, and dozing off was hardly surprising.

However, what was surprising was waking up.

I am not a good middle-of-the-night waker. I'm not sure whether I've mentioned this already, but when I get off to sleep, I can pretty much guarantee that I won't wake up until the sun is pretty high in the sky. I am not a natural waker with the dawn, like others I know. A friend used to be in the Royal Marines, and he still cannot go past five in the morning without springing from bed as fresh as a daisy. Not that a daisy necessarily occurs to me when I look at his ravaged features, beaten and moulded from rugby and boxing, as well as a long, jagged scar along one cheek from a bayonet in Afghanistan. Still, no matter what the time of year, his body clock kicks in with a personal alarm at five precisely every day. I imagine that is one reason why his wife left him – but then mine left me, so it's possible that she went for other reasons.

Be that as it may, the simple fact is that I was suddenly woken by something. It could have been the taste in my mouth – that deserved to have stirred me – but no, it was something external, I was sure.

I stretched my ears, listening intently, and I was sure that I could hear moaning, or perhaps weeping. There were voices, I thought, and I glanced at my watch to see what the time was. It was gone three in the morning, a ridiculous hour, unless it was an extension of the evening before, and I frowned, trying to discern any further noises.

There was nothing, though. I was still in my bed, I felt rank after sleeping in my clothes, and I got up and shucked off the shirt, trousers and pants, and climbed back between the sheets.

Whatever the noise had been, I was sure that I had mistaken it as being something significant.

I woke with scratchy eyes and a tongue that had been wire-woolled to remove the taste of wine. As an operation, it had failed. My mouth tasted like the floor of an eighties wine bar. In short, I hadn't slept well.

The kitchen was once more devoid of housekeeper and house owner, but I didn't let it worry me. I went to the stash of plates and peeped underneath all the crocks to see whether my cylinder of the day before had been discovered, and it was gone. Clearly Adela had been the proud owner of it, since Derek had been else-where all day yesterday. So Adela was perhaps an enthusiastic user of nitrous oxide and kept a little collection of cylinders for personal use as well as supplying Jon and his friends. Who was I to judge?

Well, if she was, as I suspected, the main supplier to Jon and his friends, I was perfectly entitled to judge. I was, after all, a parent myself. I didn't like to think of her selling drugs. Then again, I was reluctant to go making accusations to the police. She wasn't the archetypal drug dealer at all. And laughing gas wasn't illegal.

It would be interesting, though, to discover how the gas dispenser/balloon filler had appeared in the field close to where Rick had died – or where his body was found, to be fair. I was still doubtful about the actual location of the murder.

I began to make breakfast. There was a cupboard full of cereals, which I detest, but there was one packet of jumbo oats. Now, if there's one thing I can be partial to, it's a bowl of porridge. I found salt and tipped half a teaspoonful into a saucepan, and dug around for a weighing scale. It was hidden behind the breadbin, I discovered, and quickly measured a load of oats. Working on the basis of about seven times the weight of water to the weight of oats, I soon had a watery mixture. Sticking it on the heat and stirring, it slowly thickened. With a steaming bowl of porridge, happily smothered in berries and yoghurt, I went outside to sit in the sun again.

Idly, I flicked through the messages on my phone while I ate. There was nothing of great interest there, and nothing in the world that was of importance to me – the usual failing politicians, sexual liaisons, incompetent policing, all the run-of-the-mill sort of stuff that happens weekly – so I finished my meal and went back inside to rinse my bowl and spoon.

It was while I was washing up that the call came from Geoff.

'That's faster than I expected,' I said.

'Yes, well, I had a couple of trainees with bugger all to do, so I set them on it. You're right. There are some strange aspects to this.'

'Such as?'

'Well, Jez's company was absorbed into Derek's new firm, Derek Artificial Intelligence Systems, I think he called it, with AI in the middle of his initials, to be honest. He never was very good at company names – but from a close study of things, Derek hasn't fully absorbed Jez Cooper's business. It appears to have relocated to an address in Huddersfield, but when I had it checked out, there were sixty-three firms registered there.'

'It's a lawyer's office, then,' I said knowledgeably.

'No. It's a private residential address.'

'How can that be?'

'LLPs, Limited Liability Partnerships, were brought in in a bit of a hurry,' Geoff said with a note of defensiveness. 'Anyway, that doesn't matter. What happened next was that the company saw its control passing to a new address in Jersey. There, the board of partners were all employees of a Middle Eastern bank, but Derek remained the majority partner. But if you look at the firm on the internet or anywhere, you'll see it's listed still as Jez's firm. Anyone trying to sue for fraud or anything would immediately hit on Jez Cooper as the culprit.'

I shut off the call with his news whirling in my mind, as I shouldered my messenger bag and made my way back along the track to my viewpoint. For today, I had to finish this painting before I considered Geoff's revelations. Once I was done, then would be the time to reflect on Derek's business practices.

The route took me along the farm lane, leading behind the garden and out towards the farmstead in the distance. There were tyre tracks, indicating the quad bike I had seen before. I know Devon farmers use them to carry fodder and other essentials to sheep up on the moors, and I assumed this would be much the same.

I reached my viewpoint and studied the house while I set up the easel and prepared my paints. It took a little time to get everything as I needed it, and then I stood staring aimlessly at the scene while I let it sink in. Then I began mixing the lighter shades of blue, green and grey, using them to bring in tonal values, and then, while those glazes dried, I prepared the final aspects, which would be the little details that brought a painting to life: highlights on top of specific areas, little scrapes and flicks to indicate grasses or flowers, the spatters which gave rise to the sense of stones and pebbles in the foreground – all the little tricks and important aspects of good painting, in short.

By lunchtime, I was almost completely finished. The rest could wait until I got home and could study the painting in my studio with the benefit of some spare time and consistent lighting. That – and a good photo reproduced on my iPad – was all I needed.

I began to pack up my things and, as I did, I saw the quad bike making its way from the house back towards the farm in the distance. It was not terribly far away, and when I peered down, I was fairly sure that the rider was Adela. She rode past me, the engine chugging along quietly, and I watched her trundle off up the lane, standing and negotiating the wilder potholes and other obstacles on the way. She was a very competent rider, it has to be said.

Finishing my packing, collapsing the metal legs of the easel and shouldering my bag, the picture still stuck to the board under my arm, I picked up the easel's body and set off back to the house. It was not a long walk, but as I approached the garden, I heard the engine again, and paused. I had not long to wait. Adela soon appeared, riding the quad bike like a farmer's wife, her long hair blowing in the wind. She had a large cardboard box on the rear seat behind her, fixed in place with bungee cords, and I stood back to let her pass, closing my eyes and trying not to inhale the fumes from the engine, and then she was past, and making her way round to the side of the house where the bike had its little garage.

Walking up to the house, I admit I was rather thoughtful. It wasn't Adela, exactly, and it wasn't seeing her on the bike. It was more the sound I had heard, the tiny, rattly tinkle, as of lots of small metal cylinders, which emanated from the cardboard box behind her.

Adela was flushed when I walked into the kitchen. She looked over at me with a bright smile that was, well, just a little more cheery than her usual expression when seeing me.

'Have you had a successful morning?'

I pulled out my painting to show her, and she made all the right, appreciative noises about my skill and competence, and then offered lunch. There was no apology this time for my having to find my own breakfast, only a sort of hurried busyness. She offered wraps or a salad, and I could go outside to sit and she would bring it to me.

It cannot be said that I am not an accommodating guest. I walked out and stood gazing at the farm in the distance, wondering whose it was, and whether it was now being used as a storage shed for hay, tractor parts and illicit drugs. I had no doubt that Adela had been bringing nitrous oxide cylinders back with her when I saw her on the quad bike. That rattling noise was far too familiar.

The problem was, I didn't know what to do about it. Derek had told me that he was on the board of Victim Aid, and it would make sense for me to report the fact of the gas cylinders to the police – except there were some difficulties, it occurred to me.

First was, if I reported their presence here, I would be very unlikely to be popular, either with Adela or Derek. After all, if he was discovered to have been harbouring a criminal smuggler, it would open him to all kinds of investigation and accusation which he would be unlikely to appreciate.

Then again, I had no actual proof. I had heard the quad bike rattle as it passed me. Well, OK, it was the box that rattled. But she had visited a farm, and I assumed that Derek and she had responsibility for some animals on the estate. What could be more natural than that she might have a store of medicines for cattle or sheep? Or tools? But of course, there was a slight problem with that: she was supposed to be a housekeeper, not a farmer's hand. And surely there must be rules about the drugs a farm could hold? I doubted they would include nitrous oxide.

In any case, I had a clear incentive to avoid discovering proof, if at all possible. I didn't want to find something embarrassing to my employer, not when he hadn't paid me yet. This trip had been ruinously expensive already, with several hundred going into the chalet, let alone the cost of feeding Megan's drinks habit.

But when I considered ignoring the possibility of drugs, I was confronted with the memory of Rick, with the look of Al and Penny, and their friend Stan, the companion who had been at the park when I was shown the empty cartridges. And yes, I had thought at the time that his appearance could have been more than mere coincidence. After all, if a lad like him was going to try to get cheerful on something like laughing gas, he might well go to a known meeting place, such as a bandstand, where he could buy a couple of the necessary containers to share with a few friends. What was it Penny and Al had said about him? That he had been feeling rough on the Sunday when I saw them.

I pulled out my phone and started tapping. Soon I had the page up which showed the little cartridges, and I had learned that they were called *Whippets*, or *Whip-Its* after their use for making fluffy whipped cream. They could be used in small soda-syphon-like devices for cookery, or larger bottles could be bought for commercial catering firms. It was a moderately safe gas, but when I started looking through the lists of symptoms – dizziness, vomiting, nerve damage, confusion, memory loss, brain damage, hypoxia, even heart attacks – any desire to test the gas on myself soon dissipated.

It made me think about Stan, though. The boy who had seemed the more aggressive of the trio when I met them, the one who seemed to have little interest in things, who was mildly antisocial, or was toward me at any rate, and the one whom I had seen at the bandstand.

If he was using these whippets, maybe it had already caused

some mental damage? If so, with luck he might recover, but there was the other side of the coin. If Adela had a stash of these cylinders, and was providing them to the local kids, she was responsible for the damage to Stan, and if I didn't report her to the police, it was likely that she would cause similar damage to others in the area.

It was impossible. I couldn't leave the matter.

I smiled at her gaily as she brought out a superb lunch of cold fish and salad leaves. Rocket, lettuce, some chicory, with a sprinkling of fennel over the top, with radishes and cucumber slices all about the edge, and a fabulous version of French remoulade that made my taste buds dance a tango on my tongue.

Yes, I smiled at her even as I plotted her downfall.

There are ways to go about things sensibly.

First and foremost I had to find evidence to prove I was right. Secondary to that was the fact that I had to persuade the police. I was resigned to the risk of losing my fee and commission for the picture of Derek's house, but if he decided to cut up rough . . . well, there was really very little I could do about it. I could not leave a drug dealer to injure the local teens without trying to stop her.

So my decision was made. Next was, where to begin? It was possible that there was a significant number of the gas canisters at the neighbouring farm. If that was the case, it may be easy to find them. But how did they get there? Someone with a container-load? Or just four or five boxes in the boot of a car? Or Land Rover, more likely, looking at the track to the farm. If there were only a few boxes, it would be problematic searching for them. However, if she had brought a single box in here, full of a series of boxes like the one I had seen at the bandstand, which held twenty-four cylinders in each, she would need a good place to conceal them. And there had been no time to hide them before I saw her in the kitchen on my return. Only a few minutes, surely. So the box might be in the garage with the quad bike, or somewhere between the garage and the kitchen – or in the kitchen itself, of course. With all that cupboard space, there were plenty of hiding places.

For preference, I reckoned the garage would be easiest to

search. When I had finished my lunch, I took the dishes back to
the kitchen and gave them to Adela in a masterful, male manner,
and when she took them, I walked straight back out, and round
the house towards the garage.

The quad bike's shed was little better than a lean-to on the
side of the main garage. It shared its space with a variety of
power tools used for the garden, as well as old-fashioned spades,
forks and watering cans. In short, it was full of places that could
easily hide a small army of tiny gas cylinders. I sighed, and
looked about me with foreboding. It would take an age to search
it all. And then I had an idea, and began to look at the dust. All
the shelves had a fine layer. The housekeeper didn't dust in here,
tsk, tsk, I thought. Naughty, naughty. However, there were a
series of boxes on a shelf at the back of the shed. And when I
opened the nearest, you'll never guess what I found . . .

No. No cylinders, but what looked like old coins. Very old
coins.

I stared at them with a great deal of confusion for quite a long
time, until the quiet voice behind me coughed as though apologetically. 'Mr Morris, you shouldn't be in here.'

There have been times in the past when I have been seriously
surprised by events. Rarely, I have to admit, have I been so
stumped as I was there, in that shed, staring down into a cardboard box full of coins.

'What is going on?'

She walked up to me and peered down into the box herself.
Sighing, she folded over the four top flaps and pushed the box
back into its recess. 'I suppose I cannot persuade you to keep
quiet about this? I could pay you well?'

Of course, that should have put a very different complexion
on things, but just now I wasn't in the mood to play with what-
ifs such as, *what if you bugger off with all these coins and I
never see you again so you don't pay me?* Or *what if I just go
straight to the police and report this?* 'Where did you get all
these?'

She sighed and lifted a shapely buttock to perch on the top of
the quad bike. 'It's from near Tissington. I had read about the
town and I was always interested in history, so I thought it would

be interesting to come here. Derek was very kind and offered me a job when we first met, although I wasn't interested at first.'

'Why?'

'Ah, it is so difficult to get the right sort of employment, you know. I have been offered many jobs, but it is often a job that involves lying on my back. I do not want such a job. So I say no when men offer things like that. But then I realize that Derek is not that sort of a man. He is not interested in me. He only cares about other men – and his businesses. So, after a while, I think, "Why not?" The house is not a hard job, and Derek leaves me to my own interests mostly. I have to be here when he has guests, to serve, but also to make people think he is normal.'

The penny dropped. OK, the sovereign, then. It was a heavy fall, certainly. 'He's gay?'

'Yes. But this in business is not always good. If he negotiates with a Russian or a man from parts of Saudi Arabia, he finds he has a problem if he admits he is gay. So he has me to create the right atmosphere. Men who can only imagine women as chattels see me as proof of his virility, because they so rarely believe I could be here other than for his bed.'

She spoke with a degree of contempt, and I was glad I had never made that assumption. Or, at least, not made it plain to her that it was what I believed. That could have been embarrassing.

'He has many contacts in Saudi Arabia?'

She shrugged. 'Saudi, Iraq, Iran . . . he has many contacts.'

'You took the job here, fine – but where did you get all these coins?'

'I discovered them while I was walking the moors. I came across places that looked interesting. I had heard of the battle at Tissington, and when I researched that fight, I could find no mention of the hoard of money being found, so I thought it was a legend, nothing more. But when I thought about it, I realized that the army would not leave their money hidden in a castle's old dungeon. Who could tell that it would go undiscovered? Besides, if the new manor was already built, there would be no stones left in which to store money. No, I thought it was more likely to be nearby. Somewhere else. So I went to the Archive

Office, and looked at old aerial photos. Cambridge University conducted studies from the air of much of England, looking for the shadows cast by earthworks and old ruins, and they found a few interesting areas. But when I looked, there was one in particular, a hill just north and east of Tissington. And in the middle of a group of trees, I found this air shaft. I thought it was a mine, and was going to ignore it, but decided to investigate it, and when I descended, I found these,' she said airily, waving a hand at the boxes.

'But you didn't keep them here?'

'I didn't want Derek to find them. But now he has other concerns, and I have a man who is keen to look at them. It is buried treasure, yes? He wants to buy the coins. I had them stored in an old barn, but I've been bringing them back when I have spare time.'

'What if Derek finds them now?'

'Him? You think he has time to wander into the barns and sheds to look for things like this? No, he will stay near the house and avoid dirty places like this. No, he knows or guesses nothing.'

'So what will you do?'

'Sell these and return home to Poland.'

'You can't just sell them! There are laws about treasure. You have to register it somewhere,' I said somewhat incoherently.

'Where?'

'You should know that! You're the archaeologist!'

'Why should I do that? What is there for me here? When Derek goes, will I have a job? Will anyone want me? I think, no. These coins are all I have.'

'I see.' I turned to glance at the boxes once more, and then there was a sudden dull sound. On reflection, I think it was the sound of a spanner, although it could have been a wrench, hitting the back of my head. Afterwards there was a clattering noise, too, which was probably the spanner, or wrench, hitting the ground. But, to be absolutely honest, I was past all interest by that stage. All I knew was that the ground was hurtling towards my face at extreme speed, and then I found myself studying the concrete floor from extreme close-quarters. I wasn't entirely out of it. I could feel the rasp of grains of sand from the concrete on my cheekbone and jaw, and I could feel the growing bruise; but honestly, it was just so much easier to close my eyes just then.

So I did.

I came to a while later, to the sound of a vehicle starting and driving off in a swoosh of gravel. Not that I cared. All I knew was the pain of the massive lump on the back of my head, and the feeling of nausea that was pretty much all-encompassing. It was like one of those hangovers that smothers the entire body in pain. You know how I mean? A hangover ought to be a mere head and brain event, but every so often you get one which manages to encompass the legs, back and arms with a sort of equivalent anguish. This was like one of them.

My arms ached, my legs felt like boneless putty, and my back felt as if I'd managed to strain every muscle from the neck down.

It took a while to get myself on to all fours, and a lot longer to grab for a shelf and start to climb upwards to the vertical. It wasn't easy, I have to admit, but I got there, and had to stand with both hands on the shelf, swaying slightly as I waited for the world to stop spinning.

By degrees I managed to get myself to the door, with a sort of slow, shuffling gait. The light outside was blinding, and I had to stand there to acclimatize for some time before I could lurch forward towards the house.

God, that journey was hard. I could barely lift my feet, and every step induced a stomach-boggling feeling of sickness. And yes, I use that term advisedly. My mind was slow and hazy, but my stomach was well-boggled. I had to stop and throw up in a flower border when I was almost at the door.

At last I was inside, and if you guessed that the first thing I did was pick up a phone to call the police, you're wrong. First, I went through all the cupboards to find a paracetamol or aspirin. I really wasn't going to be picky just then.

There was nothing in the kitchen that I could see, so I made my way upstairs. I thought I had seen something in my bathroom's cupboard, and sure enough, when I looked inside, there were packets of both Ibuprofen and paracetamol. I took a couple of each, washed down with some tepid water from the tap, and perhaps the pain eased a little. Just then I really wasn't in a condition to judge, and all I really knew was that the sickness was fading. That itself was good news, so far as I was concerned.

Downstairs again, I sat on a barstool beside the island and tried to will the pain away. The place where she hit me was throbbing in time to a mournful dirge, and there was an impressive (to me) swelling, although I was particularly cautious about touching it. It was sore.

I had discovered a box of towels, and had just shovelled blocks of ice into it and wrapped it up, holding it to my injury with some care, when I heard a vehicle in the driveway.

Peering through the window in case it was Adela, returned with some kind of support, I was glad to see it was the Porsche. It drew up to a halt and Derek climbed out. He hurried to the door and soon he was in kitchen with me.

'Good God, Nick! What the hell's happened?'

I explained as best I could, and tried to inspire him to call the police, which he was a bit reluctant to do, but eventually, when I picked up my own phone, he agreed and put a call through.

'What actually happened here?' he kept asking, staring at my towel-wrapped ice pack. 'Why did she brain you? Were you asking her for something and she didn't want to do it?'

'Look, I saw her going to the barn over there, and coming back with a box that made a lot of rattling. When she was back, I went to look in the garage and found four boxes of ancient coins.'

'But where would she have got them?'

'She said from a mine shaft up on the hill near Tissington.'

'I just don't understand.'

We had six or seven permutations of that conversation while I sat with my eyes closed, clutching the ice to my skull, and he wandered about the room gesticulating quite wildly. Initially two constables appeared and questioned me pretty irrelevantly, as I thought, about details like where she might have gone, but all I could tell them was that she had taken her flat-bed truck and had four boxes of coins in the back.

'What sort of coins, sir?'

'I don't know! Old ones!'

'Did you see her put them in the truck?'

'I was unconscious. She knocked me down.'

'So you can't say that she took them?'

'She knocked me down after telling me she was going to see someone to sell them,' I said. 'And as soon as I woke up, the boxes were gone. Perhaps someone else came in, found me, thought to themselves that they could make a small fortune by stealing four boxes of coins – I don't know – but it's more likely that the bitch knocked me out so that she could steal them, since that is what she told me she was going to do!'

'I think it might be a good idea to get Nick here to a doctor, to make sure he isn't concussed,' Derek said, with the first helpful comment he had managed so far that day. I entirely agreed, and while the police clumped about, Derek got me to sit down in his office while he organized for a paramedic to come.

'Are you sure you're all right?'

'Yes, I'll be fine. I'll just wait here,' I said.

He left me alone and I heard his voice in the hallway talking to the police. I have to admit, this was the last thing he needed just now. With the house in the process of being sold, the business too, the poor devil could have done with a little more peace and quiet. All he wanted just now was a while to make sure that the sales all went through smoothly, and then he could leave the area and start his new life in the sun, the bastard.

It was my head talking there. I had nothing against Derek or people who make a lot of money, but it did seem unreasonable that I was the one sitting here waiting for the ambulance, while he was going to swan off with millions from the business sale.

It was a calming room. There were more rugs on the floor, and prints of flowing Arabic writing framed on the walls. A selection of blue pots sat on a sideboard, and there were two curved scimitars hanging between two windows. It felt cool and refreshing. A couple of pictures, showing scenes from some height, showed he had been making use of his skills with his drones. Wherever they had been taken, it looked like a warm country, but with orchards of various types. I closed my eyes.

It took fifteen minutes for the paramedics to arrive. The roads were clear at that time of day, apparently, according to the loquacious young medic. She bustled about methodically and gently, asking me whether I'd been sick or not, how long I was out for, and all sorts of questions about my eyesight and other things I can't remember now. The main upshot was, I may have concussion – and if I wanted I could go with them to the hospital and have a CT scan. However, I soon figured out that – whether I had concussion or not – the best thing would be to take things easy and not over-exert myself. Since that was pretty much my plan anyway, I decided to forgo the three- or four-hour wait to see a doctor at Accident and Emergency, in favour of sitting on a large cane chair in Derek's sunroom and dozing. It seemed preferable.

In a short period of time the police were gone, the paramedics had packed their bags, and I was left sitting quietly, staring at the barn in the distance. My iPad was in my lap when Derek came and joined me.

'How are you feeling?' Derek said.

'Pretty confused,' I answered.

'It's the knock on the head.'

'No, it's more the way that Adela managed to keep her activities here hidden. I mean, there were three boxes there, and I thought that she was just a normal girl who was here with a view to a different life. I mean, coming to the UK from Poland with her parents and all that. Although why a qualified archaeologist would want a job as a housekeeper never occurred to me.'

He sat in the nearer chair, staring out at the view. 'I'll miss this,' he said. Then, 'It made sense, you know. Archaeologists who get the good jobs have short-term contracts. The long-term jobs all go to people who have the right connections, and even then there aren't enough jobs to go round. They have to scrabble around for anything. It's like acting, I imagine. Too many aspiring actors, not enough TV shows. The ones who are really good will float up to the top and get the best parts, the others survive as best they can by working as waitresses – or housekeepers.'

'And she was very decorative.'

'Yes. And I daresay she told you she was safe with me,' he smiled. 'I was never going to jump on her. But it was useful to have a woman like her in the house. It helped spread the story about me that I wanted certain other businessmen to hear. If you're going to be an alpha male in business, it's best for your competitors to believe you are, well, an alpha male.'

'Yes, especially if you're working on deals in countries where gay men aren't appreciated.'

'Well, yes. I have business interests in Saudi, the Gulf States . . .'

'She told me you had dealings with Iraq and Iran, too,' I said. Suddenly he went very still, and that was when I knew.

'I've really not been terribly clever,' I said.

'In what way?'

'Mostly not realizing. I had heard that there were dodgy dealings with Iran, and I never put two and two together. But it's interesting what you can find out if you look. Little things, like taking over someone's business, but leaving him as the main contact; moving control of it offshore to a tax haven, for example; filling it with Iranian bank workers – or are they really bank workers?'

'That's an extraordinary allegation.'

Yes, it was, but he didn't bluster and deny. Rather he sat back and peered at me as though wondering whether the knock on my head had done more than the paramedic realized.

'There are lots of sanctions against Iran. Trade sanctions, which include lots of computer technology, and a lot of action against drones. Which means there's a lot of money for people who are prepared to take risks and export things to Iran that the regime wants. And if you have a nice business, with someone else listed as its head, and can sell it to a high bidder, such as a nation with lots of fossil fuel and trade sanctions against it, you can make a small fortune. Easily enough to retire on and disappear to Jamaica or the Bahamas, say.'

'Look, Nick, it's not as simple as you seem to think.' He grimaced. 'Look, you don't know what it's like, to have all your money go. I had the choice of letting it all go under or taking action.'

I think he must have seen my expression. When poor, hard-done-by men with Porsches, large mansions, regular holidays and plenty of spending money start to plead poverty, something in my gut starts to twist and snarl.

'I didn't want to do it,' he said.

'But you did. And you tried to conceal things by putting the blame on Jez Cooper, didn't you?'

'He was washed up anyway. What difference would it make to him?'

'Is that why you killed his son? Just to keep his mind off you?'

'Don't be fucking stupid!' he snapped, alarm seeping from every pore. 'I never killed anyone. Look, yes, I imported the gas, and a few other substances, but I never killed anyone.'

'Then who did?'

'There are two guys who work for another gang. They're real bastards. That's why I'm getting out of it all. I'm selling up everything.'

'Do you think they might have killed Rick?'

'Yes, but,' he began, and then a strange look came into his eyes. 'What's that?'

I listened. There was a burbling sound from the front of the house. It sounded like someone breaking wind inside a beer can. 'Motorbikes?'

'Oh, *shit!*'

He was up and out through the French windows like a sprinter straight off the blocks, and although I am generally quite a quick mover, and especially so when there is the potential of danger to myself, this once I was bemused rather than bothered. I heard the door open and close, and while I was still wondering what on earth had got into Derek, I suddenly realized that he might have had a good reason to flee.

Mainly it was the sight of Edwards coming in through the door, and seeing Pearce out in the garden.

There are times when I have been exceedingly nervous, when meeting certain people. This was no exception. I was still thinking of Derek's words. He had been involved in transporting goods into Iran, from the sound of things. Sanctions meant people prepared to take risks could earn fortunes providing the Iranian government with technology.

'Fancy seeing you again,' Pearce said. 'You seem to frequent places where there's something odd going on, don't you?'

Edwards satisfied himself with a meaningful glower as he positioned himself in front of me.

'Let me guess,' I said. 'You're looking for Derek, right?'

'Could be, sir,' Pearce said. He took a footstool and carefully positioned himself on it. His leathers creaked as he moved. Oddly enough, when Diana Rigg as Emma Peel did that, I found it intolerably wonderful. When Pearce did, it was just intolerable. It made me think more of sweat and petrol fumes than the fragrant Rigg. 'Why don't you tell us all about it, eh?'

'About what?'

'About the smuggling.'

'I don't know anything about smuggling,' I said. I was still more than a little woozy, and I doubt that the drugs the paramedic had given me were helping. In an attempt to distract myself from the thought of Edwards wielding a bike spoke, I remembered their cover story. 'Hey, have you got a warrant to come waltzing in here?'

'We don't need a warrant. We are not police,' Pearce said coolly.

'Well, I can't help.'

'Mr Morris, we have been very patient, really. But that was when we thought you were a civilian.'

'And now,' Edwards said with menace, 'it looks like you're a bleeding footsoldier.'

As I say, I was feeling more than a little befuddled, and having these two interrogate me was rather more than my head could cope with just now. I was pretty sure that pretending I still believed their story would be a good idea. 'Why don't you explain what Border Force is interested in, and I'll try to help.'

'We are interested in the shipments you have been helping market,' Pearce said, with a happy nod of encouragement. 'And we'd really like to know where they are, what they are, and where your boss is?'

'I don't have a boss. I'm self-employed,' I said. 'What are you on about?'

'We wanted to do this the nice way,' Pearce said, 'but if you're reluctant to help us, we may be able to use more persuasive methods.'

'I really have no idea what you're talking about. Wait!' Suddenly a fresh sovereign-sized penny dropped with a very loud *clang* in my skull and made me wince. 'You don't seriously believe that I have anything to do with Derek's businesses? I told you – I'm an artist!'

They both ignored me. 'You see,' Pearce said, 'it's a bit difficult to escape the conclusion you're involved since you are, as it were, here. In his house—'

'I'm painting it! Or, was. I've finished it now,' I said.

'And since we're investigating serious crime, we have to assume you're guilty of some kind of involvement—'

'I'm not!'

'And if you won't help us, we'll have to persuade you to.'

'For God's sake! I know nothing about any smuggling,' I protested, and then, because I had to say something, I told them a slightly revised version of what I did know. 'He's been doing it – smuggling. He's been supplying tech or dual-use kit to Iran, I think.'

'We think he's been smuggling arms and dual-use equipment to Iran,' Edwards growled. 'And now you seem to be implicated.'

It was then that another point occurred to me. As I say, the brain was suffering a bit. 'Hold on, you were investigating Jez Cooper!'

'It would appear that we might have been a little in error there,' Pearce said with a passable impersonation of regret. 'You were correct when you said that he had sold his business. We have investigated, and it looks rather as if Mr Swann was handling the smuggling himself, but using Mr Cooper as an unwitting partner. Cooper got nothing out of it, and lost his business, while Swann kept it all. Cooper was merely a cut-out, a distraction, to confuse investigation. And it succeeded. Mr Cooper has been eliminated from our enquiries. Now, it seems likely that Richard Parrow saw Swann with someone, and that was why he had to die. We want to find out who that person was.'

'If I could help, I would,' I said.

'Where is he now?'

'Derek? Last seen sprinting down that way,' I said, pointing to the open window.

'Why the hell didn't you tell us?' Edwards snapped.

I shrugged. 'You didn't give me a chance. You came in here, demanding to know all kinds of crap, and didn't ask where he was, did you? What do you . . .?'

But I was talking to the clear air. I rearranged the cold compress on my bruised bonce and settled back. I was not capable of chasing after anyone. Not in that condition, I wasn't.

Less than five minutes later, I heard an engine rev. Then there was a bit of a crunching sound, which sounded unpleasantly expensive, and mingled with some sort of banging noises together with loud, tinny crashes. It was intriguing enough for me to stand, wincing, and make my way to the front door.

I arrived just in time to see the Porsche throwing out gouts of gravel as Derek hoofed it up the driveway. Small stone chips clattered against windows and my face, and then he was gone in a cloud of dust.

Meanwhile, the noises were explained by the sight in the driveway. The first aspect to grab my attention was the large hammer. It looked like a sledgehammer, but one which had a pointed end on one side. Later, I was to learn that this was a log-splitting axe. The heavy, wedge-shaped head made it ideal for slamming into and through logs, and apparently made it equally effective at bashing holes into motorcycle fuel tanks. Actually, it was pretty good at destroying spokes on wheels, too. And, for good measure, it was just perfect at utterly destroying fairings, speedometers, rev counters and all the other really expensive-looking gadgetry on two modern motorcycles.

I heard a noise, and when I turned, I saw the two goons. Both were gripping their crash helmets, and Pearce looked stunned, while Edwards appeared to have lost the ability to speak.

Pearce stared at me. 'What the *fuck!* Why'd you do that!'

Meanwhile, his colleague was breathing deeply. I was reminded of a bull before charging. I haven't actually been at Pamplona during the bull run, just as I've never witnessed a bull fight – the idea of such cruelty turns my stomach – but if I were ever to stand in a ring with a matador's cape and sword, I imagine it would be a view just like this. Edwards didn't quite paw the ground, but I got the distinct impression that it was only a matter of time.

'It wasn't me,' I said, and, OK, perhaps my voice had risen a bit. I wouldn't say I squeaked, but definitely there was a degree of anxiety in my tone.

'You *bastard!*' Edwards said, and this time his foot began to move. Yes, he was just like a bull about to charge.

'It was Swann, you dickhead!' I shouted. Mainly because I wanted him to hear, rather than any attempt to intimidate him. After all, you don't intimidate a bull in the process of charging. You distract him with the cape. 'He took the hammer to your machines, not me. And now he's made off in his Porsche. You should get the local cops to catch him, they shouldn't have any trouble, after all.'

'I'm going to pull your fucking head off,' Edwards said. His arms were outstretched as though to capture me.

'Pearce, can you explain to the brain-dead Frankenstein monster you brought with you?' I suggested, because running away with my head in that condition was not attractive. I was still holding the ice pack to my skull. 'I was attacked earlier today and I have concussion. I couldn't *lift* that bloody hammer, let alone do this damage to your bikes.'

Something did seem to penetrate Pearce's brain at that, and he held up a hand to Edwards, who stood rocking back and forth on the balls of his feet like a bull entering a field with a herd of cows, not sure which was the best target for his immediate attention. 'He's right, Edwards. He was in the house when the bikes were buggered. It wasn't him.'

'I don't care!'

I looked over my shoulder at him. He just wanted to hit someone and I was convenient. 'Look, I heard the bikes being hit, and when I came out here, I was in time to see his Porsche racing off up the lane there. So yes, I would reckon it was definitely him. So call the police and get him nicked.'

'We will get it sorted,' Pearce said. He shooed his colleague back, like a lion tamer with a recalcitrant feline. 'Thank you for your help. Now, do you know where his office is?'

'Yes, I think he used his library. It's got sod-all books, just a computer or two and stuff.'

'Good. Come on, Edwards. There's nothing for us to do here.'

'My bike . . .'

It was rather like the voice of a young guy I knew, Bob. He had just bought a Honda 400 Four, which in those days was a storming machine. He adored that bike, did Bob. I recall him arriving at a friend's house at the top of a hill, and he chatted for a while before pulling his helmet back on, starting his engine, and roaring off down the hill. It was a nice, long straight with a bend at the bottom, and my friend and I could hear the engine and gear changes, whaap, whaap, whaap – *bang*.

When we had reached the bend in the road, Bob was lying in the middle of the road on his back, staring up at the sky with a perplexed expression. Meanwhile the white van driver, who had been minding his own business eating a fish and chip supper from a newspaper on his lap, was almost equally concerned.

'I was just sitting there, and then there was this bang, and me van turned round,' he kept saying.

'Is me bike all right?' Bob enquired.

I and my friend had retrieved the majority of it from beneath the van. It had hit the rear wheel of the van and bent it almost perfectly in half. 'Er, not really, no, Bob,' we had to say.

It was the same tone of voice as Bob's on that day. I almost felt sorry for him. It was hard to believe he was a grown man.

Then he caught my eye. My sympathy evaporated as he grated, 'I'll kill the fucker did that to my bike.'

I followed Pearce and Edwards into the house, but left them to it and went on through to the kitchen, where I had the freezer's dispenser chuck more ice cubes into my towel, and reset it on my bump. The coolness was not really helping yet.

Boiling the kettle, I prepared the Aeropress with coffee and stood thinking while the water boiled. There came the sounds of clattering and breaking from the library.

It was definitely a strange situation. I had never had experience of Border Force, nor any other semi-secret or secret agency. Who has? I suppose professional criminals often do, but that's more by the way of being an occupational hazard, and considered one of the risks of the job; but for an artist, it's a very curious position, to find yourself suddenly thrust into the spotlight of an international investigation.

Pearce came into the kitchen as I was pouring boiling water into my Aeropress and fitting the filter and cap on to it. He stood leaning against the counter with his arms folded. 'You know, we can't find much about him here.'

'No?'

'We need to get anything else we can about him and his business dealings.'

'Yes,' I said, nodding. The coffee should be ready soon, I thought.

'Leave that alone, I want you to listen to me very carefully,' he said.

I obeyed, turning to face him.

His face had gone all sort of empty. It's the only way I can describe it. I'm used to demonstrating how people are thinking in my art by picking up on subtle little clues from their expressions and the way they stand, how they hold their heads. I'm not the best portrait artist in the world, but I can still mix colours to create a good impression of a face. And the thing right now was, I couldn't read his expression at all. He would have been excellent at poker, I thought.

We stood there for quite a few minutes, while he clearly considered his next words very carefully; as he did so, I was struck with the idea that this really wasn't the way that a government agent should work. In fact, it was unlikely that any government staff had worked in this sort of way since the Tudors. Breaking into a private house, OK, with a warrant, but riding about the countryside on motorbikes didn't gel with my impression of normal government staff work. I suppose like the Hairy Bikers, some agency employees would rather like the idea of bikes instead of cars, but something about it seemed off, now I considered it.

And there was that matter of the warrant card and Pearce's reluctance to show one. Suddenly, standing there in front of him, I was struck with an absolute conviction that I had been a tit for believing him.

Derek had mentioned two thugs, I thought. Suddenly the brain fog seemed to clear like mist in the sun. 'Oh . . .'

His next words did not help.

'I want you to listen very carefully,' he repeated. 'Because I wouldn't want something nasty to happen to you. Your friend Swann is in trouble now, and we want to find him.'

'Have you informed the police about him and the Porsche?'

'We may have misinformed you there. We aren't actually from Border Force. We are more, what you might call, *private contractors*. Your friend undercut business partners of ours. We thought it was Cooper, but it turns out it was Swann all the time. He took the deal from our principals, and they want to discuss things with him. So I need you to think really carefully about this: where has he gone?'

'I don't know.'

He smiled then, but it was the smile of a snake. It never reached his eyes. 'I'm sorry you want to take the hard route,' he said, and stepped forward.

Now, what do you do when someone quite large starts to threaten you? In my case I picked up the Aeropress, slammed the filter end against his forehead and pressed hard.

Boiling coffee at pressure is, I imagine bloody painful. He certainly seemed to think so. His forward momentum and my own efforts emptied basically a triple-shot's worth of strong and very hot coffee over his face. It made him roar, and he had to close his eyes, grabbing for me as he did so, but while he was blinded, I took the easy approach and kicked him hard where it would hurt the most, and he crumpled with a wheeze of agony. There was no sign of Edwards, but I wasn't going to hang around to wait for him. I pelted out through the back door. It took little time to reach the Morgan where she was parked at the side of the house, spring into the driver's seat, start the engine, and sigh with relief as it caught. I was halfway up the drive before I saw Edwards appear in the doorway behind me.

How can I put this? He didn't look happy.

'You're telling me that these two are determined to find Swann?' she said.

There was a cynical tone to the detective sergeant's voice that I found hurtful. It was nearly as bad as the pain in my head. I had asked for an ice pack, and soon I was given a strange gel pack. The station's first-aider bent it, snapping something inside, and wriggled it about for a while before passing it to me. It helped a little. At least there were no hard edges, unlike the lumps of ice from Swann's dispenser.

It had taken some little while to explain to the desk sergeant what I was doing there, and then, over an hour ago, I had been brought into this little room with a table bolted to the floor and a chair which was also fixed in place. Now Ruth Daventry sat opposite me, in her hand a coffee in a large mug, stained from years of overuse and inefficient cleaning, studying me with that sort of introspective doubtfulness that I recognized from the last time a student decided to paint me.

'Look, I've told you all I know. Those two are likely very close to the house still, since they couldn't ride their bikes. The thug is dangerous, and Pearce is going to be seriously pissed off, but he may have to get to an ambulance.'

'They definitely said that Swann had defrauded them?'

'Well, they said he owed them money, and they were getting it back for their principal.'

'Interesting.'

'And meanwhile, I want some peace and quiet to rest my head,' I pointed out.

'We may be able to help you there. But I don't think you want to leave our protection just now. Not until we have caught these two men, and possibly Swann too.'

'They can't have got far,' I said with some smugness. 'Swann did you a favour when he took that sledgehammer to their bikes.'

'Yes. Perhaps he did.'

There was more I had to tell her. Before that day, I had been reluctant to drop Adela into a pothole of police interrogation, but since experiencing her spanner-handling capabilities, my sympathies were considerably reduced. 'There is one other thing about him you ought to know,' I said, and explained about the pickup truck and the dealer in the park.

'Do you know who this dealer was – the lad who took the whippets?'

I demurred, but really I didn't think I had a right to keep Jon's part secret. He had been selling drugs, but at least as a youngster he wouldn't face prison or anything. More likely, he'd just get a slap on the wrist, so I pulled a grimace and told her about Rick's brother.

'You knew this and didn't tell me?' she grated. It wasn't a nice sound. Suddenly I was reminded of the noise a metal door makes when slamming.

'I didn't think it was my secret to tell,' I said defensively. 'The boy had just lost his brother. That kind of thing can affect normal human beings. And imagine how his mother would be if her only remaining family member was taken into custody? She's just lost her other son, for God's sake!'

She stared at me for a moment before giving a short nod, as if she had decided on some course of action. 'Very well, I'll think about him. Meanwhile, do you have any idea who could have killed Rick Parrow?'

I looked down at my hands, thinking. 'Originally I thought it had to be Jez Cooper, because of the way he seemed to be dealing with Rick . . . but that was before I learned he was Rick's father. Now I have to wonder about these two: Edwards and Pearce.'

'Did you have any reason to suspect Cooper?'

'No. Nothing. Just natural prejudice against someone who dresses so badly,' I admitted. 'But now Edwards and Pearce seem much more likely. When I was thinking about Rick's body, and thought about him being killed elsewhere and dragged or carried over the next field, it seemed obvious that there would have to be at least two guys involved. I mean, Rick was only skinny, but he was still a male, and must have weighed over ten stone.'

'But you have no idea of any motive. And these two men appear to have more interest in Derek Swann than anyone else,' she noted.

'Perhaps.'

'What does that mean?'

'Well, nothing is terribly clear, is it? If Edwards and Pearce were the murderers, I suppose that might work if they still thought Jez Cooper had a hand in the business they were looking into – but why? Wouldn't they just kidnap or murder Cooper in that case? It would only make sense if they thought Rick Parrow knew something about them. Where was he killed? And if it was them, how could he have been killed and brought to the field by two guys who didn't have a car? They could hardly tie a dead body on the back of one of their bikes, could they? I don't think he'd fit on a luggage rack or in a pannier!'

'So it would be more likely to be someone with a vehicle. Someone with a car, you mean?'

'What could have made Derek want to kill the boy? The only thing I could think of was that he was scared, startled or something, and struck the boy down for no reason.'

'But what would he have used? It was a long, thin weapon. The pathologist said it was consistent with a sharpened bicycle spoke. He's heard of such weapons being used by kids and street gangs in London and other cities, but never seen anything like it here.'

'Nor have I,' I said. 'It doesn't sound a very effective weapon.'

'I imagine it would have to be used by someone who knew what they were doing,' she said. 'But all too many kids nowadays know exactly how to kill or maim. That's why we do everything we can to take knives off the streets. You only have to see a couple of victims of stabbings to never want to see one again.' She shivered. 'I'll leave you for now. I don't know that there's going to be any news today, but I'm reluctant to push you out. If the worst comes to the worst, I'll see that you get a lift back to London.'

'I have all my gear up at Swann's house,' I said. 'When can I go and fetch it?'

She shrugged. 'If you're determined, I can ask if we can send a plod with you. It should be safe enough. I doubt they'll try to return there.'

'Thanks, that would be good!'

The officer drove himself. I saw him cast somewhat contemptuous glances at the migmog when I suggested going in her, but he commented that he really didn't have time to wait. He had a lot to get on with, and sitting waiting for an elderly car to start apparently didn't fit in with his plans. In the end, I climbed into the moggie and he followed behind me in his patrol car.

Parking, it was good to see that the two bikes remained where they had been trashed. Three white-clad police investigators were wandering about them, studying the scene with deep concentration. I carefully avoided them and made my way into the house. Before anything else, I hurried upstairs to my bedroom, and gathered up all my things, throwing clothes into my bag and collecting my messenger case and assorted painting items. It took a little while, and then I checked the room to make sure all was done, including my phone charger, before making my way back downstairs.

In the kitchen I rinsed out the Aeropress, and then did a naughty thing. I was owed a cup of coffee, I reasoned, so I stole Derek's coffee. It had tasted good, and with him in his current position it didn't seem likely that he would be gaining access to a coffee machine any time soon. I stuck it in the microwave for a minute to warm through.

With my haul over my shoulders, my easel in my hand, I made my way to the front door where the bobby was waiting, but as I passed by the library, I was forced to stop at the sight inside.

The two really had trashed the place. Books lay scattered over the floor, papers were strewn widely, and pictures had been tugged from the walls to be thrown to the ground – presumably in a hunt for a safe or some similar place of concealment. The fact that they had found nothing, even after all this devastation, was proof of Swann's inventiveness, I thought. I meandered in, kicked a couple of sheets of paper aside, and wondered what on earth they were looking for. From the look of this room, it was paperwork they were searching for. God alone knew what sort of papers, though.

I kicked a few more pages around. Company accounts, letters to lawyers, letters from investors, I assumed. It was all way over my head. Much though my accountant would like me to have the problem of many investors and other professionals, there was no real likelihood of my ever getting to that sort of level.

On the desk there was a broken frame. It was one of those which had been on the wall, one of the elegantly written Arabic-looking documents had been inside on display, but the document was gone now. Only the frame and shards of glass remained.

There was nothing to keep me here. I walked out to the door, and I was faintly surprised to see that the police officer and the three crime scene specialists were nowhere to be seen. Wandering to the Morgan, I dumped my stuff in the footwell and passenger seat, and the smaller squishy bags went behind the seats, but the policeman hadn't returned when I was done. His car was still there, and I suddenly had a premonition that something wasn't good. I turned through three-sixty degrees but, at the end of that, all I could say was that the cop was not among those present.

Which was a little alarming, but not as alarming as the shaven-headed, leather-clad thug.

'Hallo again, painter,' Edwards snarled.

*   *   *

Pearce was sitting on the quad bike in the garage. I tried to hail him in a friendly manner, but the fact that my right arm was up between my shoulder blades, and that Edwards was trying, apparently, to wrap it around my throat from behind, rather took the vim and vigour from my greeting.

'You are going to regret this,' Pearce said through gritted teeth.

He had looked better. Just then his face was puffy, his eyes bloodshot and swollen, and his skin was already blossoming into blisters. That, along with the no doubt rather bruised nature of his reproductive organs, was enough to make me feel some sympathy. 'Shouldn't you see a doctor? Ow!'

That was caused by the sudden uplift of my arm. I turned a bleak eye to the smiling Edwards. 'What exactly do you want with me?'

'Just now, the sound of you in pain,' Pearce said. He stepped down from the quad bike, moving, I noticed, somewhat gingerly, and with a sort of pronounced swagger like a short, African John Wayne. I could only assume that his plums had grown somewhat.

He picked up the spanner which I assume had already given me my headache, and stood weighing it in his hand. Then he took hold of my left hand and pulled it forward. I was reluctant to agree to that, and snatched it back. That led to a sudden tearing pain in my right shoulder as Edwards lifted my arm again.

'Will you stop doing that?' I said peevishly.

Pearce had my wrist now, and he pulled it forward to the front of the quad bike. He held it there in a grip of steel and lifted the spanner. 'First, I'm going to ruin this hand, just so you can see what I'm planning, and then I'm going to do the same to your right hand, painter. I don't know, but I think you'll find it difficult to paint when your fingers are ruined.'

I don't think I said anything to that. The idea of the pain about to come was the only thing in my mind at that moment. I tried to grab my hand free, but Pearce just smiled, raised the spanner higher and began to bring it down.

In desperation I stamped as hard as I could on Edwards's shin, scraping down it and on to his boot. The boot felt like it had steel toecaps, but there was no doubt that his shins were not so well protected, and he grunted in pain, momentarily distracted. I had enough strength to pull my hand away as the spanner fell, crashing into the housing of the bike. And while I had the chance, I head-butted Pearce. As a blow to knock him out, it was a failure, but my brow managed to hit him in the mouth and the blister on his chin, and that was enough to make him drop the spanner and put both hands to his face. It hurt me too, as the shock ran through my skull, but panic distracted me from that for the present.

For good measure I stamped on Edwards's left shin as well, and when he lifted my arm higher, forcing me to bend over, I saw my chance. The spanner was in reach, and now I grabbed it and swung it as hard as I could at his knee, once, twice, again, and he howled with the third. I felt his grip loosen, and snatched my arm away, quickly knocking Pearce on the side of the head and then facing Edwards with the spanner held in both hands. Pearce fell like a skyscraper blown by demolition experts, simply collapsing vertically. My right arm was useless now, but I was counting on the fact that Edwards wouldn't know that.

He looked about him for a weapon, but I advanced. I was seriously pissed off, it has to be said. These guys had lied to me about everything, they had threatened me, and now they'd tried to cripple me and take away my only source of income. Are you surprised I was angry?

There was little for him to grab, and that made him dangerous. I saw it in his eyes. It was like watching a gunfight in an old Clint Eastwood Man With No Name movie. His eyes suddenly narrowed and focused on me, and I thought, '*Oh, shit*,' just as he launched himself at me.

I slashed wildly with the spanner, but he held up a forearm and blocked it, while his other hand bunched into a fist and moved towards me.

In the past I have been in a couple of silly car crashes. Once was because of ice, and when I hit the brakes, the car kept on going; the second was on a motorway, where I saw the driver in the middle lane dozing at the wheel, while I was overtaking in the fast lane. His car swerved in front of me, bounced off the central reservation barrier (which woke him up quickly), and ended up facing me. Every moment of that crash is imprinted on my memory, and I can still recall every split-second as I waited for the inevitable collision.

This was much the same. I saw his fingers close and tighten. I saw how the tendons at his knuckles went white, and how the fist turned slightly as it approached. It was rotating, and I could imagine how much that rotation was going to add to my pain when it connected.

And then there was a sudden thud, and a moment later I felt the punch like a physical blow that was not only to my chin, but my whole body.

But by then I didn't care. I was already on the floor, on top of Pearce, who grunted uncomfortably, I think. That was my last thought: a certain joyful delight to know I'd hurt him again. Then Edwards landed on top of me, and I lost consciousness for the second time that day.

What had happened?

Well, the gruesome twosome had seen the cop at the door and knocked him down while I was in the bedroom gathering up my things, but they were not bright enough to take away his radio. They had zip-tied his wrists and ankles, as well as those of the scene of crime guys, who were corralled into the garage next door, but that didn't stop him, as soon as he came to, from punching his radio and calling for reinforcements. There were two cars in the near neighbourhood, and they both came screaming along the lanes at full speed (which, being cheap patrol cars, probably wasn't terribly fast), and found me in a fight for my life, or at least my limbs and digits. One of them immediately flicked open his expanding baton and whacked the brute Edwards over the back of the head, which was remarkably effective at stopping his attack on me, but did result in my cracking two ribs when the bastard landed on top of me.

Still, although I was eligible for an immediate hospitalization, I decided against it. Two paramedics fussed over me, patched up the more obvious wounds, and assured me that my arm was fine. It was just deadened for a while, and soon the pins and needles started as it began to come alive again. As for the rest, I was certain that a good night's sleep, probably with the help of a good glass of whisky or three, would help. As for hospital – well, I didn't fancy waiting for six hours to be seen and told to take a paracetamol.

The two bikers, or rather bikerlesses, were arrested and guarded while they were given medical support prior to being taken to their own private accommodation at Derby's police station, because apparently the police take exception to their own being knocked down and tied hand and foot. So, as far as I was concerned, Adela and Derek would be well away by now, so the dangers to me were minimal. I did enquire about a bed and breakfast, only to learn that the chances of getting a room for the night were close to that of an ice cream's survival in hell.

However, I did know of a lady who might well have a spare room. Optimistically I took the road back to the holiday park and drove slowly up the road past the reception, and parked outside Megan's chalet.

'Any chance you might take pity on a poor bastard who hasn't even a bed for the night?'

I was graciously allowed inside, and soon had my bags dumped in the narrow hallway and the tonneau cover over the Morgan against the rain and condensation.

In the chalet, I was greeted with a large whisky. 'You look like you need it,' she said.

I eased myself into a sofa and sipped. 'Oh, yes. That already feels a lot better.' Except it didn't really. My ribs were hurting, my right arm was sore and stiff from being held at a weird angle, and my head was pounding. I only hoped that the whisky would help with all these ailments.

'Ouch.'

'You look as though you've been through the wars,' she said kindly.

In fact, she was being ridiculously generous. I looked at the French windows and saw a haggard picture of my dad. It was a bit of a shock. I felt like I'd aged a lot in the last few hours, but the image in the glass was that of a man who had gained decades in an afternoon. 'Oh, God!'

'Put your feet on the table,' she said.

'Do you have any illegally strong painkillers?'

'I know I used to be a nurse, but that's a long time ago now.'

'I can live in hope,' I said, rolling my glass around my forehead. It helped a little, but not as much as swallowing more of the liquor.

We spoke a fair bit about the bikers, and then Derek and Adela.

'So you think he was supplying the gas to kids in town?'

'Certain of it. He didn't deny it, for one thing.'

'So what were Edwards and Pearce after?'

'I think they were expecting to find a list of the goods which Derek smuggled into Iran. They said they worked for another group who wanted that business, but I don't know. I suspect the other people wanted to take over his business. He was hoping to make a killing so he could sell up here and retire to the sun, and he had it all set up very sweetly, with the company owned by Jez Cooper as a cut-out. Anyone investigating would learn that Jez was still listed as the owner of that business, and he'd be up for some interesting questions. Meanwhile Derek could catch a flight, secure in the knowledge that he had covered his tracks. I expect there will be a confusing chain of transactions with his money flitting into the Isle of Man, then to Jersey or Guernsey, up to Lichtenstein, perhaps, or Switzerland, and from there all the way to his favour bank in the Bahamas or Cayman Islands, where it could make friends with Vladimir Putin's billions. Ugh, it's just horrible to think of it. And I've got two cracked ribs and mild concussion to show for it. I don't even have the commission for the painting of his bloody house, and so far all I have is the expense of coming here.'

'And meeting me, darling.'

'How could I possibly have survived without that pleasure?' I smiled.

'So it was those two, Edwards and Pearce, who killed the boy we found, then.'

'It might have been, yes. They were strong enough to pick him up and bring him.'

'You look worried.'

'I am. I just cannot see why they would want to kill Rick. And . . .'

'What?'

'The weapon they used. Why use something like that? A sharp wire or something? I'd expect them to use a knife, or even garotte, but a sharpened cycle spoke? I don't see them getting something like that.'

'Who else could it have been, though?'

'Well,' I said apologetically, 'I've been wondering. You see, something that occurred to me was that a surrogate mother would almost certainly go through an agency. And it's not so easy to set up one of them. When I spoke to Jez, he couldn't remember the name, but it was interesting to me, so I did go and check on the agencies around at the time, and there was one which was very successful, until it hit the barriers and had some problems.'

'Oh?'

'I was thrown a little, because Jez remembered the agency nurse as being a blonde, but of course a woman can be blonde one day, a redhead the next, and brunette the day after, if she really wants, can't she? And it's easy to change a name, if you don't bother to go through all the legal rigmarole. And a first name can be changed at will, pretty much. I knew a bloke who hated his real names, which were Roy George, so he was always known as Peter. And another one who was named Rodney, but was always known as Dick. It's only the surname that needs a legal change, if you want to change your name for ever, isn't it?'

'It's all very interesting, but I don't understand.'

'What I couldn't understand was, why Pearce and Edwards would not only want to kill Rick, but how two professionals could be so stupid as to drop a nitrous oxide dispenser. I mean, they would be unlikely to use them in any case. I think that they are much more likely to reach for cocaine or something else that boosts their excitement and helps give them a certain cachet in their circles. Smoking a vape or inhaling laughing gas . . . I just don't see that working for them.'

'So it was someone else, then.'

'I thought of that too. The thing is, who? A pair of boys, perhaps. Rick's brother, his user friends like Stan, or Al and Penny – but they all seemed to like Rick. Only his brother Jon had anything bad to say about Rick, and that was based on his conviction that Rick was going to leave him and their mother. And that doesn't mean he'd be likely to kill his brother. And if he did, could he have picked up Rick on his own and carried him over a field? I doubt it. And if he did, how did he get Rick there, to the field? He isn't old enough to drive a car, so he'd have to – what? Put him on his pushbike rack? I don't think so.'

'Which means?'

'It means it was someone else, someone who found the nitrous oxide balloon dispenser, and decided to use it to implicate someone. Whoever it was, put it in the field where it could easily be discovered. And then gave me the hint that it might be there.'

'You mean me?'

'Ah, Megan, you've been a brilliant companion. Why did you decide to kill Rick?'

She sat back, her bright, dark eyes appraising. 'You're really rather cleverer than I'd expected. Yes, you're right. I was a nurse for some years, and when I decided to leave, about twenty years ago, I was keen to help women to get their own families. It seemed natural to me to help those who were desperate just to have the same right to children as anyone else.'

Picking up the bottle, she poured two more whiskies for us before continuing, 'So I got into the business. It was easy in those days. There were plenty of women who were keen to help others, and plenty more who just wanted to make a little money. I was selling their services, helping with the actual insemination. Since Jez's wife had no ovaries and had no frozen eggs, they had to rely on Helen's own reproductive organs, which was fine. It happens. And then Helen grew too fond of the child. Or perhaps she always knew she would be, and kept the money, but also kept the child.

'I was in a difficult position. I had contracts with Jez Cooper and his wife, and if they didn't get their child, they were within their rights to have their money back. But it wasn't that easy. They couldn't really fight it in court – it was illegal to pay for surrogacy. So I said I'd do my best. I managed to persuade Helen to give me the money she had taken. And waited for Jez and his wife to demand a repayment, but they didn't. They were not happy, but I think his wife didn't want to leave Helen with the fear of a court case, or with all her money gone. So . . . so I kept the money.'

She peered over my shoulder as if I wasn't there any more. This was a confessional that, for her, had been a long time coming. 'Yes, I kept all the money, and used it to build the business, but then I had the idea for a book, and just sketched it out, and to my amazement, it was a lucky success. I wrote it from the point of view of a woman smuggled to England to become a surrogate, and how she found love, and added a little element of crime by killing off two people, and it sold well, well enough that it was soon obvious that the writing was doing better than the business. And besides, the laws were getting complicated, and I could see that commercial surrogacy would soon be impossible . . . so I wrote more books. When I came here to deal with Helen, I liked it, so I've been coming back every year for some time to write my books. And all was fine, until a couple of weeks ago, when I came here for a break.'

'What happened?'

'I happened to bump into Helen in the town, and recognized her immediately. And then I saw her son, and thought he must be the boy she carried for the Coopers. Like a fool, I introduced myself to her again, and her son, and we started talking about things. He was quite cool. I suppose he thought it was odd that he only existed because I had introduced his mother to his father. And then, he obviously realized that this was a good opportunity. I am in the public eye, after all. He could use that. So one evening last week, he appeared at my chalet, and suggested that I might want to help with his future business by letting him have some money.'

'Putting the squeeze on you, then.'

'Exactly. And as I spoke to him, it became obvious that he thought I was a millionaire. The sums he was trying to extort were ludicrous! If I was Val McDermid, or JK Rowling, perhaps I could have afforded such sums, but as me? I had no chance. I tried to explain, but he wouldn't listen. And then, then Cooper appeared.'

She drank a goodly portion of whisky. 'That was just a disaster for me. I didn't recognize him at first, but as soon as I did, I knew I had to ensure he didn't speak to Rick. And when I saw Rick that evening, going to visit him I was convinced that Rick would spill the beans, and I was like a cat on hot coals all that day and the next, but it was the Thursday when I realized the fool hadn't said anything to anyone. He phoned me, and I agreed to see him, but only if he came and met me up in the corner of the park, away from everyone, and I told him to come in by the field, because I didn't want people to see us together.

'He was happy enough; I suppose he thought he was young and fit, while I was an old woman. That's how youngsters think about people like me. Old, decrepit, one foot in the grave, however you want to put it. So I went to meet him, and I was right. He was in a dreadful mood, accusing me of all sorts, from defrauding his father to stealing from his mother. Yes, Cooper had told him the truth, and he already knew his mother had made nothing. Luckily he didn't tell her that he'd learned about the money, though. He made me agree to pay him thousands. In fact twenty thousand. Otherwise he was going to tell the newspapers. What else could I do?

'As he stepped over the fence to go, I stabbed him with a sharpened spoke. Down here,' she said, indicating the hollow between neck, shoulder-blade and collar-bone. 'I learned years ago that it only takes a small puncture to stop a heart, and with him, it was almost immediate. I had to cover his mouth, but his death throes were really quite quick.'

'Where did you get the spoke from?'

'I've had it for ages, darling,' she said dismissively. 'I needed a weapon some years ago, and talking to a policeman from Basingstoke who was used to dealing with county lines gangs, I learned of these as weapons. It's amazing how helpful people are, when you tell them that you're a writer, you know. I've kept it in my handbag ever since, as a useful defence in case I need it. And I needed it with Rick. It was the only thing I could do to protect myself from his revelations.'

'So all your comments about county lines, about drug dealers, about Jez looking suspicious – that was all just to keep me confused?'

'Don't flatter yourself! No, that was me using my noodle to assess themes for a new book. It's what we authors like to call plotting.' She sighed. 'The trouble is, so often our imagination takes over and we can't remember what we have made up, what is real.'

'One thing that did occur to me,' I said.

'Go on!' She served herself a fresh glass gazing owlishly at the bottle.

'On that day when we found Rick's body – you told me that the bikers had tried to hit him, but surely Rick was already dead. Was that just to confuse me?'

'They did ride very close to him earlier that day. I don't know, maybe they wanted Jez to see that they knew about his son? That they could hurt Rick to make Jez play ball? The worst thing was, finding the body.'

'But you knew it was there.'

'Yes, but you didn't! I wanted you to see it, to report his murder. I didn't want anything to do with it – but then you walked straight past. I had to call your attention to him before we got back to the chalets.'

'Why?'

'For God's sake, I may be a murderer, but I'm not evil! Think of all the children at the park! You think I'd like one of them to find the corpse? It could give them nightmares for life,' she burst out, and then a tear sprouted in her eye. 'I couldn't bear that. Far better that you should find him. And not me. I didn't want to be too closely associated with Rick. But then you would keep on telling people it was me who found him! I could have brained you!'

There was just enough of a smile to let me know she was joking.

I think.

She continued, 'Do you know, I think I'm rather glad to have got it off my chest! I didn't like that little sod, but ever since I killed him, I've been feeling more and more despondent. It's almost as if he's haunting me. Oh, stop staring at me like that. I'm not going to attack you. Just call the police, why don't you?'

TEN

This time when he called, I told Geoff that he was buying me supper, and after the time I'd had, it would be a good one. He was good enough to ask where I'd like to go, and for me there was only one place that would suffice.

'The Savoy Grill. Nowhere else will do.'

'Bloody hell,' he muttered, but finally agreed.

We sat at a small, circular table, dimly lit by any standard, under a cartoonish picture of Winston Churchill in a bow tie. At least, I think it was him. In the near dark it was hard to see.

Geoff was there before me, and sipping at a Negroni. I ordered the same and sat down.

'It had better be good, for the amount this is going to cost me,' he grumbled.

'Since it'll be paid for by the company, you won't get me to feel guilty,' I said.

'Even so. The taster menu is a hundred and ten!'

'If you want, there's a Kitchen Table, which involves samples of everything,' I said, glancing at the menu. 'On the web I think it said a hundred and sixty-five.'

'Bloody hell!'

'Gordon Ramsay has to make money somehow. His cars cost a fortune,' I said.

'Well, you can have what you want, within reason. So long as I get a good wine out of it as well,' he said ungraciously. I got the feeling he might haggle embarrassingly with the sommelier over the best wines.

When our orders were taken, an Arnold Bennett soufflé and beef Wellington for me, and I don't honestly care what he had, we sipped our Negronis and got down to business.

'Come on, then. Give!'

I took another wonderful mouthful. 'Well, it seems that you

were quite right to be a little dubious about our friend Derek. Derek, or Del-Boy, as I prefer to call him, was not quite so successful as he liked to make out. In fact his business did fail, as you thought, and he had enormous trouble trying to rebuild it. When he did, he hit on a brilliant scheme which involved sending items to Iran which could be dual-use. That means they could be used to make drones or missiles. Iran was keen to buy, and happy to pay over the odds. He was sending computer kits to them and they paid him in cash in the Bahamas or somewhere. Oh, and he used the little sleight of hand with the business to leave Jez the named culprit in case it all went wrong, and he hoped to escape to the Bahamas or Pacific with a new identity to live out his remaining years in comfort. He was so delighted with his plan that he had a contract with the Iranian government framed and hanging on his wall. It wasn't as if anyone was likely to recognize Iranian script or be able to read it, so he felt safe enough. But Edwards and Pearce did recognize it somehow, and took it as proof of his actions. I daresay they planned to kill him.'

'Really? For a contract?'

'It's apparently a very lucrative business. He was selling microchips that could be used to make drones big enough to bomb towns in Ukraine. The Iranians made the drones and sold them to Russia. They even sent one to Swann for him to play with. He used it for filming landscapes.

'In any case, that was all fine until Jez appeared in the area. Derek had a couple of likely lads go and visit him to persuade him to go away, thinking Jez was there to cause trouble, but he wasn't, and the two heavies he sent were not really cut out for the job. Jez soon overcame them and sent them packing. Later, I saw them in the village, and it was obvious that they weren't exactly pros at the game of beating up anyone.'

'I heard they found Derek.'

'Yes, the twit decided to escape the easiest way, taking the ferry to France. In his nice, inconspicuous Porsche.'

'What about the others?'

'Edwards and Pearce, or whatever their names are, were caught at the house with the contract they'd found. Adela's truck was found in a layby, but she has disappeared. The police say that she is likely to be caught soon, but I'm not so sure. She's a bright girl, that one. A little too bright. She clearly has contacts in smuggling groups, and getting a ride on a boat going to the continent would hardly be a problem for her. Make a change to see someone going that way across the Channel! I can't be worried about that, though. If she escapes, so be it. She did at least point me towards Megan.'

'Your friend who was the killer?'

'Yes. I had heard from Jez that the agent who arranged for the surrogacy was a blonde. It didn't occur to me at the time, since Megan was so dark, but then, when Adela was bending down one day, I saw that she was actually a blonde. It surprised me, because I've always heard that blondes get more attention, but here was one trying to hide her real colour. Then again, perhaps it was just to keep unwanted attention away, I thought. She didn't want to be painted, either. Not that it means much – some women don't. But it made me think that perhaps she too wanted to remain inconspicuous. Of course she did! She was selling drugs. But before I realized that, I did start to think: Megan's hair didn't match her age or her appearance.'

'And she killed the boy.'

'She was being blackmailed. I don't think it was a premeditated act, more an immediate reaction in horror and fear when she was hit with a demand for tens of thousands of pounds. I don't condone the murder, but I can understand it.'

'The boy was stabbed to death because he wanted a few quid?' Geoff said, shaking his head. He forked another lump of food and put it into his mouth. 'Sad.'

And that was the comment that stuck with me afterwards. For a guy like Geoff, twenty thousand would be – what – a fortnight's money? As a senior banker, he'd take that much home after tax in a month. He had an expense account to wine and dine clients in restaurants that Megan and I could never hope to visit. Every year he had a holiday in the summer and another in the winter, with probably a few long weekends scattered through the year.

He would never know the stomach-churning terror of an ordinary person hit with a bill for thousands. He couldn't comprehend the sense of disaster at an increased tax bill, a surprise mechanic's bill for the car, a sudden demand for thousands for building maintenance. I could. It was the life I lived every day.

I could remember Megan telling me that most authors earned less than fourteen thousand in a year. Being hit with a demand for twenty thousand would be enough to create massive panic and fear.

At home once more, I sat in my old swivel chair by the window. The plastic cover was cracked and leaking foam. Looking around my room, I saw how the paintwork was peeling, the old table was covered in rings from hot, wet mugs. The carpet still had stains and scorch-marks from the previous owner, and the plaster on the walls had blown and was apt to wobble in a breeze. Black mould was growing in the corners of the ceiling and at the front of the room where there was little air movement.

How would I have reacted to being blackmailed, as she had been, I wondered. If someone had demanded money I couldn't possibly afford or put my hands on, what would I have done? Would I have tried to explain, to tell him I couldn't pay anything like that much, or would I have told the blackmailer, like Wellington, to go 'Publish and be damned!' Or would I have picked up the nearest weapon and struck out in terror?

I wasn't sure. And that was unsettling.

Epilogue

And that was where matters should have ended, really. All the little issues tied up neatly with a pink ribbon about them, a bow decorating the package. But there was one last chat I had, which I have to include here.

It was about two years later that I had an opportunity to go to Marbella. Yes, to the sea and sun, where I had a rare but thoroughly enjoyable commission to paint a yacht. Geoff had found a small reward for me. He is like that: he hates to think that someone could have him in their debt. If they do something for him, he expects to return the favour. I had saved him a lot of embarrassment over Derek Swann, so he wanted to give me some other business. A friend of his had an apartment in Marbella overlooking his yacht in the marina, and wanted a decent watercolour of it. So I was given a week, expenses paid, to lounge about in the sun and enjoy sunshine and painting.

It was wonderful.

OK, let's be realistic: even a large, detailed watercolour doesn't take a week. Yeah, I had to sort out the right position to paint from, get the composition right, and then paint. It took a day. The rest of the week was mine, and I spent it in the enjoyable company of some locals who introduced me to their own version of sangria.

I have heard a certain number of people say that Marbella and the Spanish coast is full of English criminals. Kenneth Noye had lived there after murdering a man in a road rage attack. I hadn't expected to meet one myself.

Sitting in my favourite spot, a glass with crackling ice before me, I was startled to hear a man say, 'Afternoon, Nick.'

'Jez! How are you?'

He lifted an eyebrow enquiringly at an empty chair and was soon sitting, a glass of sherry in his hand.

'So, what have you been up to?' he said. 'On holiday?'

'No, I'm working,' I said. 'Painting the *Scarlet Lady* over there. Handsome beast, isn't she?'

'Nice job! You over here for long?'

'No, just till the end of the week. Why?'

'I was just wondering if you wanted to come and join me. I have a small boat too.'

'Oh?'

'Yes, well, when Derek was arrested for fraud, a large part of the case was shown to be rather messy. I was paid well as a consultant by two legal firms trying to sort it all out. I was their forensic computer specialist, which was only helped by my past involvement with the firm. And then, when the business was broken up, there was still a certain amount which I could take as payment for the business takeover. So I ended up quite flush. I took three months with the Harley, and ended up here. I had planned to continue, over to Africa, and keep on going, but here things just seemed to be so easy and laid-back . . . so I stayed.'

'I'm happy for you, Jez. You needed a bit of luck. How's your head?'

'After Swann beat me up? Oh, I'm fine now. I think he had realized I had incriminating paperwork that he really didn't want to see published, so he turned up and knocked me out to steal whatever I had. It wasn't pleasant.'

'I never understood why he broke into my chalet to steal my pictures,' I said musingly.

'Yeah.' He fiddled with a napkin. 'I also have to say, Adela's really sorry she hit you like that.'

I was definitely not expecting that. 'You know her?'

'When I found where Swann was living, the first thing I did was wander over. She was there and let me in. We didn't have time to talk things through then, but she came to visit me one evening in the chalet, and we spoke about Swann and what he had done, and she helped me find out what he was up to. It was because of her I got the paperwork that proved his guilt in the takeover of my business. It was basically fraud. She was very kind.'

'I saw her truck outside your chalet. I never associated that with the affair,' I said, feeling foolish for not having considered it. 'Has she sold all her coins?'

'Coins?'

'She had boxes of them which she had discovered metal-detecting in the area.'

'Oh, those! No, they were just a layer. She collected coins, and when she had nitrous cylinders to hide, she'd put a layer of coins over the top to conceal them. It made things easier for transporting them.'

'She didn't steal the coins from Tissington?'

'Afraid not. They'd have been worth a fortune. The coins she had were only Victorian and Edwardian. Worth peanuts. But they looked good.'

He pursed his lips. 'Actually, she wanted you to have something.'

'Really?'

He nodded, and suggested we meet again the next day. I have to admit, I spent very little time painting, but instead walked about the marina and went swimming. I was intrigued as to what Adela could have which she was so keen to give me.

Next afternoon, I returned to the same bar and was sitting with, for once, a pale beer in a ridiculously small glass; in that heat I really needed at least a pint just to maintain my fluids.

Jez appeared and set an envelope in front of me before hailing the waiter. Inside I found a trio of rough sketches – the pictures taken from my chalet when it was broken into. 'She took them?'

'I gave her a bit of a bollocking afterwards. I was going to Tissington that day to talk to her. She got there before me in her truck, and she saw you sketching and painting, and grew really worried that you might show your pictures to Swann. That he'd see the truck and put two and two together. So, as soon as she worked out where you were staying, she decided to break in and look at them. One had her truck in it, and she was worried the number plate might be visible, so she stole it, and then took two others so it wasn't clear which was being taken.'

'That makes sense, I suppose.'

'She's a very sensible girl,' he said smugly.

We chatted a little more, but when he left we didn't make any plans to meet again. Why would we? He had his very delightful new life: a life involving Adela, the sea, sun and pleasantly enjoyable recreations.

And I had to get back to painting cats.